The Ga
Dark

The Gathering Darkness

**A Dolphin
Paperback**

For my daughter
LINDA CARROLL

Published in paperback in 1996

First published in Great Britain in 1995
by Orion Children's Books
a division of the Orion Publishing Group Ltd
Orion House
5 Upper St Martin's Lane
London WC2H 9EA

A catalogue record for this book
is available from the British Library

Typeset by Deltatype Ltd, Ellesmere Port, Cheshire
Printed in Great Britain by Clays Ltd, St Ives plc

ISBN 1 85881 293 3

Contents

For love is but a skein unwound
Between the dark and dawn.
A lonely ghost the ghost is
That to God shall come.
— *William Butler Yeats*

ONE

The Sickness

Across the street from Liam Cormac's apartment house stood an abandoned church of crumbling brick and stone. The remains of some scaffolding, erected several year earlier when there had been plans to restore the church, circled its spire. Pigeons strutted on the wooden boards of the platform and perched on the metal framework. When the wind blew fiercely from the west, gathering intensity as it dived into the constricted streets of New York City, loose boards grey with pigeon droppings clattered. Once, one had been dislodged and had fallen to the sidewalk below, narrowly missing an elderly couple walking their little dog. A neighbourhood organization protested about the incident to city hall but to no avail.

'Wait until someone gets killed,' Aunt Mary, his father's sister, had said grimly to Liam and his mother, Katherine, last Thanksgiving. 'Then they'll do something!'

On the September day that Liam began his first year of high school, a man looking like a scarecrow came to haunt the church steps. As people passed him by, most of them averted their heads. Infrequently, someone would drop a coin into a child's blue plastic beach bucket the man placed at his feet where he crouched on the bottom step. The hood of his ragged black sweatshirt hid most of his face.

One morning, as Liam watched him from a window of his third-floor apartment, the man took from beneath his sweatshirt a piece of cardboard that he appeared to try to smooth with a wasted hand. He propped it between his knees and the bucket and settled into his customary position, his head bowed.

Liam knew what was printed on the cardboard. He had read the few words as he passed the church one day. He had glimpsed the sparse hairs of a scraggly beard, bony hands, kneecaps poking up against the worn cloth of stained cotton trousers. It was the only time Liam saw the man up close.

On the days he went directly home after school, he found himself irresistibly drawn to look. An impulse would seize him. He would leave his homework, or whatever else he was doing, and go to a window to stare down at the man.

His mother would call out, 'Liam! Settle down, will you, please?' It was as though he couldn't see enough of that scarecrow. His mother must have seen the man, too, but they did not speak of him to each other.

The man was there every day. He stayed until darkness came. Then he would get up slowly, put the cardboard sign back under his sweatshirt, pick up the bucket, empty out what change there was, drop it in his pocket, and shuffle down the street until he disappeared from Liam's view.

On stormy days, he sat farther up the steps, where he was partly sheltered from the rain by a stone arch above the church entrance. On those days, he kept the plastic bucket on his lap and held the sign in front of it with his fingers covering some of the words. Liam felt angry at the man. Was he stupid? Who would take the trouble to climb up the steps and drop a coin in his bucket?

The sign read: I'M HUNGRY I GOT AIDS PLEASE.

In late November, on the day Aunt Mary arrived from West Virginia to spend her second Thanksgiving with Liam and his mother, the man did not appear on the church steps.

Until it grew dark, Liam searched for him throughout the neighbourhood. He went to other churches. He peered into tenement hallways and into the alleys between buildings. He checked storefront entrances. The man was nowhere to be found. Liam did not see him again.

In Springton, a village on the New Jersey shore, two hours from the city by bus, Liam's father, Philip, had been living for the past year in a small cabin. Like the man who begged on the church steps, Liam's father had AIDS.

Two
Secrets

Liam had learned of his father's sickness on a Saturday morning a year ago, a few days after his thirteenth birthday. Philip Cormac left home early to go to the Brooklyn Botanic Garden. He was a landscape architect, and he often visited botanical sites in and around the city. Liam was to meet his best friend, Luther Fahey, at the Museum of Natural History to look at prehistoric human bones.

He had been zipping up his jacket at the front door when his mother called him from the kitchen. 'Wait,' she said.

'I'll be late,' he shouted at her from the front door.

'Come here!' Her voice rose on the last word.

He went to the kitchen and sat down at the round table.

'Your father is very sick,' she said. He gazed at her silently. Her head was bent over the table as she gathered toast crumbs with one hand. The sound irritated him.

'Why don't you use a sponge?' he asked.

She looked up. Her face was wet with tears. Her hand continued to move in ever-widening circles. A pile of crumbs rose next to her coffee cup.

'Will you please quit that!' Liam cried.

'Terribly sick,' she whispered.

Fear came to him. 'Mom?'

4

'When he had his appendix out? In the fall three years ago? So we had to cancel the trip to West Virginia to see Aunt Mary and Grandpa? You remember, Liam, don't you?'

She pressed a used paper napkin against her face. She opened her hand, and the napkin drifted to the floor. 'Don't you remember that?' she cried out.

His throat had closed up. He couldn't speak.

'After the operation, he needed a blood transfusion. The blood was tainted. But we didn't know that . . . for a long while. It's very bad.'

His voice came back. It was muffled as though he were speaking through a blanket. 'Tainted with what? How bad?'

'I can't –,' she began, then stood up, circled the table, and leaned down and put her arms around Liam. Her embrace was awkward, stiff. Her elbow pressed against his neck. He sat like a stone. 'Daddy will tell you about it,' she said in his ear. He felt the moisture of her breath. He heard her walk out of the kitchen. A moment later, he heard the bedroom door close shut.

Liam walked to the museum. My mind is in pieces, he said to himself. This is what it was like to be crazy, when one part of you tried to get away from all the other parts. He did not understand what he had heard, only that something terrible had happened.

As soon as he saw Luther at the museum entrance, they quarrelled. Liam knew it was his own fault. Luther said, 'I've changed my mind. Let's not look at those dusty old bones. Let's go to Columbus Circle and watch people. Did you know that everybody sways? I'll prove it to you –'

'We're going to do what we planned,' Liam interrupted furiously. 'What do you mean people sway! You're nuts!'

'What's eating you?' Luther asked in a bewildered voice. 'They do sway! I noticed it for the first time this week. I do it myself. It's because the earth wobbles.'

Liam turned his back on Luther and walked into the great hall of the museum. He heard Luther behind him. 'No bones for me!' he said angrily. Then he was gone.

Liam went outside and paused on the steps. Luther was loping south on the broad avenue in front of the museum. Liam had no feeling about him, about the quarrel. Luther was just a boy moving fast on his way somewhere.

He saw nothing as he walked home. He felt bodies passing him; he heard traffic, its angry snarling. Suddenly he was in front of his own apartment, his key in his hand. He inserted it and turned the lock. His mother was sitting on the couch in the living room, an unopened newspaper on her lap.

'I thought you were meeting Luther,' she said listlessly.

'Are you going to tell me more?' Liam demanded.

She picked up the newspaper, then let it drop back on the couch. 'I'm not as clear about it as your father is,' she said, not looking at him, her voice oddly small, almost indistinct.

'Did you just find out? You sound like you just did,' he said.

'It's telling you,' she said, not answering his question.

He started towards his room.

'Liam? Where are you going?'

'I've got homework,' he replied harshly.

He lay on his bed, staring at the ceiling. Dread came like a slow tide, starting at his feet, closing over him.

After a while, he got up and arranged the books on his shelves in alphabetical order; then he rearranged them according to subject. He went to the kitchen and grabbed some crackers and stuffed them in his mouth. He was hungry, but he couldn't think of anything he wanted to eat. His mother was in her bedroom again. He thought of telephoning Delia, whom he loved. What would he say to her?

Their phone conversations were like a kind of singing with a repeated refrain of a few words: 'What are you thinking about . . . ?' 'You . . . ' When they laughed at the same time, it was as though a silk cloth had softly fallen over them.

Just after a noon whistle blew from somewhere, his father came home. Liam opened his door, but Philip Cormac did not see him. He was staring at Liam's mother, who stood in the bedroom entrance.

'Katherine? Did you tell him?'

'What I could,' she said.

They stood motionless, their heads bowed. The living room looked unfamiliar to Liam. It had been transformed, turned into one of those scenes he had seen on television, a picture taken after a disaster – fire or earthquake – with two sorrowful people wandering through ruins, looking for lost things in the debris.

His father suddenly looked up and saw Liam.

'Take him for a walk, will you?' his mother said coldly. 'Don't talk to him about it here.' Then, her voice louder, 'Not in our home.'

'Katherine,' his father said, so sadly.

Silently, Liam and Philip left the apartment and walked to Riverside Park, several blocks away. A few people exercised their dogs along paths glittering with broken glass. Liam's hands were cold. He shoved them in his pockets.

He was nervous. He wished he'd gone with Luther

after all. Something was coming towards him. It had no shape, but it seemed to exhale iciness like his mother's voice when she said, 'Not in our home.' In the weeks after his father's appendectomy three years ago, he and his mother carried tray meals to him, brought him books, held his arms when he practised walking around the apartment until his strength came back. What Liam knew at the moment was that this time it would be different.

His father began to speak softly, as he did when Liam, on the warm mothy edge of sleep, heard him say, 'Goodnight, sweet Liam – funny dreams, good dreams . . .'

'The sickness I have is very bad,' Philip said. 'We all die. I'll die sooner.'

'Sooner,' echoed Liam. He clenched his jaws to keep his mouth from trembling.

'No one knows, no one can predict when. It could be a year, eight years. What I've got is called acquired immune deficiency syndrome.'

Fear unfurled in Liam like a great banner. He was frightened by the wind from the river, the bounding black dog he glimpsed on a playground, the heavy monotone of traffic on Riverside Drive, but most of all, by the way his father's words reached his ears as though they travelled from a great distance.

'When your immune system doesn't work, you lose protection against all kinds of diseases, pneumonia, cancer, tuberculosis. Syndrome means –'

'AIDS,' said Liam.

His father sat down abruptly on the bench next to which they had paused. 'Yes,' he said. 'Well, I supposed you would have known about it. Everyone does now.'

Liam had read a story only last week in a newspaper about a boy in a town in the South who had AIDS, how other parents in the school he went to said he should be kept at home, and how, finally, the kid's house was set on fire in the middle of the night and the kid and his family had to move away. Where did you go when your house was burned down?

His father was telling him what he'd seen at the botanic garden that morning. Liam sat at the other end of the bench. His father's hands were gripped in his lap as he spoke of the ginkgo tree. It had existed in the Triassic period and had been saved from extinction by Buddhist monks. Liam had learned the Latin names of plants long before he knew the common ones. Often his father had taken him to sites where he was working.

Once, he remembered, his father had told him, 'The earth is so intimate when you touch it and lie upon it. It's a body. It seems to breathe. The whole earth breathes.'

Liam wanted to cry out loud. But there were no words for what he felt.

How was it they were sitting on the bench like two acquaintances who might, or might not, talk to each other?

He hadn't asked Liam what he knew about AIDS. He hadn't said anything about tainted blood transfusions. But if he had, Liam would have known his father was lying to him just as his mother had lied to him.

Blood transfusions were safe now. They had been safe for years. Liam knew that from the sex-education class in school, what Luther called, 'Learning how if you're so dumb you didn't guess.'

'They burned down somebody's house because their kid had AIDS – they made them leave the place where they lived,' Liam burst out.

'The stupid and cruel love their stupidity,' his father

said. 'It gives them immense power. Let's go home now. Do you want to ask me anything?'

Philip turned and held out his hand as though he wanted Liam to take it. Liam couldn't.

'How long have you had it?' he asked.

'I'm not sure,' his father said, his voice calm, as though he were continuing to talk about the history of a tree. He was staring at a nearby maple, at its few yellowed leaves. 'I've had a related illness, HIV, for quite some time. Then it changed into this other thing a short while ago.'

They both stood up. They walked home as silently as they had gone to the park.

Liam was thinking about the past year, about how he had noticed things without questioning what they meant – his father's increasing thinness, how often he came home early from his office to rest in the afternoons, his frequent colds and fevers.

There had been something else. It had weighed on Liam, but each day when he went to school, he had thrown off the weight, left it at home. The three of them weren't together as they had been. At supper, each of them gave reports of the day, his about school, Daddy's about some job he was doing in Westchester, Mom's about the classes she was taking to become a librarian.

When the reports were over, the dishes washed and dried and put away, each of them went off to his or her room and closed the door.

Liam had been glad. In a way, he wasn't very interested in his mother and father – not the way he always had been. He guessed it was partly because of Delia, who had come to live in his mind and in his dreams at night.

They stood at the door to the apartment. His father said, 'Please. Look at me.' Liam turned to him but took a step backwards. 'I know how terrible this news is that I've given you,' Philip said. 'There was a moment in the last two weeks when I thought I wouldn't tell you at all. But I knew that would be worse – when you found out.'

'You weren't on drugs or something?' Liam asked. As he waited for his father to answer him, he felt a faint stirring of hope that he would say, '*Yes* . . . yes, I'm a heroin addict.'

His father stretched out his arms towards him. Liam moved farther away. 'No drugs,' said Philip curtly. He unlocked the door and they went in.

For a few days, Liam forgot his father and the sickness for moments at a time – when he was working on a maths problem or reading a story that absorbed him, hanging around with Luther, and especially when he looked at Delia in the classes he had with her.

But before he fell asleep at night, he felt a black panic that enclosed him like hot tar. Once, just at dawn, he awoke hearing his mother cry out, 'Do you know what you've done to me? To Liam?'

He opened his bedroom door. The apartment was silent. In the living room, the lights of passing cars flickered and faded on the white walls. He felt his beating heart, a thumping in his throat.

He went back to his bed and fell into a dozy half dream of himself on a hospital trolley when he was six, felt the trolley move slowly as his mother leaned over him, murmuring something, as his father rested his hand on Liam's brow and an attendant began to draw him farther away to the operating room, where his tonsils were to be removed, and the coverlet of drowsiness, induced by a drug they had given him, lay over his terror, muffling it, as he was pushed into a white room, where he fell into the eye of a huge radiant light.

He started and woke up completely. The room was pale with grey daylight. Rain tapped against his window. For a short while he was comforted, shut in by rain, warm beneath his old red blanket.

Only a few days later, there was another shock. The three of them had finished, supper. There had been no conversation at all that night. Then Philip said, 'Liam, I'm going away for a bit. Not far. Do you remember Springton, where we once rented a cottage for two weeks, a couple of years ago?'

'It's almost Thanksgiving!' Liam cried out, thinking to himself, Half-wit! What's the difference!

'It's better for all of us,' his mother said.

They're enemies, Liam suddenly knew.

'Better? Why?' he asked. They wouldn't tell him. They were going to lie.

'There's a good doctor down there in the Springton hospital. He's a specialist in what I've got. I need to be near a hospital. And I'll be able to work on a book I've been thinking about.'

'There are hospitals here! What book?' Liam demanded. His mother rose and began to take plates and cutlery to the sink.

'A history of botanical gardens.'

'You can write a history here,' Liam cried.

There was a clatter of knives and forks falling into the porcelain sink.

'Liam. I need to be by myself. It takes all my strength to live with this thing I've got. After a while, you and Mom can visit. It's not a long bus ride, about two hours. I'll need the car to get to Springton from the cabin I rented –'

'What cabin?' Liam shouted his question, frantic. 'When did you rent a cabin?'

His mother began to weep. For a moment, Liam felt quieted, as though her tears were falling inside him, cooling a fever.

'Could you *not* cry?' his father pleaded.

'Oh? It's the time to laugh?' his mother exclaimed.

'Who knows?' Liam asked. 'Does everybody know?' He imagined the burning house in the Southern town, the boy with AIDS and his family in their nightclothes, carrying whatever they'd been able to rescue from the flames.

'Your aunt Mary,' his father said. His mother held her face in her hands. 'A few old friends. Not Grandpa. He can't remember anything now anyhow.'

'What do I say about you?' Liam asked. It was as though the three of them were conspirators.

His mother and father spoke at the same moment.

'AIDS,' Philip said.

'Cancer,' Mom said.

There was a stricken silence. His father reached out and touched Liam's hand. Liam snatched it away and got up so quickly, he overturned his chair. No one spoke as he righted it. He went to his bedroom.

In the end, he lied, too. He told Luther and Delia that his father was very sick, a kind of cancer. Delia cried and leaned her head against his shoulder. He held himself stiffly. He'd extracted tears from her with a lie. He hated himself.

It was two months before Liam and his mother visited Philip Cormac in his rented cabin a mile or so from Springton. After that they went regularly once a month to see him. Liam didn't ask why the visits started so long after his father moved away. He didn't want to watch his mother's scared eyes as she cooked up some story to tell him.

In the cabin, his mother always made large quantities of vegetable soup, most of which she stored in the small freezer of the refrigerator while his father pretended to read a book. Liam noticed he never turned a page. There wasn't much conversation.

Liam spoke carelessly about school, making up things. He was bored and frightened at the same time. He longed to be on the bus heading home. He shut his ears when his parents spoke to each other. He felt he was in a play in which the three of them said words someone else had written. It was the same when he talked to his father on the telephone from New York. When the visits were over, when he and Mom settled into the cracked plastic seats of the bus, and the driver worked the gears and headed north, Liam was nearly happy.

In the summer of that year, Philip was in the Springton hospital for a month with pneumonia. Katherine visited him once. Liam talked to him on the phone. His father's voice was scratchy like a defective tape. 'I think I saw an eagle yesterday from my window,' he told Liam.

Liam was silent. Three years ago, when they rented the cottage in Springton, he had taken with him a kite shaped like an eagle. When he heard *eagle*, a door in his memory cracked open. What he saw beyond the door grew clearer every moment like a photograph negative in a developing tank.

'There aren't eagles down there,' he said gruffly.

'It could have been a falcon,' his father's voice rasped.

'I've got to go,' Liam said, and hung up the phone.

His father had given him the eagle kite for his tenth birthday. They had taken their two-week vacation in the cottage in August. Early one morning, Liam set out for the beach, carrying the kite. He hadn't had a chance to fly it until then. The city parks were full of trees in whose branches the kite could have become entangled.

A west wind blew steadily, raking the tall dune grass. The glint of sun on the water made daggers of light. Liam had the flying line wound around a bobbin he carried in one hand, the other fingers bunched carefully on either side of the kite's cross piece. The thin brilliantly coloured paper rustled and crackled in the wind.

It was too early for swimmers or sunbathers. Far in the distance, Liam saw a man walking a dog on a leash at the water's edge. The dog would dash forwards to snap at the foam left by the waves, dragging the man with him.

He came to a place where the dune rose abruptly, then folded back on itself, making a kind of shadowed passage. Liam smiled when he saw his father standing at the passage entrance, gazing into it. He could recall the pleasure he had felt finding him there. He had thought he'd gone into the village for groceries, or to the brightly painted farm stand not far from the cottage.

An instant later, his father drew to himself, as though from the wall of hard-packed sand, a long pale arm whose covering of blond hairs Liam could see from where he stood. His father draped the arm around his own shoulders like a scarf of flesh, then leaned forward and pulled into the light a young fair-haired man in bathing trunks who rested his head against his father's neck. Liam saw his father place one hand on the man's head and press him so close it seemed only one person stood there.

Liam must have made some sound carried to his father by the wind.

Philip Cormac turned and saw him. The young man sprang backwards into the passage, his disappearance marked by a thin shower of sand. Philip started to walk quickly in Liam's direction.

Liam ran down the beach. A gull cried somewhere. His fingers broke through the paper of the kite. He dropped it on the sand. He caught sight of a flight of wooden steps, and he raced up them, gulping for air, until he reached a narrow platform halfway to the top of the dune.

He paused, tried to catch his breath, heard himself groan. There was no one now on the beach. He stared at the vast platter of the Atlantic Ocean with its crinkled rim of sand.

No distant blur of sail or bulk of working boat broke the line of the horizon. The world was empty.

It might have been a solar wind that blew against his face and ruffled his hair, stirred the raggedy, tangled carpet of orange day lilies that grew on either side of the steps. For a moment, he could not recall a human face. His hands, gripping a wooden railing, looked strange to him, as though they belonged to somebody else.

He turned and stared up at a huge frame house that the steps led to. 'A Victorian pile' was how his father had described it only yesterday as they took a twilight walk on the beach.

His father told him everything – about the Hanging Gardens of Babylon, about desert plants that sent their roots miles to find water, about how pearls grew in oysters, about the dangerous, interesting world beyond the rooms of their apartment, their neighbourhood, their country. He had read Liam a thousand books, and kissed his head and eyelids before he tucked him beneath his blanket at night.

He had drawn pictures of a tiny foetus at stages of its development, right up to the moment when it squirmed, howling, from the womb into the world.

'You were really pissed off,' his father had told him, grinning. 'I saw your little ancient man's face, all squinched up. Yelling. That's how we all come – pissed off to find ourselves in this cold world.'

In this way, Liam had learned of his beginning. In this way, too, he had learned the sound of truth, a larger thing, a presence existing beyond all facts, all opinions – the truth in his father's voice speaking from the deepest part of himself.

But his father had not spoken of men who loved each other as men and women were supposed to. Yet, in a way he did not understand, Liam had known something about that for a long time. Other children had spoken of it. He had heard, without much interest, discussions of it on television. He had seen articles in newspapers. There was a word, *gay*. Once that word had meant merry, lighthearted. The meaning of words could dissolve, change.

He knew other words, the ones kids sometimes called one another for the angry thrill of it – *faggot* and *fairy*, *pansy* and *queer* and *dyke* and *nellie*. Fighting words.

He glanced up at the old house. It looked empty, but there might be someone inside it, waiting for him to take one more step up and become a trespasser so that someone could shoot him.

After a while, he went down to the beach and headed towards home. He caught sight of the kite where he had dropped it on the sand. The paper popped and rippled in the wind like a small fierce fire. He tore off the eagle's yellow beak and threw it into the water, and then, without knowing why, he dug a hole, smashed the crosspiece, and buried it all, coloured paper and laths and string and bobbin.

His father arrived home an hour or so after he did, his arms loaded with bags of groceries. His mother was frying chicken for a picnic they planned to take to the beach later on.

Philip didn't look at him right away. But as Liam stood at a window, watching cardinals fussing at the bird feeder outside, he suddenly appeared at his side. 'That was a friend I ran into . . . Geoff,' he said.

Ran into, Liam thought, and felt his mouth twist. He said nothing.

That evening, as the three of them sat on the beach, a fire of driftwood warming their legs, Liam felt he was saying goodbye to them. Something had happened. It was as though he were remembering them from a past time.

He had tried telling himself that Geoff *was* his father's friend. He had seen men hug each other before.

But, oh! Not like that! He drew away from the fire just as his mother reached for his hand. 'It's so lovely here,' she murmured. 'Look at the moon. It's nearly full.' Liam buried his hands in the cool sand. He raised his head and saw his father staring at him, his eyes sockets of darkness.

Later, on the day that his father had left the apartment carrying two suitcases, and a duffel bag, two years and three months after that picnic on the beach, Liam made the first of several visits to the public library in his neighbourhood. Each time he took from the shelf the same heavy medical encyclopaedia. The pages he studied were smudged, he was sure, with his own fingerprints.

He flinched when he looked at the photographic plates that showed ailing human bodies in violent colours. He read more and more about his father's illness. On the fourth afternoon, he came across the words *brain seizures*, and he fled the library, leaving the encyclopedia on a table, and went into a small Greek fast-food place a block from home, where he drank cups of black coffee until it grew dark.

He was thinking, his stomach fluttering as caffeine washed through it in thick waves, how he had managed to forget for so long what he had witnessed on the beach. He couldn't recall the name of the man his father had embraced, although on the evening of the picnic, he had thought he would never forget it.

By the time school started that year, he had slid back, so easily it now seemed, into his familiar life. The summer vacation in the cottage in Springton had dropped away just as a book in which he had found nothing to interest him might have fallen from his hand.

Yet all the time, the memory of what he had seen on the beach had remained, coiled, in his head. Now it had unwound, sprung up like a jack-in-the-box, every detail of it as clear as it had been when the sea wind had rustled the paper of the eagle kite as he stood frozen, looking at his father and a man locked together as though nothing could separate them.

He had broken and buried the kite. Nothing much of it would have survived the years. He had buried the memory. Everything of it had survived.

He thought of the sex-education classes in school, in which what he heard had a peculiar familiarity like faces in dreams that you know but can't name. After the classes Luther would make him laugh, and their hilarity would release them from the room of facts and embarrassment.

'Now, children!' Luther would say solemnly. 'Don't ever be naughty. There's death in these here parts!'

They would walk away from school, bent over with laughter. 'They're doing *it*,' Luther would say, pointing up at the window of some building.

'That's an office!' Liam would cry.

'Everywhere – they're always doing it,' Luther would intone. 'Between wars, what else is there to do?'

With Delia, it was different. If they spoke to each other in the corridor right after the sex class, there was a strangeness between them, a sense that they were nothing more than the bodily parts the teacher had drawn on the blackboard, that could make babies or kill with disease.

Why did the teacher smile as she wrote the words *needles, blood, bodily fluids* in differently coloured chalk? She spoke so cosily. Teddy bears having sexual intercourse. Sex wasn't cosy. It was a precipice that drew you to its edge, closer, closer.

The next day, the fifth and last that he went to the library, he found *brain seizures* again. He couldn't read what was written there.

The knowledge he had gained stuffed his mind. Luther's jokes didn't penetrate it any more than did confidences exchanged with Delia. He could never tell them what he knew about his father.

There was no one who would answer the questions that haunted him.

Had his father done it once with the man on the beach? Had there been other men? Why had he got married? Was it that he had wanted to try *that*, too? He had, after all, done it with *her* once. 'Because I'm here,' Liam said aloud. A man reading a newspaper on the opposite side of the library table looked at him disapprovingly.

'So I see,' he said.

Liam returned the encyclopaedia to its place on the shelf and went home.

'Hello, darling,' his mother called out from the kitchen. He went straight to his room. His father would die.

A thought came to him, so terrible a thought, he flew to the kitchen. His mother was scrubbing small red potatoes with a brush at the sink.

'Are you all right?' he cried.

Startled, she dropped the potatoes and turned to him.

'I mean – you're not sick, too, are you?'

She studied his face for a moment. Then she went to him and took his shoulders in her hands. 'I am absolutely all right,' she said forcefully.

The second Thanksgiving of his father's absence had come. Aunt Mary arrived two days before the holiday, complaining about the fresh chestnuts and pecan pie she had had to carry along with her luggage. She announced that the nurse she had found to stay with Liam's grandfather while she was away wore too much makeup. She taught chemistry at a junior college in West Virginia. Liam could imagine her classes – formulas hurled like thunderbolts at students crouching at their desks.

'You need family around you in these troubled times,' she had insisted last year.

In the old days before his father's illness, when his mother still spoke to Liam about her thoughts and feelings, she had once said she didn't like Aunt Mary one bit, but you had to put up with people in your family, even when a relative was a crocodile.

Liam had discovered some time ago that if he said, 'You're right,' to whatever his aunt said, she'd leave him pretty much alone.

'My sister belongs to the blamist party,' his father had once told him. 'She found out when she was above five – when I was born, as a matter of fact – that you can blame other people for everything rotten that happens to you. It's a quick fix for making your life simple.'

One day before Thanksgiving, Liam woke and sat straight up in his bed. He wanted desperately to see Daddy.

During the year he'd been away, Liam had had no desire to see him at all, not even to talk to him on the telephone. The visits he'd made with his mother to the cabin in Springton had been wearying and lifeless. They were always followed by a kind of self-disgust in Liam, as though he'd cheated on a test or lied stupidly about something that hardly mattered.

Now he heard Aunt Mary rearranging the furniture in the living room. She was a person who always had a better idea than anyone else had.

Barefoot, in his pyjamas, he went to the kitchen.

'Wear slippers,' Aunt Mary called after him.

'I want to see Daddy,' he said to his mother.

'Well – you can see him. We'll go down in a week or so,' his mother said in a vague voice. She was staring at a small turkey in a plastic bag that lay on the counter. 'It'll never thaw,' she muttered.

'I mean today,' Liam said.

'I don't know about the bus schedule,' his mother said.

'There are buses all the time. Can I?'

She turned and clasped her hands and stared down at the floor. 'All right,' she said. 'Do what you want.'

'Maybe he really was a dope addict. Maybe he got it from a needle, and you don't want to tell me that!' he cried.

'From the blood transfusion,' she said as though reciting a rule she might forget at any moment.

She raised her head. Her blue eyes, so like his own, gazed at him with apparent calm. 'I'm sorry,' he muttered for no reason he could think of. She reached out and touched his cheek with her fingers. He realized how rarely she touched him any more.

'I'm glad you're going to see him – if that's what you want to do,' she said. She glanced away for a moment. She whispered in the direction of a narrow broom closet, 'He must be lonely.'

At that moment, Aunt Mary plodded into the kitchen.

'I want you to get some Brussels sprouts, Liam,' she commanded. 'How did the sprouts get forgotten?' she asked the room. 'Well, Liam?'

'Liam's going to Springton to see his dad,' his mother said.

'I'm absolutely against it!' Aunt Mary cried. 'I've always been against it. And I've dragged all this food up from home for tomorrow! You're not going to stay overnight down there, are you? What about the trouble I've gone to for our Thanksgiving?'

'I don't know if I'll stay the night,' Liam said.

'No one has proved you can't get that revolting disease from drinking glasses and utensils. You should make your own meals while you're there. Take a towel from here! Really, Liam! You might think of our feelings!'

'Mary!' His mother's voice sounded like a trumpet call.

'Why is it that you dig up the stupidest things people tell you? What are you saying? How dare you presume I'd let Liam be exposed if there was any danger?'

Liam had to press one bare foot on the other to stop himself from jumping around in a crazy way. He was suddenly happy! He'd forgotten what it was like – to be with his mother in this way, united, defended.

Aunt Mary looked bewildered, if only for a moment. She said sullenly, 'You can probably get it from tears.'

'Tears!' exclaimed his mother. She shook her head as though in disbelief at her sister-in-law's words. But then her shoulders slumped, and she turned to the counter to press a finger against the turkey's breast.

'Tears, tears!' Aunt Mary repeated impatiently. 'When people cry.'

THREE

The Two Women

'Well – and how are the two women?'

'Okay.'

'You're some great reporter.'

'I'm not a reporter,' Liam said. He dropped his backpack on the bare floor of the cabin. Dust rose and settled.

'Everyone is a reporter in one way or another,' his father said. 'Your face tells me they're grim.'

'If I look grim, it's because of the way you ask about them. Why do you call them "the two women"? It's Mom and your sister, Aunt Mary. You remember them, don't you?'

His father smiled faintly. A large black cat waddled into the room and sat down, staring at Liam.

'Where did you get *that*?' he asked. But why had he spoken so scornfully? Why had he come at all? He felt his glance sliding about the room as though his eyes had come loose from his head.

'That is Julius. He came tearing out of the woods a month or so ago, just after your last visit. He was thin as a wire, and a large yellow dog was chasing him, snapping its fangs.' His father paused and drew a deep breath. 'I named him after you.'

As far back as Liam could recall, his father had made such jokes, crazy jokes that used to make him laugh wildly just because there was no explanation for them. He didn't laugh now. The joke – if that's what his father thought it was – was senseless.

'You feed him too much,' Liam said. 'He's the fattest thing I ever saw.'

'Somebody has to eat around here,' his father said mildly. 'I ordered take-out for our supper right after you phoned.'

Liam shrugged. He didn't care about food. He didn't want to talk about food.

'But really – how are they? Is your mom holding up against Aunt Mary destroying the furniture?'

'What do you care?' Liam burst out. 'They won't ask me about you!'

'I bet they won't!' his father said sourly.

They had never talked to each other this way. The visits with Mom had been polite and soft and dim. But now he felt the way he had one late bitterly cold afternoon when he'd taken a shortcut home from school across an empty lot and seen a figure covered with rags rise up like an apparition from the weed-and garbage-covered broken earth and wave its arms at him. The very air of the cabin felt raw and chill. If he left now, he knew he'd not be able to come back again.

He looked at his father directly for the first time.

Philip was sitting in a brown wicker chair that creaked with his every slow movement. His hair, once so thick, was like a handful of dry straw. His nose looked longer, his teeth larger. But it was his thinness, the flesh barely covering his bones, that made Liam's heart grip in his chest.

He had told Liam on the phone that he wouldn't be able to meet him. So Liam had walked the mile or so to the cabin, looking at nothing, kicking the road, wondering at the impulse that had brought him to Springton.

'Am I supposed to walk into town and get the take-out?' he asked. He tried to keep his voice low, ordinary.

'I'll be better by the time we should go,' his father said. 'I wasn't feeling so good this morning.'

The cabin was barely furnished. Between two small windows stood a bed covered with a dark grey blanket. There were a few wooden chairs, a table, a small sofa bed draped with a faded green cotton spread, and two architect lamps craning from a wall like nosy people peering over a fence. The shade on a standing lamp was torn. Against one wall of the room was a sketchy kitchen. What seemed like dozens of medicine bottles were lined up on an open shelf above a small sink. A few garments drooped from nails on another wall. There was a brown tweed jacket Liam remembered. A door led to a bathroom with a toilet and shower.

There was beauty in the landscape Liam could glimpse through the windows, a farm field, islands of trees, leafless now, and the heavy branches of a tall blue spruce that stood outside the cabin door. A few hundred feet from the cabin, the tea-coloured waters of an inlet wound to the ocean a half-mile away.

There were piles of books on chairs, on the floor. Liam bent to pick one up. It was a collection of poetry by William Butler Yeats.

Philip was staring at Liam's backpack. Liam grabbed it and took it to the sofa bed, where he dropped it. As he passed the round table, he ran his hand across it. Dust.

'Have you talked to Mom about Ireland? I've been working out the trip ever since we spoke about it last month. I've figured out what we can do in a week. The sooner I make plane reservations, the cheaper they'll be. Your spring break isn't that far away.'

Liam had forgotten all about Ireland, all about the conversation they had had on the telephone. He hadn't even mentioned it to his mother.

'How can you go anywhere?' Liam asked.

'I'm better than I was last week. It's the nature of this thing – you can be so awfully sick, then you get better.'

'You look worse than when Mom and I came last time.'

'What a brute you can be, Liam!'

Liam's throat seemed to hollow out and go dry. He stood without speaking, his bones like lead.

After a moment, his father said, 'I'm sorry. You're not a brute. I am. Sickness changes a person.'

'Okay,' Liam said, his voice just above a whisper. He turned his back on his father.

'Liam, please . . . I'm really sorry I spoke that way. I only want you to understand that I will get better. I've thought so much about this trip, you and me. We'll go to Clare and Galway. I want to see the tower where Yeats lived. In Ireland, they call it "tour". It's right beside a river. And we'll go to his grave and to pubs in Sligo, and a few days in Dublin so we can walk around St Stephen's Green . . .' His voice was thinning, running out. It stopped all at once.

Liam sat down next to his backpack on the sofa bed.

After a while, his voice stronger, his father said, 'I want us to do something together.' He plucked at the cloth of his jeans. 'If it's possible.' Then, with sudden irritability, he said, 'I don't want your mother along this time.'

Liam watched how slowly he stood up. 'I really am better. I'm trying a new drug.' He walked to the kitchen counter and pointed at a pot. 'I actually made soup yesterday. And I have a loaf of very good bread if you're hungry after your walk. I should have asked you sooner . . . There's a very good baker and cook in Springton. That's where we'll get supper. And there's a place near here I want you to see. I found it when I was walking one day. My God, it's Thanksgiving tomorrow, isn't it? I keep losing track. It was so good of you to come to see me – though maybe you won't mind missing Aunt Mary shouting at the turkey to cook itself properly.'

Liam didn't know whether he'd stay the night. Julius suddenly sped across the cabin floor and leaped to the sofa.

His father let out a small gasp of laughter. 'Poor Julius. He clears off when I start moving. I've stepped on him a few times.'

He opened the tiny refrigerator beneath the stove and turned back into the room, holding a long loaf of bread. 'See? It's like the bread you can buy in Paris,' he said.

There were tears running down his cheeks. He brushed his face with one hand.

'Someone I know died a while ago,' he said. 'A friend.' He sighed and put the loaf back inside the refrigerator. 'Let's sit down. Did you want to try the bread?'

'Don't open the refrigerator again,' Liam said. 'I'm not hungry.' He went to the table and pulled out a chair and sat down, his father sitting across from him.

'Who died?' Liam asked. 'What friend?'

His father got up, took out the loaf once more, and held it out to Liam. 'Please. Break off a piece. It's really good.' Reluctantly, Liam tore off the heel and chewed it. His father was wiping his face with both hands now. 'A young friend,' he said in a muffled voice. He watched

Liam closely as though waiting for a significant judgement about the bread. When he spoke, his voice was stronger. 'Anything interesting in school these days?' he asked.

'Science,' Liam replied.

'Isn't the bread good?'

Liam thought he might go crazy if his father said *bread* one more time. 'It's okay,' he said.

'Anything you'd care to add about school?'

'We get searched for weapons.'

'Every day?'

'Spot checks.'

'You must think the world is a war. How do the kids feel about that?'

'I don't know. They found three knives on one guy. He said he had to be ready.'

'For what?'

'They never say.'

They fell silent. Liam had trained himself to move across the surface of their time together like a cautious ice skater. It was different today. He sensed a widening hole in the ice. He and Daddy could fall through it into the deathly cold water.

'Listen!' his father said suddenly, holding a finger to his lips. 'Can you hear it? That drone like sleepy bees?'

Liam did.

'Those are molecules. Someone named Brown discovered them, so, of course, they're called Brown's molecules. They knock against one another. You can't always hear them. It's a comfort finding out things, and finding out how much you don't know.'

'Yeah,' said Liam. 'I know people who get a lot of comfort out of not knowing anything.'

'That's not what I meant.'

Liam had known that. He said nothing for what seemed an hour.

'Liam? Will you walk with me?'

'Arf! Arf!' Liam barked, and got up from the table abruptly.

A while later, as he stood staring out of a window, he heard his father moving about the room, hesitantly, like a very old person. He felt a flash of pity. But his mother's words, heard in the night, came back to him. *Do you know what you've done to me? To Liam?*

He hadn't come down here to feel sorry for his father.

He turned to see him pulling on the sleeves of a thick sweater. When he saw Liam looking at him, he smiled in the old way, tenderly, with a kind of – what? Challenge?

'Did you notice the sun has come out? I'm ready to go for a drive now. I want to show you something. Are you ready?'

'Does it matter if I'm ready?' Liam asked.

His father leaned against the wall among the clothes hanging from the nails.

'I've never in my life had anyone so angry at me as you are,' he said in a matter-of-fact voice. 'Not counting my sister. Liam. I didn't choose to leave this life.'

'Could we go now?' Liam asked. In his own ears, he sounded three years old.

Down where the inlet broadened, narrow roads wound through farms and among reeds and patches of woods. The reeds bent to the wind. Because Philip was driving so slowly, Liam could hear the rustle of their long fronds. They brushed away his fretful, nervous thoughts that had, since his arrival at the cabin, been unable to form one simple thing he could state to Philip. He had been fresh, balky, sneering. Now there was only the soft rhythmic whispering outside the car, along with the low monotone of the engine. His father's thin wrists protruded from the sweater sleeves. His long thin fingers rested lightly on the steering wheel.

Years later, whenever Liam saw reeds bending over a narrow country road, he would recall this pause, moments of quietness, when he'd been emptied out of anger and pity.

'I've taken two wrong turns,' his father said. 'I think I do it on purpose to stay longer near the reeds. I love them so – genus *Phragmites*. There it is.' He gestured with one hand towards three small cottages that sat prissily on their lots. The road was about to end in sand. Liam could see the autumnal sea, the colour of gun-metal. The sky had clouded up again; the sunlight was weak.

His father parked on a grassy verge across from the cottages. A sloping path led through a stand of trees. A historical marker stood where it began. Liam read: SLAVE GRAVEYARD: IN 1847, HERE WERE BURIED ELWOOD BECKER AND HIS WIFE, LETITIA, AND, AT THEIR REQUEST, THEIR 19 SLAVES.

'I didn't know they had slaves this far north,' Liam said.

'There was slavery nearly everywhere – from the beginning of human community. I read somewhere that ten thousand Greeks were sold into Roman slavery on one afternoon on the island of Delos in Greece, thousands of years ago.'

They started to walk down the path. Liam suddenly recalled a curious story Philip had read to him several years ago. It had told of an old Amazonian Indian who had captured an English explorer and forced him to read all of Charles Dickens's novels over and over again. He was about to ask his father the title of that story, and the writer's name, but found he couldn't. He rarely, except by accident, referred to the time before Philip had told him of his sickness.

They arrived at a small white picket fence bolted on either end to two large boulders. An oblong space was enclosed by a drystone wall, itself enclosed by evergreens and maple and oak trees. Two small crumbling tombstones stood like sentries. Before them, at intervals, were nineteen rough stones, the kind you could have found in a field.

A heavy silence was gathered there, a hush. Liam listened as though something might speak to him. The bare branches of the deciduous trees rattled faintly. He and his father leaned against the picket fence.

After a while, Philip went back up the path. Liam lingered. He looked at each unhewn stone, at the two small tombstones. He was trying to gather up the whole place to keep in memory. It was haunted, echoing with lives now gone and all their suffering.

At the thought of remembering the graveyard later, the knowledge of his father's death that was to come struck him with such force that he fell forwards against the sharp fence stakes, and the pain they caused made him rear back. He wanted to get away now, and he ran up the path to the car.

His father sat in the driver's seat, the door open, smoking a cigarette.

'Since when do you smoke?' Liam asked.

'I just took it up,' Philip said coolly.

Liam got into the car. How dare his father speak to him

that way? It was his fault. He'd brought this terrible thing into all their lives, that forced everyone to tell lies and be alone in fear.

Philip drove fast along the roads among the reeds. The cigarette had gone out but still hung from his lips. He parked on the dirt road behind the cabin, turned off the motor, and seemed to throw himself out of the car only to fall against it limply.

'Are you okay?' Liam questioned, alarmed, imagining an ambulance drawn up to the cabin, his father on a stretcher.

'Of course I'm all right,' Philip replied irritably. 'I wanted to get home. That's all.'

Liam kicked at the dirt road. Dust and sand flew up into the air. 'Why are you yelling at me?' he demanded.

'I wasn't yelling,' said his father. 'I don't want to be asked if I'm all right a hundred times.'

'What are we going to do now?'

'What did you expect? There's no television. Pretty soon we'll go into Springton and pick up our supper. We might even have a conversation. At the moment, I have to lie down.'

Liam kicked at the road again. His father started towards the cabin. Suddenly he turned. 'Don't do that,' he said.

'Why not?'

His father stared angrily at him.

'Because it bothers me,' he said.

His jeans had slipped down to his hips. His shoes looked too big for his feet. Liam could see the cords of his neck muscles.

They seemed to be facing each other across an empty world into which, slowly circling, a brown leaf from a nearby tree fell at Liam's feet. He kicked again at the road, violently. A cloud of dust rose up and then settled.

'Liam!' His father's voice rang like a shot. All at once, he clutched his waist and crouched.

He looked like a dwarf with features carved cruelly by a knife.

A hood seemed to slip over Liam's head. He heard shouting. It was his own voice.

'I know how you got it! I saw you on the beach with that man. Hugging. Hugging! You all lie. Everybody is lying, lying! You know I saw you! You know it!'

His voice, which had begun to deepen this last year, cracked, and to his horror, it rose high, a small child's screech of temper.

His father slowly straightened up and stood unmoving, his expression unreadable.

'You don't know anything,' he said quietly.

Gasping, Liam said, 'I know everything.'

'Nothing.'

'You killed our family.' Tears burned his cheeks. For a moment, silence closed them in. He could hear their breathing.

His father said, 'Nobody is killed except me.'

Liam kicked again and again at the dirt until a wall of dust rose and held between where he and his father stood. It was as though a horse had galloped frantically between two fires.

'Your own sister won't have anything to do with you because you're an old queer. . . . What about my mother! What about her! Has she got it? Have I got it?'

'No,' said his father, and walked away to the front of the cabin.

'Damn Ireland!' Liam shouted at his retreating back. 'Damn Yeats and Ireland!'

Liam yanked open the car door and flung himself into the back seat. His nose was running. He raked his face with open fingers. He heard himself whimper. His fingers were wet and sticky, and he wiped them on his jacket. He had lost everything, everyone. He'd done it to himself. If only he could go back in time a few minutes!

The best thing was to know nothing. And he'd given up the second best, to know and not tell. It had done him no good. There had been one moment of elation when he'd shouted at his father and delivered himself of the burden of what he'd witnessed on the beach years ago. Now there was desperate regret. What would he do?

A rattling noise broke into the silence and distracted him from his misery. He looked through the back window. A beat-up little foreign car pulled in to park behind him. He could make out an old woman behind the windshield, in the driver's seat. A car door creaked. The old woman stepped out, drawing after herself a large canvas bag. Liam got out of the back seat at the same time, and she saw him and smiled.

Her little teeth, pale yellow like the kernels of early corn, gleamed in a big soft face framed by hair the colour of cigar ashes. Thick glasses sat on her fat nose. Her shabby dark coat was buttoned to beneath her chin. She wore hightop black sneakers, and as she came towards him, she favoured one broad foot, canting forwards with each step.

'You must be Philip's son,' she said in a gravelly voice. 'I brought his reading matter. It's hard for him to get to the library now and then. How is he? Last week was pretty bad. I'm Mrs Sigurd Mottley – called Sig for short.'

She was standing in front of him, peering at his face. She was shorter than he was. She must be very old. Probably in her eighties, he thought.

'Are you? His son?'

'Yeah,' he said. He smelled strong sweet powder. Lilac, he guessed.

'You don't waste words,' she remarked. She continued to look at him closely. Could she see he had been crying?

'He's told me about you,' she said. 'That is to say, he refers to you often in our conversations. Liam, isn't it?'

He nodded.

'I help out here and there. Your father doesn't always get around too easily. We don't have much of a community. Too isolated, only a few people in the winter. I'm in a church group. Very small congregation, but we try to keep an eye on one another.'

He had to say something. She was waiting.

'Thanks . . . for keeping an eye on him.'

She laughed. 'No thanks asked for. Going around like this keeps my mind off my troubles.' She started down the slope to the front of the cabin.

'He showed me a drawing book of his garden designs,' her voice trailed back. 'Wondrous. What you can do with a hedge here and there.' She seemed to be waiting for him. Reluctantly, he walked to her side. He was being drawn back into the cabin. She rested a hand as light as a leaf on his shoulder. 'He wants to go to Ireland with you,' she said softly. 'But you won't count on that, will you? Poor man. AIDS is the pits.'

Liam shuddered. His curses came back to him, shouted at a place he'd never been, at a poet he'd never read. But there was a surprise in the way she'd said the name of the sickness so plainly.

She halted for a moment and spread open the canvas bag. 'Books about Ireland,' she said. 'I found him a street map of Dublin. That's all he wants these days. *Gaelic Twilight* – he'll be pleased I got that. Who am I to tell him he won't be able to go? He'd appreciate it if I knew something about Ireland besides shamrocks, and car bombs in the North. It gives him relief to talk about it. He told me his grandfather, your great-grandfather, was a veterinarian in Donegal. I didn't know there was such a place. And the vet packed up and emigrated and came here to settle. Well – it must be dreadfully hard on you and your mother. It would make me cry if I could. But I seem to have lost the knack for crying.'

He realized she was the only person besides Aunt Mary and his mother who knew what his father's sickness was. The only person he knew anyhow. He didn't know the doctor who treated his father, or doctors. When old friends of his mother and father's came to the apartment, they didn't say *AIDS* right out as Mrs Mottley had. 'How is he doing?' they might ask.

'You coming?' Mrs Mottley inquired, her hand on the door.

He would have to go in. Either that or walk to Springton and wait for the bus back to the city. But he couldn't do that. His return ticket was in his backpack.

He followed Mrs Mottley into the shadowy room, where his father sat in the wicker chair, his head against the backrest, just as he had been when Liam had first arrived.

During the few minutes Mrs Mottley talked to his father, she handed him one by one the books she had brought, pronouncing the titles aloud as though it gave her pleasure. Liam leaned against the kitchen sink. Julius wound himself around the old woman's ankles, and, groaning a little, she stooped to pat him. Philip would look at each book and let it fall from his hand to the floor.

'They may turn up that story you wanted by Flann O'Brien, was that his name?' Mrs Mottley asked. 'They've got that system, you know, the computer they can do a search on. But I did dig up a map of Dublin. Here. I thought you'd like it.'

'I love it, Sig. You're an angel.'

'Don't call me that. It drives my mind towards my failings. Are you all right for everything else now that your son has come? The church is giving a little Thanksgiving dinner tomorrow. I could drop by some turkey.'

'Sig, I hate turkey. But Liam?' His father looked over at him. 'Will you be here tomorrow? Would you like some turkey?'

Liam said no, not sure which question he was answering.

'Not even apple pie?' Mrs Mottley asked, looking from Liam to Philip. Then, as though their unanswering silence was of no consequence, she said, 'Well, since you're together, apple pie can't count for much, can it? I'll be back next Wednesday, Philip.' She stooped once more to touch Julius's big head before she went to the door with her shambling, forward-leaning walk. She paused there and looked back at Liam.

'I'm glad to have met you,' she said in a serious way. 'I hope I'll see you again.'

After she had closed the door, after Liam heard the car drive away, his father began to speak, tiredly, calmly.

'When she first turned up,' he began, 'I was appalled. I thought she'd kill me with the sort of goodness you're

39

supposed to praise constantly. But she's not like that at all. She's a smart old person. She's poor as a mouse, lives on a few dollars from Social Security. She used to work in the Springton pharmacy until she retired. She was married once, she told me, years and years ago, but only briefly. No children. No family left at all. I've driven by the shack she lives in. She keeps a few chickens, an old brown dog, and lots of cats. Some of the summer people, the ones who rent houses in July and August, abandon the poor things when they've finished playing with them – like toys – and she gathers the strays and orphans and shelters them. She looks in on sick people, like me – not that there are many around here like me. She's merciful. She hasn't the least idea that she's a hero.'

It was as though nothing had happened earlier on the road behind the cabin. How could that be? Liam wondered. How could it be that after such violence of feeling, such terrible words, they were still together?

The room was nearly dark. Liam was thankful for that. A light might dispel the easing of tension between them. He had begun to feel a delicate, mysterious touch of comfort as he listened to Philip.

'And the library books she brings. I'd be lost without them,' he went on.

'You said you were going to write about the history of botanical gardens,' Liam said. His voice sounded strange to him, faintly rusty.

'Yes, I really was. But I found out it takes physical strength to write. I didn't know that. And you have to have the intention and keep it. I lost that. This sickness interrupts everything.'

Julius was purring loudly. 'He sounds like Brown's molecules,' Liam remarked.

Philip laughed. 'It's such a lovely sound,' he said. 'When I wake during the night, he's there on the bed, weighing two hundred pounds, it feels like, all of it shoved against my leg. I feel desperate sometimes, all that weight on me. But he and I – we travel through the dark together.'

He'd been alone until Julius came. Then there had been only a cat, purring, for company. But it was all his own fault.

'Mom and I came – when you'd let us.'

'Let you!' his father exclaimed. 'What gave you the idea it was up to me?' He seemed to hesitate a moment, to struggle for words. 'It could have been different when you did come if you'd talked to me as if I was real.'

There was a hardness in his voice, resentment. Liam went to the lamp with the torn shade and turned it on. For a moment he was blinded. 'Don't say that to me,' he said, and turned to face his father. 'It wasn't up to me either.'

Philip groaned. 'Oh, I know that. What I said was wrong. But, Liam – because something took me by surprise doesn't change everything. I'm your father. You didn't become someone else's son. Your mother didn't vanish from my history. If I could explain what happened, I would. Mom told me you tell your friends I've got cancer. Sometimes she even seems to forget – and tells *me* I've got cancer. But secrets have a way of telling themselves despite the efforts we make to conceal them.'

'Why did you come down here? Why did you just leave us?' Liam shouted, startling himself.

'Listen! Every time your mother looked at me, she thought of how I'd wrecked everything for her. Your mother is naturally a kind person – in the same way that your aunt is naturally unkind. Although unkindness seems to have no end, there is a limit to kindness. And I couldn't bear her suffering! I had to get away from it – to keep some strength for myself. And there was something else . . .' He looked away from Liam and fell silent.

'Did you tell her?'

'As soon as I knew.'

'Knew what?'

'That I was sick,' his father said with a touch of crankiness.

'I mean – about him.'

'I thought, at first, it was a kind of aberration –'

'I don't know what that means.'

'A singular thing, a one time thing.'

'But you had to tell her, didn't you? How you got it?'

'We always told each other everything. But this time – I couldn't speak of it until the sickness forced me to.'

'So you did tell her, about him?'

His father nodded.

'Why didn't you lie!' cried Liam.

'How? Tell her I was a drug addict? Do you think she could have believed that? And it would have killed everything between us if I had lied.'

Julius was pacing back and forth in front of the refrigerator.

'There's an open can of cat food in there. Feed him, will you?' his father asked.

Liam took the can from a shelf and dumped the cat food into a plastic dish on the floor next to a bowl of water. Julius began to eat, purring between bites.

'Liam? Does your mother know what you know? Did you tell her that you saw me on the beach with Geoff?'

Liam, watching the cat, shook his head. 'Doesn't she tell you everything?' he asked. 'That's what you just said.

How come you think she wouldn't have told you that?'

'You never said a word?' his father asked wonderingly. 'How have you kept it to yourself all this time?'

'Get off my back, will you?' Liam said. 'What do you care?'

'Tell her,' Philip said. 'As hard as that will be for you both, it can't be as terrible as her finding out you've known all along. Please. Liam, look at me!'

Reluctantly, Liam looked at him. Philip was pulling up one trouser leg. There was an irregular blotch like a flattened pinkish leech on the pale skin near his shin.

'That's Kaposi's sarcoma,' Philip said. 'And it is a kind of cancer. They treat it with a drug that only weakens the immune system further. It's the nature of this awful thing. It's like a nightmare octopus that grows two tentacles to replace the one you cut off.

'What you've been telling people is a part of the truth. I won't ask you to change that story. But you must tell her!'

'I'll tell her what I want to,' Liam cried. 'And if you say one word to her – about the beach and all and me being there, I won't come here again. Never!'

'Can you tell me why?' his father pleaded.

Liam couldn't answer him. He didn't know why. He only knew that to tell his mother about the blond man was the worst thing he could think of except for an imagined scene that came to his mind from time to time – a scene in which he stood up in the school auditorium and announced to everyone that his father had become one of the statistics about AIDS written on the blackboard in the sex-education class.

'How come he isn't here?' Liam asked, his voice shaking with anger. How he hated it all! Grown-ups and their messes!

'He was,' his father answered in a low voice, almost a whisper. 'I took care of him until he went to the hospital to die.'

'That's why we didn't come to see you the first months you were here?'

His father nodded, not looking at him.

'And he's dead?'

'Yes. After a long time.'

Liam was silent a moment. A shameful gladness filled him. Good!

'That's who you meant when you said a friend had died,' he stated.

'Yes.'

'He died from what you've got,' Liam said.

'Don't be glad about anyone's death,' his father said sharply as though he'd read Liam's thoughts.

'I'm not,' Liam said. But he had been. He glanced around the room, thinking, *He* was here, sick, getting thinner like Daddy until finally he was too thin for living. A thought struck him. 'Would you have left us? Gone away with him if he hadn't died?' he asked.

'I don't know what I would have done,' his father replied slowly.

'Don't you know anything?'

'Each time I think that I do, find some knowledge I can grip and hold on to, it's a path opening into all that I don't know,' Philip said.

'Even that old woman, Motter . . . whatever . . . knows we aren't going to Ireland or anywhere else. You can't even feed the cat tonight! Don't talk to me about trips any more.'

'All right. I won't,' his father said.

Maybe Aunt Mary was right, Liam thought. The world

was a leaking sore, and you'd damn well better have your own towel!

When Luther or Delia asked how his father was, he'd answer, 'He's doing okay.' Sometimes he felt swollen with the lie.

He was thinking now of how it was with Delia when they could find a place, a time, to be alone. He thought of the breath-stopping weight of breast and bone against him. And at such a moment, he'd recall the long arm with its blond down, reaching out of the shadows of the dune to clasp his father's neck. He'd see the broken sticks of the eagle kite that he'd stamped into the sand. Then he'd let go of Delia, and he'd talk to her indifferently, as if she didn't matter to him.

He'd move far away from her into that world of cold talk about sex that went on in the boys' cloakroom at school. Or when they were all together, he and his friends, after classes, a small mob moving down the street, showing one another how much they knew, sneering at Harriet Varney, pregnant, famous in the sophomore class because of her huge belly, her grim-faced mother coming to get her every afternoon, laughing cruelly when nasty Eric Bleidel said, 'The barn door was locked after the whore got away.'

How superior they all felt! Kings of nothing! What if Liam had said on one of those afternoons when they bawled and shouted their way from school, scattering the grown-ups who passed by like scuffed pebbles, 'My father is a faggot!'?

He thought he would fall to the floor with the horror of the thought.

'Can't you say anything?' he asked, his voice trailing off.

For the second time that day, his father wept. As tears coursed down his gaunt face, he said, 'You lose your skin between yourself and the world when you're sick the way I am. There's nothing between you and it. I can say – are you ready for supper?'

Oh, God! thought Liam, staring at his father's face. He looks like an eagle . . . a sick eagle.

His father was fiddling with a string bean, turning it over and over with his fork. Liam, who had thought he had no appetite, had eaten everything, cold roast chicken, the bean salad, a thick chocolate brownie.

In Springton, Liam had wandered about the main street while Philip got their supper from the take-out bakery. There were a few stores, the pharmacy where Sig must have worked, a hardware centre, a dress shop in whose single display window a dusty wedding gown hung from the shoulders of a mannequin, some ramshackle houses, a small movie theatre with one poster advertising an old Disney movie, a seafood restaurant closed for the winter, and a dark narrow pizza place, in its gloomy depths a red neon sign flashing MEATBALLS!

Despite the mournful, half-deserted look of the street, the air was crisp and faintly salty. Liam thought of how it would look in summer, everything open and busy, people strolling with children. He felt he'd been let out of a locked, airless cellar for a little while.

He looked across at his father's nearly full plate.

'Aren't you going to eat any more?'

'I'll try,' Philip said. He gave a slight cough. A moment later, he was coughing convulsively. He staggered away from the table and stood in a corner of the cabin. Liam wanted to cover his ears.

The realization of his father's physical suffering entered his consciousness. Until that moment, everything about him, the leech-shaped mark on his leg, the slowness of his movements, had been simply more proof of his father's responsibility for the misery he had caused Liam and his mother.

'Can I do something? You want a glass of water?' he called out.

He thought he saw him shake his head. After another moment, the coughing ceased and Philip returned to the table. He ate one string bean, his face full of distaste.

'The body closes up like one of those sow bugs you find under a board,' he said. 'Its tiny legs fold in, and it turns into a dark grey ball. No room for food. I'm okay now. I want to say that I know we can't go to Ireland. It's been a wonderful story, a daydream I've been having.'

He took a crumpled pack of cigarettes from a shirt pocket and got up and opened the small window over the sink. He stood there blowing smoke out into the night. 'Maybe you can come down here for a few days during your spring break,' he said.

'That's months away,' Liam said. He regretted his words at once. They mustn't talk about 'months away'. But his father seemed not to have heard him.

'I may be stronger. We might drive south, perhaps to Cape May. Even to North Carolina. Julius likes the car. He sits in the back window and dozes. There are splendid beaches in the South.'

They wouldn't be able to go anywhere. Liam didn't want to say that, although the words seemed to press against his lips. He changed the subject.

'Grandpa called last week and I answered the phone. He was okay at first, then he said, "Who is this calling me?" '

'I'm glad his memory is shot,' his father said, his voice a little stronger now. 'He would have been so bewildered and frightened by what's happened to me. You know he was a mechanical engineer? Not only in his work. He insisted that all trouble was structural. When your grandma died twenty years ago, he shrank into himself. But he worked in a frenzy. I suppose he found comfort in the way things could fit one another and answer a purpose you could see right in front of you. But what you can do with engines you can't really do with living. My mother was sick for a long time. He couldn't solve that, though he felt he ought to be able to solve it. It's when he began to be forgetful.'

He had never spoken to Liam about his own father before. Liam strained to understand what he was being told about an old man he had liked but who always seemed to be thinking about something else, not the person standing in front of him. Now his grandpa couldn't think about anything much.

Philip turned on the tap to extinguish the cigarette. 'God! It tastes awful! I think I'll give it up.'

Things had changed again. Liam felt the difference in his legs and arms, all through his body; it was an ebbing away of raw strain.

'Will you clean up, please?' his father asked in the familiar, confident voice Liam had heard all his life, up until a year ago. 'I'll lie down for a while. I see the sky has cleared. We can go for a night walk.'

Liam carried plates to the sink. His father moved out of the way, saying, 'I'm glad you'll be here tonight. And there should be some compensation for you. You won't have to find Aunt Mary waiting behind the door to give you the third degree.'

He picked up the small plastic salt and pepper shakers

from the table and held them to his eyes as if they were binoculars. 'Wickedness is everywhere!' he said in a falsetto voice. 'That brother of mine . . .' He faltered, returned the shakers to the table. Somewhat reluctantly, he said, 'I'm not being fair.'

They looked at each other, both, perhaps, thinking about being fair, what it meant.

'When I was a little kid, I loved Mary so, my big good-looking sister who knew everything. She hasn't spoken to me since I became sick.'

Liam hadn't known that. He'd not given a thought to what went on between his father and his aunt, not even thought of them as brother and sister. They'd simply been there.

'She began to be disappointed so early.' His father frowned. 'Now she's stuck with the care of our old man. I can't lift a finger to help her.'

'Does she know about it? How you got sick?'

'Your mom wouldn't have told her. But Mary has antennae. She has suspicions. It's a matter of principle with her, to believe only her own explanations for whatever happens, in her family, in the world. I don't know what she knows – or guesses. I'm so sorry about her. About the two of us, more than ever now.

'We got lost in the woods once. Dad and Mother had taken us to a state park somewhere for a picnic. We wandered off. She's only five years older than I am. But she carried me on her back when I was too tired to walk. I guess she was about eight then. I can still feel it, her braid, my cheek resting against it, my legs hanging down her back. She must have been scared, but she was trying to keep me from being scared. Now I'm lost in the woods again – and she's so angry.'

Liam turned on the tap, holding a plate under the weak flow of tepid water. The sadness in his father's voice was hard to bear. He made himself think of something funny, that time when his father had removed Liam's little cap with the propeller on top of it that whirled when he moved, and put it on the head of Julius's predecessor, a large, solemn orange cat named Sweeney, who died some years past.

Liam smiled, visualizing a cat's indignation when it's made to wear human garments. He must have been about three. Mom was out somewhere. It had been he and his father, laughing together helplessly. He turned off the tap. The cabin was so silent. Did Brown's molecules sleep at times like everything else? His father was gripping the back of a chair. His hair was as thin as old Sig's.

'I could make you toast,' Liam said urgently, glancing at the barely touched food on his father's plate.

Philip raised his head. 'I haven't got a toaster,' he said, gently as though he were speaking to an infant. He smiled; his eyes seemed enormous to Liam, the way your own eyes feel when you look up at the sky.

'But thank you,' he said in a grave, formal voice. He made his way slowly towards his bed.

Who are you supposed to pity? The thousands drowned in a tidal wave in a far-off country you have trouble finding in an atlas? Children starving in places that have become deserts because rain has ceased to fall?

As Liam cleaned up the supper dishes, he thought about himself and Luther and pity. A week or so before, he and Luther had gone to a big record store on lower Broadway to see if they could get a videotape they both liked of a small new band called Slave Ship. Near the store entrance, a man was sitting on the sidewalk with a cigar box opened on his lap. His face and bare ankles were grimy with dirt.

For a second, Liam thought he was the beggar from the church. But it was someone else, much older. He paused. Luther grabbed his arm. 'Come on,' he said impatiently.

Liam had taken change from his pocket, and he dropped it in the box, which held a few coins, some of them pennies.

'What did you do that for?' Luther demanded as they entered the store.

Liam shrugged.

Luther didn't notice. 'He ought to get a job. Some of them make two hundred bucks a day,' he said.

'Maybe he can't get a job. He's old.'

'Yeah. Well, tough! There are plenty of jobs.'

'How do you know?' Liam asked.

'Because I know! I'm not feeling sorry for someone like that. What about people getting killed in earthquakes, that kind of stuff? It's not their fault. That guy screwed up his own life.'

In the record-store window stood a full-scale cardboard figure of Elvis Presley in a white satin suit trimmed with gold braid. HE'S BACK! said a sign at the foot of the figure.

'There's someone you've got to feel sorry for. Elvis had everything, and he lost it all.'

'Because of an earthquake?' Liam asked sarcastically.

Luther ignored his words. 'Look at this mob,' he said resentfully. 'We'll have to spend the whole day in line.'

'God! I hate Elvis Presley!' Liam exclaimed.

Luther laughed. 'Don't say that so loud, man. Around here, they'll tear your head off! Elvis is what they know!'

*

'You've already got on two sweaters and a jacket,' Liam observed.

'The outside of me gets very cold,' his father said.

Philip had rested an hour on his bed, his eyes closed, one thin hand upon his forehead. Liam had looked at the street map of Dublin without much interest and opened a few books of poetry. He didn't read in them.

They went outdoors. A streak of black cloud like a line of tar marked the horizon. Directly above, the stars were thick and brilliant.

'When I was lying down, you know what I was thinking about? How you keep things to yourself,' his father said. The silence all around them, the chill air like cold cloth, seemed a well into which his father's words fell, distinct, each one like a stone.

'I didn't know what you'd told her, what she knew,' Liam said. 'But one night I heard Mom say to you something about what you'd done to us. Everything was smoky. I couldn't figure it out. Then I'd stop thinking about it for days –' He fell silent.

'Then – you'd remember what you'd seen on the beach,' his father said.

'Yes. I'd sort of remember. When you were in the hospital this summer and you talked about the eagle you thought you'd seen from the window, or the falcon . . . whatever . . . I suddenly thought of that kite you gave me for my birthday.'

'What did you do with it? I wondered where it was when you came back to the cottage that day.'

'I broke it. I made a hole and buried the pieces in the sand,' Liam answered with a kind of ferocity. It wasn't directed towards his father. He felt clear and righteous as though, at last, he'd been able to claim a truth of his own, an action of his own. There was nothing murky about it.

'How did you put everything together?' his father asked sombrely.

'Maybe I wouldn't have. But you went away. Mom was so quiet. When we came here to see you, it was like there was an elephant in the room and you both acted as though it wasn't here. Everybody knows about AIDS now. How you can get it . . . all that. I've just listened to her lie – talk about a blood transfusion.'

His father's voice rose sharply. 'What's that scorn I hear in the way you're talking?'

'You people. You all lie. In the government, the police, the whole world, lying, lying . . .'

'You lied, too,' his father said. 'You lied by not saying what you suspected.'

Liam was silent. After a moment, he said, 'Are we going for a walk?' Trouble was coming back, a little lash of anger, like a wave breaking at his feet.

'The reason you know about everyone else telling lies is because of your own lies,' his father persisted. 'Do you want me to remind you of the whoppers you've told?'

'It's not the same!' Liam cried out at the injustice.

'Don't get mad. I know it's no way near the same. It's wrong to lie and people do it. It's a kind of choice human beings seem to be able to make even when they're little. Just don't let yourself off the hook.'

'Why didn't you tell me yourself? I had to try to figure things out all on my own,' Liam heard himself wail. It surprised him as much as it appeared to surprise his father, who froze into a statue.

Was there going to be another fight on the road? It was much too late to get a bus back to the city. Liam saw himself trying to sleep in a cold field.

The statue suddenly moved and held out both his hands. 'I didn't know how to tell you,' his father said. 'How could I explain what I didn't understand?' He began to walk towards the road.

'I've tried to find some part of me that isn't sick,' he went on. Liam caught up with him but kept a distance between them. He was stirred and frightened.

They gained the road, and as though they had reached a silent agreement, each went to an opposite side. There was no breeze. Starlight illuminated the dun-coloured autumn fields around them upon which fell the shadows of trees like reflections on the surface of a muddy lake.

'Sickness swallows you up,' Philip said. 'I keep trying to find a thing it can't touch. When I imagined going to Ireland with you, it was a wish to be as I once was.'

They walked along the road for a few minutes, not speaking. When his father spoke again, it was in the most dejected voice. 'I know we can't really go anywhere.'

Liam supposed he had thought being grown-up only meant doing whatever you wanted to do. The things children wanted to do were almost always what they weren't supposed to do. He had thought there was one world for grown-ups, a different one for children. He had thought grown-ups were never helpless.

The misery of the beggar had touched him lightly, not his heart but his curiosity, because he had the same sickness his father had.

Philip was still talking to him from across the road. He listened reluctantly.

'When you were little,' his father was saying, 'around four, I think, you asked me, "Do you know about the stars?" I said yes, I knew about them. You were lying on the floor, your chin propped up on a hand, and you asked me then, "What's behind them?" '

'What did you say?' Liam asked. He had always loved hearing about times when he was very young. Even now, when his head was so heavy, his brain so cloudy and confused, he felt the familiar love of hearing his own history. It was as though he could visit his earlier self and feel what he had felt then.

'I told you that nobody was certain. That scientists, astrophysicists, had ideas about it.'

'That would have cleared it all up,' Liam said.

His father laughed. 'That's my boy,' he said softly.

'We've been reading about the universe in school,' Liam said.

'And now do you know what's behind the stars?'

'Infinity. The universe is supposed to be growing all the time.'

Now his father burst into laughter. 'Listen to this,' he said in the buoyant tones Liam had all but forgotten, it was so long since he'd heard them. 'I read in the paper last week that there'd been a supernova explosion that happened fifteen million years ago, but the light from it only reached the earth on Saturday. *Saturday!*' his father shouted into the night. 'Poor little earth and its tiny weekdays. Fifteen million years ago!'

He laughed again. Liam, glancing at him, had a fleeting impression that he was strong, that he had been almost restored.

Energy is like a flame, he thought, and even as he said this to himself, his father seemed to be extinguished, to become insubstantial like a shadow.

'Do you believe in God?' Liam asked him suddenly.

'Yes,' his father said. Liam was astonished for some reason. He waited for an explanation, for some of the things he'd heard other people say – that God was nature or a universal force or an invisible presence in all life.

His father said, 'A Scots philosopher, Hume, I think, said we can't know.'

'How can you believe in something you can't know?' Liam asked.

'It's done all the time,' his father replied. Liam thought he heard a note of mockery.

'You're laughing at me,' he said.

'Oh, no! Not at you. Never at you!'

They stood still, looking at each other. Though they had both spoken with strong feeling, they had kept their voices low. There was something about night in the country that made you feel like whispering.

He observed that his father had his hands in his pockets just as he had. He felt the increasing chill in the air. The branches of a nearby maple looked like a chart of bones, one of those Liam had seen in the medical encyclopaedia.

'Have you called me a queer to yourself?' his father asked almost lightly.

'I hate that!' Liam flashed out.

'It's only another word for what isn't understood.'

'Can you say how it was? What it was?' Liam asked. He heard a tremor in his voice. Did he really want to know? It was more as if he had to.

'It breaks over you like a huge wave,' his father said. 'You go under. Some people swim out of the wave. I couldn't. It wounded your mother dreadfully. Some-times it was worse for her – about Geoff – than the fact of my sickness. She felt I had chosen someone over her. No. That I'd chosen a man over her. But I think it's different now for her. She's had to go through so much.

'I'm not sure of anything, Liam, except that you're here, and I'm glad for that.'

Liam could see his father shivering. And his breath, as he spoke, was uneven, as though he'd been running for miles.

'We'd better go back,' Liam said.

He turned towards the cabin. When he glanced over his shoulder, he saw Philip following him almost meekly.

They hadn't fought after all. There was some comfort in that. It was as though, finally, they had entered an empty room from which all the old things had been removed so that there was nothing left except bare floor and walls.

Imagining that room, Liam began to put things in it, a poster of a mountain range in Alaska, a big table upon which he could place books and paper and pencils, a chair he could sit on, a good radio, shortwave maybe, a photograph of Delia, her head turned in such a way that her dark hair fell against one cheek.

They were going down the slope to the cabin door when his father spoke. 'About the stars. Did you know it's really true – that the light we see is from the past? That when we look up at the sky, all we can see happened millions of years ago? That it took all that unimaginable time for the light we can see now to reach us? It's all in the past. It's all over.'

The cabin had no shades. The moon had risen and pools of light lay upon the dusty floor. Liam had been listening to his father's breathing from across the room. He slipped out from under his blanket on the sofa bed and went to the other bed. Julius was lying curled at its foot.

Liam stood motionless, looking down at one of the two most familiar faces of his life, its features sharpened by illness, softened by moonlight.

He thought of the invisible pores of flesh, the caverns of ears and nostrils, the complex, intricate mesh of bone and socket. He thought of entering human bodies.

Language, the capacity to speak, was in a person from the very beginning. Somehow, you knew about what bodies could do, too. Your own body told you. What you did to it and with it told you.

In the classroom with the jolly teacher, even as she wrote out the information, the warning words that appeared so quickly on the blackboard – *blood, bodily fluids, needles* – it met some knowledge that was already in you, that uncurled like a blossoming leaf.

There was the laughter, too, and the rough stuff. Sex was comical even as it was thrilling. And no matter what you knew about it, there was always much you didn't know.

He and Luther, hee-hawing like donkeys . . . Luther saying something like, 'Bottle up! Keep those bodily fluids to yourself, boy!'

But all that was funny faded away when Liam glanced at Delia, sitting at her desk. She might turn her head briefly towards him. He would see, and feel like a knife thrust into his belly, the way her eyes were set so deeply in their sockets, see the high cheekbones, the sudden downward sweep of her thick, rather short eyelashes, the puffy upper lip drawn over the lower lip, even the down on her arm. His gut would sink. He could feel it even now as he stood in the cold cabin.

He wanted to touch his father. Even more, he wanted to crawl under the blankets with him as he had years ago when he was little. Tentatively, lightly, so as not to awaken him, he touched his father's shoulder beneath the blanket with a finger, let it rest there a second.

He gazed at a window. The moon appeared to hold still against the glass. But, of course, it was moving. Everything, the earth, the universe, was moving all the time. The light that glimmered on his father's face had travelled ninety-three million miles.

As he stared down, shadows moved slowly across the blade of his father's nose, across his sallow, sunken cheeks, until, at last, only one ear showed, perfect, pale, like a seashell bleached white by waves over thousands of years.

FOUR

The Plague

Let's skip a Christmas visit. You know it's not because
I don't want to see you. I'm studying health. It takes all
my strength. No presents wanted or needed. I won't be
lonely – I have so much to do. I asked Mom to get you
something you've wanted, I think. I'm concentrating
on March, when you can spend a few days with me.
I'm making plans! Love, Daddy

This note to Liam came a week or so before Christmas.
His mother handed the envelope to him with a preoccupied frown as though she were thinking of something else. He did not quite believe that look of hers. But
he did not want to show the note to her. She had already
told him Philip wanted to be alone this Christmas. When
she said it, Liam sensed she thought it had something to
do with her. He knew it didn't.

It was the first written message Liam had received from
his father from the outside – from the world beyond
home. He was startled as he looked at the firmly written
words. He read the note often during the day, in his
room, in the kitchen while he was eating an apple, going
down in the elevator. He knew what the words meant: *I
have so much to do.*

His father was doing something when he sat in the
wicker chair, his head against the backrest. He *was*
concentrating, trying to get better in his body.

The knowledge of his father's struggle was new to Liam, like the handwriting in the note. It was after he had come home from his visit to Springton that he'd realized Philip was not idle, that it was the life in him that reached out to take hold of the big cat, that reached for books on Ireland. He was in a battle against what was trying to kill him.

He had bought his father a present. One afternoon just before school closed for the holidays, he discovered a bookstore that specialized in foreign books. He had found a collection of Irish folk-tales. On one side of each page, the text was in Gaelic; on the other, in English translation. As the clerk wrapped the book, Liam imagined how his father would smile when he unwrapped it. He would take it to him in January, when the holidays were over.

Aunt Mary had returned. Seeing her so soon after Thanksgiving made it seem she was living in the apartment. When his mother said, 'Philip wants to be by himself,' Aunt Mary made no comment.

But she had plenty of comments about other things. Where was the Christmas tree? The good ones would have been bought by now. Why hadn't Liam cleaned his closet in two hundred years? Why didn't he have writing assignments to take to school in January? His teachers must be lazy. Liam spent too much time on the telephone. His friend, Luther, had the manners of a lout – he hadn't stood up when she came into the living room while he was visiting Liam. Why shouldn't they have turkey for Christmas dinner? What was wrong with turkey?

At their mealtimes, she complained about what she called 'consumerism'. 'Buy! Buy! Buy!' she exclaimed. 'Nobody knows what Christmas is about any more.'

'It's about charity and hope, too,' his mother said on one such occasion. His aunt raged on as though she hadn't heard.

She's like a car whose brakes are shot, Liam thought to himself. He began to watch her with a certain interest.

'How's Grandpa?' he asked once.

'You have no idea what I have to put up with,' she replied. 'Wait till you grow up and have responsibilities!'

Before he had thought, the words were out of his mouth. 'I won't be able to take care of my father when he's old,' he said.

She sagged in her chair and said no more.

On a corner a few blocks from the apartment, Christmas trees huddled together as though terrified by the wild howls of music that issued from a boom box on the sidewalk. The men who sold the trees warmed their hands over a fire in a steel drum, darted to customers, then back to the warmth.

Liam and his mother picked out a small pine tree and carried it home. 'What a runt,' Aunt Mary said, poking her head out of the kitchen. The old box of decorations Liam had seen every Christmas as far back as he could remember was on the sofa. Liam found a snapshot in it of himself when he was in nursery school. There were little paper angel wings pasted to his shoulders. Who was he then? Were you only one person? Or were you different people who became one person at some point when you were grown-up?

'We'll decorate the tree tonight,' Aunt Mary said.

'We'll do it now, Mary,' his mother said pleasantly as if she were commenting on the weather. There was no answer from the kitchen.

As Liam separated the strands of tinsel, he remembered

how Daddy had stopped him from tossing handfuls of it on the branches of a tree. 'When you put each one on a branch, you have to think first about where it should go. It looks very different than if you've just got rid of it all, higgledy-piggledy, so you can get at the presents,' he'd told him.

Liam smiled now as he hung a small wooden Santa Claus on a branch. His mother was testing the strings of Christmas lights, whose wires were tangled on the floor like sleeping snakes. She must have seen him smile.

'What's so funny? What are you thinking about?' she asked.

'Something Daddy said once.'

She replaced one of the dead green bulbs that were supposed to look like pine cones. 'I think of things Daddy would say,' she said.

Last Christmas, Daddy had not been with them. But he hadn't been alone. He had been taking care of the blond man, Geoff. Had there been a tree in the Springton cabin? Liam felt a powerful impulse to say out loud what he was thinking about.

At that moment his mother plugged in the socket and the twisted lines of lights went on, green and yellow, red and blue.

'It's nearly the best moment of Christmas. When you've tested the lights and they actually work,' she said. He felt weak with relief that he had not spoken of his thoughts. He had come close to some danger; he had passed it, but it left a chill, and the living room, with its familiar, somewhat shabby, furnishings, seemed a place he didn't know. Still, it was better in a way than last Christmas, when he'd felt he and his mother might suddenly throw tree and presents out the window.

You could get used to nearly anything, he thought.

'Maybe we should leave the lights on the floor,' he said.

'No, we won't do that,' his mother said as though he had made a serious suggestion. 'But let's skip the stuff that's supposed to be a carpet of grass.'

'Okay,' he said.

When they'd finished decorating the tree, his mother went into her bedroom and returned shortly, carrying wrapped presents. Most of them, he noted, were for him. He wasn't much interested. It was strange not to really want anything.

'You had a letter from Daddy,' she said. 'He must have explained why he didn't want us to visit him. He was never crazy about Christmas, and now . . .' She fell silent. There was a blank look on her face. He knew that look – she was feeling something she didn't want him to know. He stifled an impulse to tell her that in hiding what she was feeling, she *was* telling him something.

She began to speak again with a kind of brightness he didn't like. 'We'll go down to Springton in a few days, shall we? When Aunt Mary goes home.'

As though summoned, Aunt Mary came to the kitchen door, drying her hands on a towel.

'Poor Father,' she said, sighing. 'Of course, he doesn't know it's Christmas. But still . . . Well. The tree looks all right. I'm sure it's more than most people have.'

'Most people don't celebrate Christmas,' Liam said with a touch of sarcasm.

'I was hardly referring to China and Pakistan and such places,' Aunt Mary snapped.

His father's present to Liam was a shortwave radio. Mom had got him a few tapes, including a video of the group

64

Slave Ship, which he and Luther had not been able to find that day at the record shop, four sea stories by a writer named Patrick O'Brian, and two flannel shirts.

Aunt Mary picked up the video and turned it around in her hands. 'I suppose this is one of those songs that tell you to go out and shoot everybody in sight.'

'It's rock, not rap,' he said.

Her present to him – she must have found it in a store in ogre-land – was the thickest, woolliest, ugliest sweater he had ever seen. She insisted he try it on for size. 'Perfect fit!' she said triumphantly as he pulled it over his head. He felt he'd instantly joined an order of monks devoted to itchiness and slow suffocation.

For a while during the long afternoon, after presents were opened and dinner was eaten, Liam fiddled with the shortwave bands on his new radio. He heard and was absorbed by jazz music from Jerusalem, a British news broadcast, and voices speaking in languages he didn't recognize. As the day darkened, as evening fell, he went to stand idly at the living room window. In other apartments across the street, he saw the flickering lights of Christmas trees, hills of bright crumpled wrapping paper. But the rooms appeared empty of people. He felt dull and tired.

His mother called to him. 'I've got Daddy on the phone. He wants to speak to you.'

Aunt Mary was looking through a book of quilts Mom had given her and sat only a few feet from the phone. Liam took it as far away as the cord would reach.

'Hello, Daddy.'

'Liam, dear,' said the faint voice. 'Has it been all right? The day?'

Liam wanted to say, Not without you. 'It's been okay.'

'Did you reach paradise on your new radio?'

'Just England and Israel . . . a few other places.'

'We'll have to settle for those places then . . . I can't talk for long, although I'd like to.'

'Is it bad?' Liam whispered urgently.

'A little setback,' said his father, so weakly, Liam pressed the phone against his ear. 'Goodbye, my duck.' There was a click. Liam waited for the dial tone and hung up. He went to his room as Aunt Mary said, 'He didn't want to talk to me . . . Afraid I'd tell him about our father.'

Liam turned to her from his doorway. 'You could have asked to talk to him,' he said.

'Did he ask for me in the normal, civil way a brother should?'

Liam slowly closed his door, hoping she would not hear the click of the latch.

But he could still hear her, reciting the list of her trials. 'My father, for whom I am entirely responsible . . . late papers handed in by totally insufficient students . . . the house that the nurse is far too superior to even dust . . .'

She was leaving on the twenty-seventh. It was something to look forward to. She had never been so cross and disagreeable, even when Liam had come home the day after Thanksgiving and she had followed him from room to room, carrying most of a pecan pie, which, she insisted, he should eat out of courtesy to her, who had made it especially for him.

The day after Christmas, as the three of them ate breakfast, his mother told Aunt Mary she was taking Liam to a winter jacket sale at Macy's. It was news to him.

'I'll enjoy a few hours alone,' Aunt Mary remarked.

'But I'll put it to use and clean out your fridge. There isn't room for a grape. Liam's old jacket looks fine to me.'

'I suppose it does,' his mother said vaguely, taking the dishes to the sink.

They left a few minutes later. As soon as they were on the sidewalk, walking towards the subway, Mom said, 'We've been sprung. She's going tomorrow, thank heavens!'

'Why won't she speak to Daddy?'

She said nothing. He took hold of her arm. 'Mom?'

She handed him a subway token. 'I don't know why really. I've asked her to write to him. I don't think she has. Not that she'd tell me.'

They had reached the subway entrance. 'I hate her for it,' she said fiercely. A second later, she cried, 'I'm sorry, I shouldn't have said that!'

'Move on, folks,' said a man behind them.

Katherine Cormac grabbed the railing by the stairs that led downwards. The man hustled by, muttering something. As they descended into an unpleasant warmth smelling of cement and metal, his mother said, 'She's not dumb. She knows how impossible she makes herself. And it's real and constant, you know, her responsibility for Grandpa. We've all been shattered by what's happened. It's terrible for you. I'm ashamed I can't seem to talk about it more —' Her voice seemed to plead.

They went through the turnstile as their train pulled into the station. Liam said nothing, and once they were standing in the crowded car, there was no use in trying to talk. What could he have said anyhow? He glanced at his mother; she was holding on to a strap, her face turned upwards, her lips moving as though she were continuing the conversation silently.

The relief he had felt getting out of the apartment, and the anticipation of spending some time with his mother, faded as soon as they went into the store. It was a madhouse of shoppers, shoving and elbowing one another around the counters. There actually was a jacket sale, but neither Liam nor his mother lifted a single one from the racks. They looked at each other. His mother shrugged, smiled. 'Well, it was an excuse to get away,' she said. 'Your old jacket looks fine.'

He was standing beside her. Past the people who milled close by, he glimpsed a long mirror in which the two of them were reflected. He was at least two inches taller than his mother. A strange thought came to him – that the tall, very young man in the mirror was actually his own father, that he, Liam, hadn't been born yet, that everything that was to happen was contained in this moment like a seed in a pod. He felt dizzy. His mother gripped his arm firmly. 'I think you need lunch,' she said.

They ate tacos, standing up at a round counter. Afterwards, they walked along Sixth Avenue until the raw wind drove them into a subway station. He was glad Christmas was over.

Aunt Mary announced as they came in that she had made a chicken salad for supper. She hoped that would do. Later, Liam went into the kitchen to get a glass of orange juice. Aunt Mary was setting the table. He watched her. In her busyness, she seemed unaware of his scrutiny.

Her mouth, so often tight with resentment, was relaxed. His father had said she was good-looking. Her dark hair was lustrous and thick and bound around her head. A few tendrils escaped from the black hairpins he had first noticed when he was small and had asked his father if she'd been born wearing them. He remembered his father laughing as he said, 'I hope not!' Her eyes were like her brother's. And she had his eagle nose. He had not realized until that moment how much she resembled Philip.

She looked up at him suddenly. She must have realized he had been observing her. She smiled so faintly, Liam wasn't sure it was a smile.

'Looking over the ruins?' she asked amiably.

'You're not a ruin,' he replied. Hope touched him lightly like a leaf. She looked so much like Daddy. Perhaps they were alike in other ways, too, ways he didn't know about. He felt a longing for friendliness from her. From the strain in his shoulders, he realized he was leaning towards her.

'What would you know about ruins?' she said brusquely, and turned to the sink to fill glasses with water.

There was little conversation at supper. Aunt Mary asked without interest if they had found a jacket for Liam, and when Mom said no, she remarked that you never could find much at sales.

After supper, the three of them watched an old movie adapted from *A Christmas Carol* by Charles Dickens.

'Tiny Tim is really too much,' Aunt Mary muttered. Liam had seen the movie so many times, his attention drifted away. The actors were buried in their costumes. Only their heads and their faces, which seemed to have been fashioned out of grey clay, suggested there might be living flesh inside the dark frock coats and huge scarves.

Suddenly, as though imposed on the screen, Liam saw naked bodies entwined like the muscular, snaky limbs of a wisteria. He put his hand over his face. He hardly breathed until he heard the click of the television remote. His mother pulled at his hand. He looked at her blankly.

'Are you all right?' she asked.

He nodded. It seemed to him that at that moment they were inside the same thought, that she had seen into the picture in his head, that it was in hers, too.

'Oh – I forgot,' Aunt Mary was saying. 'There was a phone call.' She was removing cushions from the sofa bed in an alcove in the living room where she slept when she visited.

'What phone call?' his mother asked.

Aunt Mary yawned. 'It was when you were out. Some person named Sig. She said my brother had to go to the hospital again.'

'Mary! My God! Philip doesn't go to the hospital just to get a pill! How could you not tell us! Liam, go get the address book on my night table.'

'He's always going to the hospital,' Aunt Mary said resentfully.

Liam stood next to his mother when she called the Springton hospital. His hands were damp. He heard the squeaking of the sofa bed as it was extended on its metal legs. Mom was bent over the phone, and he couldn't see her face. Her arm was trembling.

She spoke, she listened. Aunt Mary smoothed down her sheets. Mom made two more calls, one to the bus company, the second to the Summer Dreams motel, where she made a reservation for three rooms. She hung up and turned to Liam. Her eyes were wide, staring. 'There are no more buses tonight,' she said. 'We'll go down in the morning. Pack a few things. He's very sick. It's bad.'

'What about me?' asked Aunt Mary.

'I made a reservation for you. But do as you like. Liam, we'll have to get up at five.'

Liam knew it was coming. He felt it as a gathering darkness around their small family. He imagined Julius alone in the dark cabin. But Sig would have taken the cat.

His mother asked him, 'Do you know who Sig is?'

'An old woman down there,' he answered. 'She helps him.'

His mother put her hands over her face as Aunt Mary went, very quietly, to the bathroom and closed the door.

Aunt Mary went with them. There was no conversation in the taxi to the Port Authority or on the two-hour bus trip.

They were each locked into themselves, Liam thought. He felt he was a twig being carried on a fast-moving stream. Perhaps that was why the trip seemed the shortest he had taken to Springton.

They walked from the bus station to the small motel. Only two cars were in the parking lot. A red neon sign, raised over the entrance to the motel office, flashed the name, SUMMER DREAMS. The sign was like a swollen vein pulsating in the oyster grey light of this early hour.

Liam's room was next to his mother's. He didn't see where his aunt went. The room had a smell that was both clean and stale. Until he turned on a light, it had the aspect of a warehouse, perhaps because the furniture was so big. A television set sat on the bureau, and he turned it on. At the sound of a loud hectic voice, talking about some food product, he turned it off. The huge bed was covered with a spread the colour and texture of dried oatmeal. In the bathroom, the toilet seat had a plastic cover powdered with dust. A small bar of soap was stuck to the floor of the shower. Liam put all his clothes in one drawer and one of the novels his mother had given him for Christmas on the bedside table.

Christmas felt far in the past. He was barely thinking of what might lie ahead. He noticed things and didn't reflect upon them.

There was a knock on the door. He opened it and his mother stood there, her skin ashen, her mouth tight.

'I won't forgive her for this,' she said, looking over his shoulder as though she spoke to a person lurking in the dim interior of the room. 'To not tell us that someone had phoned! I hadn't guessed at how angry she is.'

Liam hadn't guessed at how angry his mother was. He was suddenly frightened. Her eyes focused on him. 'We'll go to the hospital now,' she said.

As she spoke, Aunt Mary, who must have approached them on tiptoe, said in a low voice, 'I'll come, too.'

They walked silently to the hospital six blocks away, on a narrow road parallel to the main street Liam could glimpse through the backyards of the houses. It had been only a few weeks ago that he had looked into stores on that street while his father picked up their supper at the take-out bakery. The line between *then* and *now* had vanished. Time made no sense to Liam.

Two cars were parked in the space reserved for doctors. In the hospital, a receptionist sat at the information desk in front of a switchboard. A large fake plant stood next to a stand upon which rested a few paper plates holding muffins wrapped in plastic. Looking at them, Liam wondered if the muffins were plastic, too.

Breakfast had been hurried. The three of them had stood in the kitchen, eating what they could find. But Liam had no appetite. He felt hollowed out. He heard his mother asking for a Dr Parikh at the reception desk. Aunt Mary had gone to the large window near the entrance doors. There wasn't much for her to look at except a squat wooden house with a lopsided FOR SALE sign nailed to the front door.

'Go sit, Liam,' his mother ordered him in a sharp voice. 'We'll talk to the doctor before we go up.' She waved towards several chairs grouped around a table. A few torn medical journals lay upon it.

A large woman carrying an infant came into the lobby and walked purposefully to a door, which she pushed open with a grunt. The infant let out a thin cry. Then the quiet returned until a short man in a white coat stepped out of an elevator.

'Mrs Cormac?' he asked, looking from Aunt Mary to Liam's mother.

His mother stood up. 'I'm Mrs Cormac,' she said. She put her hand over her mouth as though she feared she'd spoken too loudly.

'I'm Dr Parikh,' he said. He had delicate features, and his eyes were deep-set and dark. A stern haircut had shaped his hair into a black cap. His fingers were long and thin and browner than his face.

He glanced briefly at Liam. When he spoke, his voice was faintly accented. Words seemed to curl out of his mouth.

'Your husband is very sick,' he said. 'We've been treating the lymphoma with chemotherapy. But it has advanced. It's in his liver, his lungs. You must be prepared. He's not always conscious. We are doing what we can to make him comfortable.'

Aunt Mary had turned away from the window. She stared at the doctor. Her hands were tightly gripped beneath her chest as though she were secretly trying to tear something, cloth or heavy paper.

'I didn't know he had lymphoma,' Katherine Cormac said. She seemed to shrink away from the doctor. Liam thought he'd gone deaf. He didn't know what lymphoma was, yet the word filled his ears like a soft poisonous wax. He followed the doctor and his aunt and mother into the elevator, which rose slowly, with much creaking, to the second floor, where they got off. The doctor preceded them down a silent corridor.

Liam knew his hearing had come back when he heard Aunt Mary whisper to his mother, 'Where do they get these Indian doctors?'

'From India,' his mother said flatly.

Dr Parikh paused before a door. He looked directly at Liam. 'Talk to him,' he said. 'Talk as if he can hear every word you say. I'll be back later.' He pushed open the door. Katherine Cormac went in, and Liam followed her.

'I'll wait out here a few minutes,' Aunt Mary muttered.

A nurse stood in front of a window. The light was behind her so that Liam couldn't see her face. She came towards them, and he had to turn to the narrow hospital bed.

Philip Cormac looked like an inert, withered child. A tube led from his left arm up and over a metal bar on a stand to connect with a large plastic bag containing liquid. Another tube came from beneath a white coverlet and emptied into another bag half full of a cloudy yellow water. He heard his mother groan. Or was it he himself who groaned?

They stood next to the bed and looked down at his father. His eyes were closed. His mouth was slightly open, the lips like two lines of dusty chalk. They could hear his slow uneven breathing. His skin was blotched and flaking.

'Philip . . . Philip . . .' his mother called softly.

'Daddy,' whispered Liam. His father's eyelids twitched. The chalky lips moved slightly. One eye opened, then the other, very slowly like tiny crinkled shades pulled up by an unsteady hand.

'Hello,' he said so faintly it was like thin paper, or a dry leaf, rustling.

Liam and his mother stooped over him at once, both of them listening intently as though more words would follow, as though everything would be made clear now, that, at last, they would understand what had happened to him.

Philip's lids closed again. For a while, they stood there, watching him.

When Aunt Mary entered the room half an hour or so later, she stayed close to the door. She was silent as she stared at her brother. After a few minutes, she left. The nurse was in and out of the room, her hands busy with small quick movements as she checked the valves on the tubes, touched Philip's wrist and his forehead. Once, she took hold of one foot and held it in her hand.

She had a stern, sad face. When she looked at Liam, she did not smile. Unexpectedly, she reached out and took his hand as she had taken hold of his father's foot and held it in a firm clasp for a second.

Philip, like a rudderless boat, drifted in and out of consciousness. Once he murmured, 'So dry.' Liam's mother held a glass with a bent straw to his mouth. He turned his head away, frowning. She went out of the room then and was gone for half an hour. When she returned, she was holding a bag of green grapes.

She held one against his lips. 'Can't,' he muttered. She put the grape into her mouth and pulled the skin off with her teeth. With two fingers, she pressed the pulp against Philip's lips. It slid down his chin. She skinned another grape. This time she kept it between her teeth, bent, and pressed her mouth against Philip's. His whole body seemed to strain as he took the grape pulp into his own mouth.

Dr Parikh came from time to time. Aunt Mary remained outside the room, going from window to window. Liam wandered down the corridor, glimpsing at patients through half-open doors. He saw a woman with her plaster-covered leg in traction; a very old man, hunched on the edge of his bed, his head bowed; and other patients lying motionless in their beds. He went down to the lobby and discovered Mrs Mottley sitting on a chair, her coat buttoned to her chin. She nodded when she saw him. 'I thought I'd come by,' she said.

'You could come up to see him,' Liam said.

'I'll just sit here a while,' she said.

'He's dying,' Liam said.

'I know,' she said. 'The plague has taken him.'

He thought of the beggar on the church steps, the boy whose house had been burned down, his father. 'There are so many who –' He couldn't finish his sentence.

'Yes. Thousands upon thousands,' she said. She touched his arm briefly. 'I've got Julius. He doesn't like the other cats, but he's taken a shine to an old Labrador. They sleep together. It's a sight.'

He had forgotten Julius.

'I'd better go back,' he said.

'Yes,' she agreed. 'I expect he knows when you're there.'

When he was in the room with his father and mother, time stopped. When he went to the bathroom, or looked through the local newspaper in the small waiting room on the second floor, or walked up and down the corridor, passing his aunt without a word exchanged, it dragged interminably.

'I noticed a pizza place when I went to get the grapes,' his mother said to him as dusk began to fall. 'Go and get yourself some supper there.'

'What about you?'

'I'll get a sandwich or something later. I can't leave now.'

'Can't I bring you something?' he asked. She shook her head.

In the pizza place he had seen a few weeks ago, where the sign flashed MEATBALLS! he ate half a pizza. The waiter, a boy not much older than he was, said, 'Pretty dead around here this time of year.' His voice held an inquiry.

The word *dead* stood out like a boulder in a stream. Liam paid for his pizza and ran back to the hospital. The small building was lit up by now. People milled around the lobby, waiting for the evening visiting hours to begin. He took the stairs, two at a time.

There was a different nurse in his father's room, her fingers on Philip's wrist. His mother was sitting in a chair next to the bed.

'Did you get something to eat?' she asked in a low voice.

He nodded. The nurse looked at him blankly before she left. She was young, with a small pouty face beneath her frilled cap.

'I didn't see Aunt Mary,' he whispered.

'She's gone back to the motel to rest,' his mother said.

He looked at the bed. His father's eyes were half-open. His fingers plucked at the coverlet.

'Daddy?'

'Are you okay?' his father asked in a voice so cracked and small, Liam wasn't sure if that was what he had really said.

'I'm okay,' he answered.

Philip's eyes closed. The hand that was free fell slowly from his thigh. The fingers of his other hand, which was held rigid by the needle from the tube, continued to work at the coverlet.

Liam looked at his mother. Their gaze held for a minute. She smiled very faintly as though she saw him from a long distance away. 'It'll be soon,' she said.

He left the room, went to the bathroom, to the waiting room, back to his father's door, where a small card read *Philip Cormac*. Minutes passed, or hours. A young woman pushed a cart past him, holding emptied supper trays. The pouty nurse sat at the nurses' desk, reading a magazine. The old man he had noticed earlier lay groaning in his bed. In one room, he glimpsed the sludge grey light of a small television set with the sound turned off.

A few minutes after a large clock on a wall near the bathroom read ten o'clock, Aunt Mary stepped from the elevator. Liam was standing next to the door of Philip's room. She touched his shoulder.

'Is he still alive?' she asked.

Liam didn't answer. He went inside. His mother lay back in the chair, her eyes closed. He looked at his father. His face was swollen. He bent over him, hearing a thin whistle of air.

He went back into the corridor. Aunt Mary was leaning against the wall. Tears ran down her face, like a thin rain falling on a rock.

It had grown quiet in the hospital. How old was his father? he asked himself in sudden panic. When was his birthday? He couldn't remember.

'How old is he?' he asked his aunt.

'Thirty-eight,' she said, and covered her face. Liam noticed a small ring on her finger. The stone it held suddenly flashed, and he turned to see a light go on over his father's room. A nurse went in. He followed her.

His mother and the nurse stood close to the bed. His mother looked up at him. She was holding his father's hand in both of hers. As she gazed steadily at Liam, she placed the hand carefully on the coverlet. She walked to Liam and put her arms around him.

'He's gone,' she said into his ear. He looked over her shoulder at the bed, at a body that was utterly still. He couldn't bear the weight of his mother's arms. He moved slowly from her embrace. He remembered it was Saturday.

Saturday, a name for a day. It blew away like a wisp of paper in a flame and disappeared.

Suddenly the room was filled with people, two nurses, Dr Parikh, and Aunt Mary, her tears dried. Liam went out to the corridor. It felt different to walk there. He wanted to be outside the hospital. He felt strong enough to walk miles.

He was filled with relief. The year was gone, lifted from his back like a boulder he had been carrying. He wanted to leave Springton at once, to be back in the city, to see Luther and Delia. School was little more than a week away. He had things to do.

He went to the big window at the end of the corridor. Although the sky was black, the light outside held a faint luminous shine. He saw trees, a few houses, the amber glow of a street lamp, a car moving slowly. He realized with surprise, as though he'd forgotten all about seasons and weather, that it was snowing.

As he pressed his face against the cold glass and heard the tick of snowflakes, he began to cry.

Ordinary, familiar time resumed like a clock that had been rewound. One thing followed another. Aunt Mary, after making a phone call to her home and then to Pennsylvania Station in New York, said she'd have to leave them as soon as they returned to the city. The nurse she'd left in charge of Grandpa had a family emergency and couldn't stay on after tonight.

Liam and his mother found Mrs Mottley still sitting in the hospital lobby. When Liam told her his father was dead, she stood up. 'Free of suffering' was all she said. She drove them to the cabin in her rattling old car.

On the round table in the chilly dusty-smelling room, Katherine found a note written in pencil on a page of Philip's sketch pad.

She and Liam read it together silently.

Dear Katherine, dear Liam, Cremation for me as we've always agreed. No funeral. Sig will keep the cat and return a few books to the library for me. Please give her whatever she can use for herself or others. My two dears. There's hardly anything left of me. I'm glad to let go of that little bit. Not frightened at all. Tired.

Katherine and Sig made small piles of clothes and dishes and books, a few groceries. Liam swept the floor with a worn broom. After they'd done their work in the cabin, Sig drove them to the motel.

Mom took Sig's hand in her own. 'I don't know how to thank you,' she said.

'Then don't,' Sig said. 'I liked your husband, Mrs Cormac.'

They returned to the city. Aunt Mary left them at the bus station to go and catch her train home.

The next evening when Liam answered the phone, an agitated old voice spoke into his ear, 'Can you tell me what's happened to my son? Who is this? Mary is keeping something from me.' The voice rose to a cry. 'Everything is kept from me!'

'Grandpa,' Liam said. His mother came to the bedroom door.

'Is it Liam?' the voice quavered. 'You'll tell me, won't you?'

He looked helplessly at Mom.

'Liam?'

'Grandpa, he was very sick.'

'Lord,' said his grandfather. 'Oh, oh, he's dead. Awful! That I should live —'

Suddenly Aunt Mary's voice came loudly over the phone. 'Katherine, for heaven's sake —'

'It's Liam.'

'Why did you tell him?'

He heard sobbing in the background. 'Poppa, sit down!' his aunt called out.

'He seemed to know,' Liam said.

'He certainly does now!' she said. 'Well, the damage is done. All I can hope for is that he won't remember in the morning.' She hung up abruptly.

'But he *did* know something,' Liam said to his mother.

'You did right,' she said firmly. 'No matter what kind of a haze he lives in, he would have sensed it. In her own indirect way, she must have told him something – though she'd never admit to that. You told him what he needed to know. Now. It doesn't matter if he forgets it.'

But later, Liam cried in his room. Why had he told Grandpa? Whatever his mother said, he'd made trouble. Would life ever get better? Would there come a time when his thoughts would be clear and simple, when this awful tangled mess of feeling would go away?

Two days later, some friends of the Cormacs gathered in the apartment. Aunt Mary had managed to find a student to stay with Grandpa, and she came, too. What Liam recalled later was the moment when one of her black hairpins fell on the cold salmon lying in a platter on the table. He saw his mother carefully lift it off. And in the kitchen, his aunt had looked at him almost triumphantly. 'Father forgot,' she said.

People spoke to him gently. He must have talked to some of them. He didn't know what he'd said. There was some laughter, some conversation. His mother was pale. She looked calm, but she seemed to have to sit down frequently. Afterwards, when the guests left, Aunt Mary washed dishes in the kitchen. As Liam and his mother returned chairs and tables to their accustomed places, they were both transfixed by her loud cry, 'Oh, God! It's over!'

The night before school began again, Liam lay sleepless in his bed. He imagined his father's hands. He thought of ash, of dust, and of something less visible, a thing no human eye could see. Dazed with studying death for so long, he got up and stood motionless. It was as dark as a room can be in the city. He set himself the task of gathering what he needed for school. He found socks, underwear, jeans, a flannel shirt, a sweater, unable to see the colour of his clothes. He put them on a chair in the order he would dress himself. Books were harder to collect. As though he were sightless, he felt book covers, ran his fingers across pages, and packed what he thought were the right ones in his backpack.

At some point, his fingers drifted across a package on a shelf; he felt the twist of Christmas ribbon around it. It was the collection of Irish folktales he'd meant to give his father in January. He stood motionless, listening. He thought he heard someone wailing in the distance. He touched the wrapped book with one finger just as he had touched his father's shoulder a few weeks ago while Philip Cormac lay sleeping on his bed in the Springton cabin. The wailing ceased. It must have been an ambulance. He did not think he would ever be able to unwrap his father's present, crumple the paper and ribbon, open the cover, look at what he'd written there: *For my father, love from Liam*. He dropped on all fours. On the floor beneath his desk, he found a ballpoint pen and wiped the dust from it on to his trousers.

He knew what he was doing was strange, but it didn't matter to him. He never reached for the light switch or raised a window shade. It seemed to him that he must do everything in this darkness, that his slow, nearly silent groping for his things would lead him into sleep. The strangest thing of all was his sense that his father watched him, and that if he turned on the light, that presence, which was without weight or shape, would vanish.

When he had done all that he could think of, he crawled beneath his red blanket and fell asleep at once.

FIVE
Revelation

On a Saturday morning in the second week of June, Liam and Luther went downtown to Greenwich Village to look for a pet shop that sold exotic birds. Luther had heard from someone that toucans, parrots, and macaws flew freely about the shop. His mother had warned him that the largest bird she'd allow him to keep in his room was a budgerigar.

'What I'd like is a condor,' Luther said to Liam as they emerged from the subway. 'Can't you see it? A bird with a ten-foot wingspan following me to school like Mary's little lamb? It'd be like having your own personal bomber. They eat deer. I could train it to eat people.' Luther laughed.

It had been several months since Luther, or anyone else, had spoken to Liam as if he was pitiful. Listening to Delia, a few weeks after his father had died, tell him how terrible he must feel, he was seized with impatience, as though he were being forced to listen to a dull story about someone else. He had wanted to interrupt her, tell her she had it all wrong. But he kept his mouth shut. He sensed that if he said one word, if he told of the unaccountable feelings he had about his father, everything would unravel, and he'd tell her the whole story.

He felt it packed inside of him like a furled parachute, grief and anger and puzzlement. A touch on the rip cord, that one word, would release the whole of it.

At first, he and his mother had spoken constantly of Philip Cormac, always the Philip of past years, when he'd been well. Gradually, their conversations dwindled. Now they rarely mentioned him. And gradually, as Liam woke up and did the things he had to do, he stopped thinking about him. The first mornings of his father's absence, which had filled him with such an ache, were erased like words on a blackboard, leaving only a ghostly mark or two, here and there, beneath the new writing of his daily life.

Last week, he had tried to visualize his father's eyes. When he couldn't, he told himself, He's really dead.

'It's supposed to be closer to Hudson Street,' Luther said as they walked along Bleecker Street.

A young man wearing loose soft trousers and only a deerskin vest over his chest was coming towards them. Lined along the edge of the sidewalk behind them, Liam noticed a few small trees with green leaves. Ginkgoes, he recalled. Saved from extinction by Buddhist monks, Daddy had told him. Between each tree, large black plastic garbage bags appeared to lean over the kerb like heavy people looking vaguely for their feet. A scent touched the air briefly as the young man passed them. Lilac. Liam thought of Sig Mottley. She wore lilac talcum. Was she alive? And Julius?

At that moment, Luther cried, 'Ooh! Liam! Did you see that cute boy?' His voice rose on the last word like the shrill cry of a bird caught in a net. He bent double with laughter.

With no thought, hardly aware of where he was or what he was doing, Liam seized hold of Luther's thick arm. 'Don't laugh at him! Don't *ever* laugh at him!' he shouted.

Luther swung at him and hit his head. They grappled fiercely on the sidewalk. 'What are you!' Luther gasped, twisting a handful of Liam's T-shirt until Liam felt his ribs compress. 'One of them? A nasty faggot?'

They fell into the street, their limbs tangled, pounding at each other. A car honked. Liam heard shouts from somewhere nearby. He felt himself violently shoved. His face was pressed to the kerb, where he tasted something bitter, acrid, damp butt ends of cigarettes. He got dizzily to his feet. A clump of people stood half a block away looking at him with disgust and fear. The driver of the car that had honked at him called out, 'You ought to be in jail, you thug!'

Luther was nowhere to be seen. The car moved on with an enraged roar of shifting gears. The people who had been watching him crossed the street and went their way. The young ginkgoes fluttered in a faint breeze. Someone came out of a shop. Others walked along, looking in windows.

Liam had no idea how long he stood there, still dazed, hearing not the echo of Luther's words but of his own. *Don't laugh at him!* What *him*? What had he meant, *ever*?

He went on towards Hudson, pausing when he came to the exotic bird shop he and Luther had been searching for. In the display window, a great scarlet-and-yellow macaw stared at him from one eye. Parrots preened on swinging perches. Birds he'd never seen strutted and squawked and groomed one another. He stared into the depths of the shop, where he could make out a counter, a customer perhaps, a man carrying a sack, probably seeds for the birds. He rubbed his face and felt wetness on his cheeks.

In his inner vision, the eagle kite he had never had a chance to fly spread its paper wings. The living birds in the window seemed a mass of violent colour, painful to his eyes,

It was not Delia or Luther, or anyone else, from whom he had most wanted to conceal the source of his father's sickness. It was from himself. The condemnation and scorn he had so feared in others had been in him all along, ever since he had seen Philip embracing the other man on the beach.

He took the subway, rode up in the elevator in his building, found the front-door key in his hand, unaware of anything he had seen along the way, just as he had been unaware that morning one year and seven months ago when he had come home from Riverside Park with his father.

His mother was in the kitchen, reading the newspaper.

'I know how he got it,' he said, surprised at the quietness of his voice. The words he had spoken had risen in him like a tidal wave.

Her mouth moved but formed nothing. Her shoulders slumped. He heard her sigh as she folded up the newspaper. Whatever had passed through her mind, she only nodded.

'I saw him on the beach. It was the summer after he got me the eagle kite,' he went on. 'I took it down to fly it. Daddy was there with the man. They . . . Daddy held him.'

'Geoff Chaffee,' his mother pronounced slowly.

'Yes. Geoff. He told me.'

She looked up at him. 'He told you?'

'Yes. He's dead, too.'

'I know.'

'Did you ever meet him?'

'He worked at one of the sites where Philip had a contract to do the garden planning. I went once. I met him.'

Liam pulled out a chair and sat down across the table from her. 'Did you know then about him and Geoff?'

'I don't believe Philip had fallen in love with him yet,' she said. 'Maybe he had. I don't know.' She got up and turned on the flame beneath a kettle. 'Even if you try,' she said, 'you can't tell everything.' She paused and came back to her chair. 'Because you can't know everything.'

'Did Aunt Mary know – about him?'

'She guessed. We didn't speak of it. It was impossible for her to talk of such things.'

'What about you?'

'It was a different kind of pain.'

'I wish he'd had a funeral,' Liam said with sudden intensity. He hadn't even known he'd wanted that. 'Was he ashamed?'

'No. I was, at first.' She smiled a little grimly. 'When you get left, you feel shame as well as anger. But he'd never wanted a funeral. We used to talk a lot at night. It was one of the things he told me.'

He was thinking of them, talking at night in the room next to his.

'Why didn't you tell me?' she asked. 'I mean, that you knew?'

He thought for a minute. He said, 'If I had told you, then it would have been really true.'

They were silent for a while. The water in the kettle boiled. She made herself a cup of instant coffee.

'I've been thinking,' she said at last. 'I don't start my new job until September. Maybe we could go to Ireland for a week. It was where he wanted to take you. There's a special fare I read about last week in the Sunday paper. Just a week. We don't have a lot of money, but Daddy did his best to leave us afloat. I was thinking of some time in August. Would you like that?'

As she spoke, she reached out and took his hand firmly in hers. Then, as she had when he was little, she pulled gently at each finger.

'Yes,' he said.

'There's something I didn't tell you,' she said. 'About his ashes.' She smiled slightly. 'I think I did something illegal. I took them to the New York Botanical Garden. It was very early, and I'm pretty sure no one saw me. I dug snow from around the roots of a Japanese maple tree. I sprinkled them there.'

'Would you show me the tree some day?'

'Yes,' she said.

They went on talking together quietly. It was a day in June, and the light would last a long time.

Cassia retai...
with difficul...

'I don't need this lecture... I'm not just out of a convent, although you seem to think so. Compared with other people of my age, I've been around more than most.'

'Geographically, yes. Not emotionally. It wouldn't surprise me if you've never been kissed,' Simón said, smiling.

'Of course I've been kissed!' she exploded indignantly.

'Like this?' He cupped her chin and her cheek in the warm curve of his palm and, tilting her face up, put his lips lightly on hers. For a moment, while her heart bungee jumped, his mouth remained on hers, motionless. Then, softly and slowly, it moved in a kiss so gentle yet so subtly arousing that her response astonished and horrified her.

'Not like that,' he said mockingly.

Anne Weale was still at school when a women's magazine published some of her stories. At twenty-five she had her first novel accepted by Mills & Boon. Now, with a grown-up son and still happily married to her first love, Anne divides her life between her winter home—a Spanish village ringed by mountains and vineyards—and a summer place in Guernsey, one of the many islands around the world she has used as backgrounds for her books.

Recent titles by the same author:

NEVER GO BACK

A NIGHT
TO REMEMBER

BY
ANNE WEALE

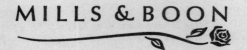

MILLS & BOON

All the characters in this book have no existence outside the imagination
of the author, and have no relation whatsoever to anyone bearing the
same name or names. They are not even distantly inspired by any
individual known or unknown to the author, and all the incidents are
pure invention.

MILLS & BOON and the Rose Device
are trademarks of the publisher.
Harlequin Mills & Boon Limited,
Eton House, 18-24 Paradise Road, Richmond, Surrey TW9 1SR

© Anne Weale 1996

ISBN 0 263 79476 8

Set in Times Roman 10 on 11¼ pt.
01-9605-58410 C1

Made and printed in Great Britain

CHAPTER ONE

THEY arrived at a quiet time of day, when everyone staying at the hotel was either up on the ski-slopes of the Sierra Nevada or out on a sightseeing excursion.

Sitting behind the reception desk in her neat black dress, with her long mane of light brown hair brushed smoothly back from her face and fastened with pins and a black bow attached to a comb, Cassia was reading a French novel left behind by one of the guests and given to her by their room maid who had found it in the waste-paper basket.

The book was propped on the shelf beneath the counter, and as soon as Cassia heard a car drawing up to the entrance she raised her head and returned to the real world.

The car was a Mercedes sports coupé. Its driver, visible through the hotel's glass doors which would slide apart when he came near them, was a tall, dark man, casually dressed in a sweater and jeans.

She watched him walk round the front of the car to open the passenger door for a girl with long, sexy legs revealed by a very short skirt. It rode even higher up her thighs as she twisted round to reach for something on the back seat. The something proved to be a fur jacket. When she was on her feet, standing almost as tall as the man, she slung the fur round her shoulders, over the red cashmere sweater defining her voluptuous breasts.

They were a spectacular couple, whose looks suggested that they might be show business personalities. But they wouldn't be adding their names to the long list of stars

5

and directors who had stayed at Granada's most expensive hotel.

Tonight the Castillo del Sultán was fully booked. Only one suite was unoccupied, but that was reserved for the Marqués de Mondragón, who was driving down from Madrid and wasn't expected to arrive until shortly before dinner.

When he did, he would be welcomed by the manager, Señor Alvarez, and conducted upstairs with the ceremony befitting a grandee of Spain whose high rank had been conferred on an ancestor by Queen Isabella I, whose statue, on a high plinth with fountains playing round its base, was one of the most photographed monuments in the historic city of Granada.

As the newcomers entered the lobby the girl's eyes focused on the windows of the small shop, closed until four p.m., offering a selection of expensive souvenirs and gifts. She made a beeline for the enticing displays, leaving the man to approach the desk on his own.

Speaking Spanish with almost no trace of her native language, Cassia said pleasantly, 'Good afternoon, sir.'

'Good afternoon.' His voice was deeper and quieter than the opulent car and the ostentatiously glamorous girl had led her to expect.

Before she could tell him that unfortunately they were fully booked, and offer to ring up one of the other hotels for him, he said, 'My secretary booked the Mirador for us two or three weeks ago.'

His Spanish was pure *castellano*, like that of the aged professor who, to supplement his pension, had taught Cassia to speak as he did, not with the more guttural accent of the *granadinos*.

'You weren't expecting us till later,' he went on. 'But I changed my plans and left Madrid this morning.'

The Mirador was the name of the hotel's most beautiful suite. But it was seldom occupied by beautiful people. Most of those who could afford to enjoy its luxury were middle-aged, if not elderly. Cassia had assumed that the Marqués would be many years older than this man, who looked to be in his early thirties, with thick dark hair and an aura of health and vigour, not to say animal magnetism.

She was not often disconcerted. Her life, with its many upheavals and fluctuations of fortune, had made her unusually self-possessed. But something about the way he was looking down at her from the other side of the counter threw her into confusion.

However, she tried not to show it, saying politely, 'Would you sign the register, please?' and offering him a gold-nibbed fountain pen filled with black ink, one of the many small touches of style which combined to give the Castillo its reputation as one of Spain's finest hotels.

Given the opportunity to live at the level of the Castillo's guests, Cassia would have chosen to stay at a smaller and quieter establishment, once a monastery and now a State-run *parador*, inside the walls of the Alhambra. But the Parador San Francisco was always booked up for months ahead, especially as its charges were not high in relation to the exorbitant rates charged by the Castillo del Sultán.

Even though the cost of living in Spain was no longer as low as when she and her father had first come here, on what this man would be paying for his week here she could have lived well for months.

The Marqués took the pen in his long brown fingers and signed his name—or part of it—below the previous entry in the leather-bound, gold-stamped register. She knew that written in full his name would occupy two or three lines. Acquired over many generations, his family's subsidiary titles had become almost as numerous as those of Spain's best known grandee, the Duchess of Alba.

But all he wrote was one word—Mondragón. Like 'Alba', it was enough to identify him to anyone with the smallest interest in Spanish history.

As he signed Cassia pressed two bells—one to summon a baggage porter, the other to alert one of the attendants responsible for parking the guests' cars in the hotel's underground garage and bringing them to the entrance when they were needed again.

It was a measure of the efficiency with which the Castillo was run that, although it was a slack time of day, there was very little delay before both men came through the staff door behind the imposing marble staircase, their uniforms immaculate, their expressions friendly but respectful.

Although she knew it wasn't the first time that the Marqués had stayed at the hotel, Cassia was surprised when he greeted José, the senior car valet, by his name, and even shook hands with him before handing over his keys.

As she opened the gate of the area behind the reception desk Manolo, the oldest of the hall porters, returned to his desk on the opposite side of the lobby. He had worked at the hotel for years and had many tales to tell of gala occasions, scandals discreetly hushed up and outrageous behaviour by people who should have known better.

He also received a cordial greeting from the Marqués, who enquired after Manolo's wife and family but did not present the porter to his own companion, Cassia noticed. Whoever she was, she was obviously not the Marquesa. Perhaps he wasn't married yet. In which case there was no reason why he shouldn't amuse himself with whoever was willing to partner him on a temporary basis.

Although she worked in a milieu where such liaisons were commonplace, Cassia herself marched to a different drummer. She was a romantic, with high ideals and probably hopeless expectations. The man who captured *her* heart would not be one who regarded women as playthings.

She waited until the two men had finished talking before stepping forward to say, 'Unfortunately Señor Alvarez isn't here at the moment. May I show you to your suite, Excellency?'

'Thank you, but that's unnecessary, *señorita*. I've been staying here since I was so high.' The Marqués indicated the height of a small boy. As he spoke he gave Cassia's figure a brief but comprehensive appraisal.

Although she wasn't as tall as his long-stemmed girl-friend, in proportion to her own medium height her legs were equally long and slender. But, while some of the maids wore short skirts under their uniform overalls, Señor Alvarez wouldn't have approved of one of his receptionists showing her knees. It was Cassia's willingness to conform to his somewhat old-fashioned standards, as well as her fluency in several languages, which had made him promote her from her first lowly job as one of the early-morning cleaners.

Holding out his hand for the key to the suite, the Marqués glanced over his shoulder. 'Come along, Isa.'

As Isa turned from her inspection of the wares in the shop Cassia asked him, 'Shall I send up a valet and maid to unpack for you?'

'A valet, no. But Señorita Sanchez has more luggage than I have.' As she joined him he said, 'Do you want your gear unpacked for you, Isa?'

'Of course... and I shall need some clothes pressed.' She slipped her hand into his and gave him an intimate smile.

The smile he gave her had a predatory gleam, making Cassia think that it wouldn't be long before the glamorous Isa was called upon to justify her existence in his scheme of things.

It might have been that they had only recently met, and this was his first opportunity to take her to bed. Cassia wished them joy of each other. The idea of having sex—one couldn't call it making love—with a partner for whom one had no tender feelings disgusted her. She knew lots of people did it, but that didn't make it a good or wise way to behave.

The strength of her intuition—that before Isa had had time to admire the panoramic view of Granada from the windows of the Mirador suite she would find herself gazing at the ceiling above the vast double bed—brought a slight flush to her cheeks as she handed the Marqués the key with its *taracea* tag—an example of the fine marquetry crafted in the city for centuries.

To her discomfiture, he noticed. She had read what was in his mind, and now he was reading hers. She was almost certain of it.

'I hope you enjoy your stay with us,' she said stiltedly.

Normally when she said that to guests she was sincerely hopeful that they would enjoy their time in Granada. This time the words were mechanical, and not accompanied by her usual warm smile. There was something about this couple that made her uncomfortable with them.

'Thank you, I'm sure we shall. Señorita Sanchez will let you know when she's ready for the maid.'

Confirming Cassia's hunch that between the arrival of their luggage and the arrangement of its contents the Marqués had another priority, he steered his *amiguita* towards the waiting lift.

'*Ay, ay* . . . what it is to be young and handsome.' As the lift was taking its passengers to the top floor, where the best suites were located, Manolo was crossing the lobby to join Cassia at the reception desk. 'Every time he comes here he has a different girl—each one more beautiful than the last.'

'But only interested in what they can get out of him,' she said caustically, turning the register round to look at the swift but easily decipherable signature 'Mondragón'.

'No, no. There you're wrong,' said Manolo. 'Maybe that will be true in thirty years' time, when he's an old rake like his grandfather. I was here when the old Marqués brought his last mistress to stay with us. A lovely little creature, she was, but May to his December. On their third day here, she killed him.'

'I'm not surprised,' said Cassia. She was about to add that she couldn't imagine anything more horrible than going to bed with an old man in his sixties when she realised it might offend Manolo, who was himself nearing retirement. 'Did she stab him or shoot him?'

Either way, it must have caused the hotel a lot of bother and expense to keep the scandal out of the newspapers and refurbish the scene of the crime.

Manolo's face crinkled into a network of laughter lines and his chest heaved with the wheezy mirth of a heavy off-duty smoker. 'She killed him with kindness, *chica*. Not a bad way to go, if you ask me...in the arms of a beautiful girl. I should be so lucky!'

His chuckles were infectious, and Cassia couldn't help smiling. Besides, he was only joking. She had met his plump, loving wife, and knew that they were deeply devoted to each other and to the progeny of their teenage marriage—five children and numerous grandchildren.

'Did you also know the Marqués's father?' she asked.

The porter shook his head. 'He never came to Granada. The family has many estates all over Spain but no property here. The *papá* of the present Marqués was thrown from a horse soon after this one was born. He struck his head on a rock and his brain was damaged.

They say his wife had him packed off to one of their smaller *palacios* with a couple of nurses to look after him. After that she kicked up her heels until this young fellow was almost grown up. Then she divorced his father and married a rich American.'

At this point a florist's messenger entered the lobby with a lavish basket of flowers for one of the German guests. After that answering the telephone and attending to other duties prevented Manolo and Cassia from continuing their conversation.

During her father's last months, at the end of every work-shift she had hurried back to their studio apartment in the Albaicín, the old Moorish quarter of the city, to spend all her free time with him.

Now she was on her own she did as much overtime as possible, partly because the apartment was full of painful memories, and partly to earn enough money to return to the country of which, having been born there, she was officially a citizen but where she had never lived.

Cassia's father had been English, her mother French. Without any effort on her part she had grown up speaking both languages and, until she was seven, absorbing both cultures. Then her parents had split up, her mother running away with a lover who hadn't wanted to be encumbered with another man's child. The arrangement had suited Cassia, who had always adored her father and had found her mother disturbingly volatile—sometimes extravagantly affectionate and then, without reason or warning, impatient and even unkind.

Now, fifteen years later, she understood the wisdom of the French adage—*Tout comprendre est tout pardonner*. Understanding *did* bring forgiveness. In some of his moods her father would have tried the patience of a saint. With hindsight, it wasn't surprising that he had driven his much younger and equally mercurial wife to leave him.

The only surprising thing was that Cassia was so unlike either of them in temperament. She was forced to conclude that her own more phlegmatic and practical nature must be an inheritance from her grandparents. But if they were still alive she had no idea where they lived, so that was a conjecture which would remain unproven.

In order to add to her savings, she was still on duty in the now crowded lobby when, at nine o'clock that evening, Isa Sanchez stepped out of the lift and drew the eyes of every man there to her beautiful, lissom body, only partly concealed by a sliver of thin silk velvet, hand-painted with jewel colours.

Tonight her arresting legs were hosed to tone with the dress and her matching slippers. Her black hair, earlier hidden by a Hermès silk scarf, was now a cloud of silky curls round her exquisitely made-up face.

No wonder they're all gawping at her. Physically, she's a knock-out, thought Cassia. Whether she has any brains in that beautiful head... *quién sabe*? But, looking like that, does it matter? Except that she won't always. Beauty fades. Intelligence lasts.

The lift was full, and it wasn't until two other women had emerged that Isa's escort stepped out. He too caught and held attention, not because he was also dressed to kill, but because of his height and physique.

Nearly all the young men in Spain were taller and better built than their fathers and grandfathers, whose growth had often been stunted by the inadequate nutrition of earlier decades when Spain had been a poor country. Even now the average height of the Spanish was still below that of more prosperous parts of the European Community. Heightwise, the Marqués had more in common with the tall Scandinavians than with his own countrymen, and few men in any country carried themselves with that proudly upright bearing.

Tonight, as it had been earlier, his style of dress was casual—designer jeans and a blazer over a dark blue shirt, the button-down collar unbuttoned at the neck. From the open collar of his shirt down to his polished black loafers he could have been an Ivy League American, a member of the French *gratin* or of almost any élite social group the world over.

From the neck up he could only be Spanish. Those fiery black eyes, the aquiline nose and haughty cheekbones had their origins in the time when the great red-walled fortress overlooking Granada had encapsulated what had been then the world's most advanced civilisation.

The Moors, who had built the Alhambra and the ancient part of the city where Cassia lived, had eventually been driven out. But they had bequeathed to the Spanish not only some of their knowledge of science, philosophy and art, but also their exotic dark looks.

Somewhere, far back in the lineage of the tall man now crossing the lobby in the direction of the bar, there had to be a link with the Moors who had dominated Spain for hundreds of years.

Half an hour later the Marqués and Isa emerged from the bar, and she went to the ladies' cloakroom, crossing the lobby with an arrogant, hip-swinging walk copied from the catwalk strut of the supermodels.

It was early January, and although the day had been sunny and warm, at this time of year the nights were cold. The Marqués was carrying his girlfriend's fur jacket for her. Cassia recognised it as wolf fur, presumably made from the pelts of animals bred in the wild. The thought of their suffering after they had been trapped would have stopped her buying and wearing such a coat, even if she could have afforded it.

But in Spain furs were much in evidence during the winter months, when parts of the country were under snow and the wind blowing over the high sierras was often bitterly cold. Guests passing through the lobby were frequently swathed in luxurious, ankle-length mink coats.

She was waiting for Isa Sanchez to re-emerge from the cloakroom when the Marqués suddenly swung round and walked towards her.

'Still on duty, *señorita*? You work long hours. Do you live in the hotel?'

Surprised that he should take the trouble to speak to her, she shook her head. 'But I don't have far to go home, *señor*.'

Switching to English, he said, 'I think you're British, aren't you?' Before she could reply, he went on, 'It's your beautiful skin and your eyes which give the game away. Your Spanish is very nearly perfect. You can even roll your Rs to the manner born... an astonishing accomplishment for a Brit.' He smiled at her. 'If you don't mind my saying so, most of your compatriots are hopelessly bad linguists.'

'I'm afraid so,' she agreed, trying not to show her amazement, not only at his compliments but at his command of English. If her Spanish was nearly perfect, his English *was* perfect.

She had heard that in Jerez de la Frontera, the home of sherry, the children of families whose wealth derived from the wine had always had English nannies and, in times gone by, English governesses. But she couldn't believe that a nanny could have taught him the flawless and idiomatic English he spoke now. Perhaps his amorous conquests had included an English girl.

'How long have you lived in Spain?' he asked.

Isa appeared at his elbow. 'Come on, Simón... I'm hungry.'

He turned to her, holding out the jacket. As the Spanish girl put her evening bag on the counter, and turned her back in order to slip her bare arms into the satin-lined sleeves, they were both given a view of her beautiful bra-less bosom inside the low *décolletage* of the velvet dress. For the Marqués, being taller and closer to her, it must have been even more revealing than Cassia's glimpse of his *amiguita*'s ripe golden breasts.

As Isa picked up her bag she flashed a brief glance at Cassia, in which the English girl read the arrogant condescension of a glamorous playgirl with a ten-out-of-ten escort for one of the world's little people.

'Let's go!' Smiling gaily at the Marqués, the Spanish girl flashed her teeth, snapped her fingers and did a brief, sexy shimmy. 'I want to eat and dance.'

'Just as long as you remember that tomorrow, at eight, no later, we leave for the ski-slopes. If you aren't up, I'll leave you behind.'

Although the Spaniard spoke lightly, there could be no doubting that he meant it.

'Why must we start so early?' Her tone was faintly petulant.

'Because that's why we're here...to ski. Not for the discos.' Turning to Cassia, he said, 'Goodnight, *señorita*.'

Watching them walk away, she was surprised that he had remembered to wrap up their conversation with a courteous goodnight.

Then she heard Isa ask, 'What were you talking to her about?'

Whatever the Marqués replied was drowned by the conversation of a group of people descending the staircase.

Many foreigners who came to Granada were nervous of venturing into the Albaicín district unescorted. They felt safer going there with a tour group, or on a minibus excursion which would take them to selected vantage points without the risk of having their pockets picked or their bags snatched.

In fact, the modern part of Granada was no more dangerous than any big city anywhere, and the Albaicín was safe enough during the day. At night it was not advisable for lone tourists to wander there. After working late, even Cassia went home by taxi rather than on foot. As she had her main meals at the hotel, the apartment was now a place where she only slept and had breakfast.

The following morning, wrapped in a warm wool dressing-gown and wearing a pair of gaudy, plaid-patterned carpet slippers bought at the Saturday market in the Plaza Larga, she took her breakfast onto the little roof terrace from which her father John Browning had painted dozens of pictures of the Alhambra's towers and battlements silhouetted against the snowy peaks of the Sierra Nevada.

It had to be one of the world's most magical views, especially at sunrise and sunset, or on a hot summer night with a full moon riding the sky. Sometimes Cassia thought that she must be crazy to be planning to leave this beautiful place for the cloudy skies and long, cold winters of northern Europe.

But her father's lease on the apartment was running out, and the owner wouldn't renew it. Nor could she find another apartment nearby. To live amid the noise and air pollution of the modern city was not an attractive prospect. The alternative was to go to England and find out if that was where she really belonged.

After breakfast she had a quick shower. Then, wearing a Turkish bathrobe which had belonged to John Browning, she started to make up her face. It didn't take long. Apart from using a sunblock to shield her fine, creamy skin from sun damage, and spending five minutes on her eyelids and lips, she didn't go in for the sort of complicated *maquillage* she had seen on Isa Sanchez the night before. *Her* eyes had been works of art, and her

mouth outlined, rouged and glossed to look like the
petals of some rare and exquisite orchid.

'It's your beautiful skin and your eyes which give the
game away. Your Spanish is very nearly perfect.'

The Marqués's startling compliment echoed in Cassia's
mind as she dabbed blobs of sunblock on her forehead
and cheeks. Did her skin deserve such an accolade? Being
fair, it was finer in texture than the olive skins of most
Spanish women, but it wouldn't necessarily wear as well
as their oilier complexions. And surely grey eyes were a
common feature among all the Western nations?

She was forced to conclude that the Spanish lord's
compliments carried as little weight as the term *guapa*,
applied to girl babies regardless of whether they really
were pretty infants.

She was due on duty at eight, but arrived a quarter
of an hour early. The lobby was full of people in
colourful ski-suits, some with the ski-passes called
taquillas clipped to their jackets or on wristbands, many
with goggles round their necks and carrying heavy ski-
boots. Perhaps the Marqués and Isa had already left for
Pradollano, the complex serving the *pistas*.

Annoyed with herself, Cassia realised that the reason
she was here ahead of time was that she had hoped to
catch sight of them before they went off for the day.

She was on the telephone, taking down the name and
address of someone who wanted to book a room for the
following month, when she saw the Marqués coming
down the staircase. He was wearing a black salopette—
the close-fitting, chest-high trousers held up by shoulder
straps favoured by the most active skiers. He was carrying
a discreet black and grey ski-jacket, and at present the
upper part of his body was clad only in a bright, coral-
coloured T-shirt, with a cotton scarf of the same colour
knotted round his throat. His brown arms were bare to

the point where the swell of powerful muscles was visible between elbow and shoulder.

Without glancing towards the reception desk he crossed the lobby to the newspaper kiosk. Moments later Isa appeared on the staircase, stifling a yawn. She was wearing a shimmery pale yellow all-in-one ski-suit with a deeper yellow peaked cap, and yellow hoops in her ears.

The Marqués came away from the kiosk with several women's magazines which he handed over to Isa, presumably for her to read on the drive to Pradollano. Perhaps he didn't find her conversational abilities matched her talents in other directions.

Watching them leaving the hotel, Cassia suppressed a sigh. She had always longed to try skiing. But, even though they lived within an hour's bus ride of the slopes, the cost of hiring the necessary equipment had been beyond their means. Besides, her father hadn't been interested and would never have allowed her to try the sport on her own.

In the middle of the afternoon the switchboard operator rang through to Reception.

'Cassia, the Marqués de Mondragón is on the line. He's asking for Señor Alvarez, but I know he's having a family party for his wife's birthday today. I don't want to disturb them unless it's essential. Can I put him through to you?'

'Of course.' As she waited to be connected Cassia was aware of an involuntary quiver of excitement. 'You have a problem, Excellency?'

'Señorita Sanchez has hurt herself,' the deep voice said in her ear. 'Nothing serious. Another novice cannoned into her on the nursery slopes. They both fell over and got their skis in a tangle. I think it's merely a sprain, but rather than taking her to the first-aid clinic up here

I'd like the hotel doctor to look at her. Can you arrange for him to be there when we get back to the hotel in about forty-five minutes?'

'Certainly, *señor*. We have an excellent doctor on call. He has a lot of experience in dealing with skiing injuries.'

'Good.' Instead of ringing off, he said, 'You're the British girl I spoke to last night. What's your name?'

'Cassia Browning, *señor*.'

'Any relation to Robert Browning, the poet?'

'I shouldn't think so.'

'But you know his work?'

'Of course.'

'Unusual!' was his reply. 'Most girls of your age have only heard of pop stars.' And then he did ring off.

After she had alerted the hotel's doctor Cassia returned to the novel she had been reading when the Marqués arrived the day before. But it didn't hold her attention, which kept switching to Isa Sanchez's accident.

Such mishaps were common on the nursery slopes, before the beginners learnt control. According to Señor Alvarez, now that skiing was the sport of the masses all ski-resorts everywhere were too crowded for comfort and safety. He always advised guests at the Castillo not to go skiing on Saturdays and Sundays, when the *granadinos* were out in force. A few years ago even the king, Don Juan Carlos, himself an expert skier, had been in collision with a schoolboy learner.

The week before, a Swedish guest at the hotel had chipped a bone in her shoulder, and had had to spend the rest of her holiday with her arm in a sling. It might be that Isa Sanchez had also been put out of action. If she had, Cassia wondered if the Marqués would change his plans and keep her company, or leave her behind while he went skiing on his own. If she was a beginner and he an experienced skier, they wouldn't have seen much of each other anyway. Most of the difficult red

and black *pistas* used by the experts were a long way
from the nursery slopes. Perhaps today, being the first
day, he had returned to have lunch with her.

The doctor was waiting in the lobby when the sleek
car with the Madrid registration glided up to the entrance, and a porter pushed a wheelchair down the ramp
provided for disabled guests. When Señorita Sanchez was
wheeled into the lobby, her smeared mascara showed that
she had been crying. Cassia wondered if she was in great
pain, or if the Marqués had been unsympathetic, even
impatient with her. He didn't look as if he would have
much time for weaker beings, especially if their shortcomings interfered with his enjoyment.

About fifteen minutes later the doctor returned to the
lobby. Normally in Señor Alvarez's absence he would
have dealt with the assistant manager. But as he was away
on his honeymoon the doctor spoke to Cassia.

'The young lady has wrenched the muscles of her inner
thigh. A few days' rest is the cure. I'll look in on her
tomorrow.'

Presently Cassia wrote a brief report of the incident
to give to the other receptionist, who today was replacing her at four. In spite of his family party, it was
likely that during the evening the manager would ring
up and expect to be informed of any untoward events.
It was his obsessive attention to every aspect of the
running of the Castillo that had put it ahead of its rivals.

Just before she went off duty she was summoned to
the housekeeper's room.

'As tomorrow's your morning off, I thought you might
like these flowers to take to the cemetery,' Señora Ortiz
said kindly, indicating the florist's basket on her desk.
'They were only delivered the day before yesterday, but
the lady they were sent to didn't want to take them
with her.'

All the flowers in the public rooms were supplied and refreshed by Granada's best florist, but those left over from special occasions or discarded by guests were one of the housekeeper's perks, sometimes shared with her minions.

'That's very kind of you, *señora*. They're lovely.'

'It gets dark early at this time of year. Why not take them home and enjoy them yourself tonight? You can take them to your father in the morning.'

The quickest way from the hotel to the Albaicín quarter was by the wooded road passing the Alhambra. Restfully shady in the heat of high summer, this afternoon the tall trees cast gloomy shadows. An elderly vagrant who frequented the area, muttering to himself, glowered at Cassia as she passed him, and she felt very conscious of the abyss separating him from the hotel guest from whom she had inherited the flowers she was carrying.

She was halfway down the hill when she heard a whistle of the kind meant to call attention. Turning, she was astonished to see the Marqués loping towards her.

'I thought it was you by the bow in your hair,' he said, catching up with her. 'I'm going down to find a pharmacy. The doctor has prescribed a gel for my friend to rub on her sprained leg.'

'We could have sent someone to fetch it for you,' she said.

'I needed some more air and exercise. Let me carry that for you?' He took over the basket of flowers. 'You said you hadn't far to go home, but isn't there a bus you could catch? This is a dismal walk, and I just passed a drunk who gave me a mouthful of abuse.'

'He doesn't swear if you say good afternoon to him. He must be very unhappy, poor old fellow.'

'No doubt his troubles are of his own making,' the Marqués said drily.

Coming from someone born with a silver spoon in his mouth as well as exceptionally good looks, Cassia found his reply deeply irritating.

'Not necessarily. Life can be hard for the strong...for the weak, impossible,' she answered. 'You don't know what pressures have brought that man to his present state...and you obviously don't care either,' she added impulsively.

Matching his stride to her shorter steps, he looked down at her, one eyebrow raised.

Suddenly switching to English, as he had the day before, he said, 'Do you care, Miss Browning?'

'Yes, I do. I feel very sorry for people like that. It may sometimes be their own fault that they've hit bottom, but not always.'

'And what, if anything, do you do about it?'

'Not very much,' she admitted. 'But at least I don't dismiss them as garbage.'

'Is that what you think I do?'

The truthful answer was yes, but her spurt of anger had died down, and she was becoming aware that she shouldn't have let it flare up. He was accustomed to deference. He wouldn't like being criticised, not even by an equal, and much less by an inferior.

'For all I know, you may be exceedingly generous to the poor and the misfits,' she said quietly. 'How is Miss Sanchez feeling? What bad luck for her to be hurt on her first day here.'

'She would have done better to spend the days shopping,' he said. 'But she was keen to learn...or at least to have a reason to dress up in the last word in designer ski-kit. I left her in the care of an instructor and came back at lunchtime to find her a casualty. Do you ski, Miss Browning?'

'No, I don't.'

If her reply surprised him, in view of the nearness of the Sierra Nevada, he didn't query the reason for it, but repeated his question of the night before. 'How long have you lived here?'

'In Granada—four years. In Spain—since I was fifteen.'

'How long ago is that?'

'I'm twenty-two. Before we came here we lived on the seaward side of the Sierra. Then my father became ill and needed complicated hospital treatment so we moved here. Unfortunately he died. I'll be leaving Spain soon. There are many things I shall miss. Which is your favourite part of Spain?'

'It depends on my mood. Sometimes I like Madrid. Sometimes I like Galicia . . . even though it rains a lot there. Even Extramadura, so arid and parched in the summer, can be beautiful in the spring. I like most parts of my country . . . but sometimes I want to get out of it and enjoy other places. Where are you going when you leave here?'

'To England.'

'To relations?'

'No, both my parents were only children. I'm on my own now.'

'That can be an advantage. Families aren't always the support they're supposed to be. I have no brothers or sisters, but I do have numerous more distant relations and they're mostly a pain in the . . . neck.'

By now they had passed the souvenir shops near the bottom of the hill and were in the Plaza Nueva, not far from a chemist's shop. Cassia showed him where it was, and would have retrieved the basket and taken her leave.

The Marqués had other ideas. Keeping a firm hold on it, he said, 'If you don't mind waiting while I buy this stuff for Isa, I'll walk you home.'

Why he should wish to do so was a puzzle she couldn't fathom. Then a wild possibility occurred, which made her heart lurch with apprehension.

CHAPTER TWO

COULD it possibly be that with Isa put out of action by her wrenched thigh muscle the Marqués had it in mind to make a pass at herself?

Cassia had read about men with insatiable sexual appetites. If Simón de Mondragón's grandfather had died because of that predilection, perhaps it was a family trait.

The chemist's shop was an old-fashioned establishment, its walls lined with mahogany lockers topped by ceramic jars painted with the names of the physics they had once contained. Having recently reopened after the afternoon closure it was crowded, mainly with elderly people who knew the chemist and his assistant and liked to have a chat while they made their purchases.

Standing at the side of the shop while the Marqués waited his turn, Cassia expected to see signs of impatience on his face. But in fact he appeared to be interested in the conversations going on at the counter. More than once the grooves down his lean cheeks deepened with amusement as he listened to forthright opinions on the government and the city fathers from people whose lives were at the opposite end of the social spectrum from his own.

Among Cassia's neighbours in the Albaicín, many of the older ones could remember the civil war in the thirties. It was probable that, being aristocrats, the Marqués's family had supported the Nationalists led by General Franco. Acts of heroism as well as many terrible atrocities had taken place on both sides. In the public cemetery near the Alhambra, where her father was buried, more than two thousand *granadinos* had been executed, most of them long forgotten. Only the brutal execution by Nationalist partisans of Granada's young but already famous poet, Federico García Lorca, was a war crime still widely remembered.

Thinking about the poet, Cassia wasn't aware that the Marqués had finished being served until he said, 'Sorry to keep you waiting so long.'

She came down to earth with a start. 'It doesn't matter.'

Outside the shop he said. 'You were looking very sad in there. Were you thinking about your father? Tell me about him.'

'He was an artist. Not a very successful one. The things he wanted to paint didn't sell. To keep us housed and fed he had to paint what would sell—picturesque views of the Alhambra and the Generalife gardens. I liked them, but he despised them and the people who bought them. It's a difficult life, being an artist. I'm glad I haven't inherited his gift. I can't draw for peanuts,' she said lightly.

'Nor can I, but I'm interested in art. I've inherited some fine paintings and I'm adding to the collection. Do you have any of the paintings your father did to please himself?'

'A few.'

'I'd like to see them, if I may.'

'They're not for sale,' said Cassia, in case he had hopes of buying the works of an undiscovered genius for bargain prices. 'I shall never part with them.'

'I'd still like to see them.'

A woman from the gypsy community in the cave-houses on Sacromonte, the hilltop above the Albaicín, approached them, offering a sprig of heather.

'To bring luck to you and your pretty young lady, *señor*,' she wheedled.

Cassia expected him to ignore her, or to wave her away with a gesture. To her surprise, he took some coins from his pocket. 'People make their own luck, *señora*,' he said, putting them into her hand and taking the already wilted sprig.

'But they aren't all born with your looks, handsome,' she quipped, with a flash of gold teeth. She turned to Cassia. 'You've picked yourself a fine fellow, *señorita*. But when they're as fine as this one they have many opportunities. Don't give him all he wants. Keep him guessing. Remember, the fruit on the tree inside the locked patio always looks more delicious than oranges growing in a roadside orchard where anyone can pick them.'

'You should be writing poetry, not selling heather,' said the Marqués. With a bow he presented her with a flower removed from the basket he was carrying.

'She'll need a strong will to resist *you*!' Laughing, the gypsy touched the rose to his cheek before going on her way.

'I hope you don't mind my giving away one of your flowers,' he said, reverting to English. 'I've always liked the gypsies. They're part of the Spain of my childhood, which is rapidly disappearing. Every year we become more like the rest of Europe. A homogenised world may have some advantages, but it isn't as colourful and interesting.'

He handed the heather to her. 'Do you believe in luck and fortune-telling and all those gypsy stock-in-trades?'

Cassia shook her head. But she did believe that gypsies were shrewd judges of characters, able to gauge at a glance a great deal about the people they accosted. Clearly the gypsy had recognised that the Marqués was a practised charmer, and also that she, Cassia, lacked the experience to handle him.

They were now at the point where the New Square merged with the old Plaza Santa Ana. A few yards further Cassia would be turning off into the labyrinth of narrow streets and steep alleys, where the churches had once been mosques and many of the little squares still had the public wells known by the Moorish name *agilbes*.

She said, in a businesslike tone, 'It's a long trudge up to my place. I doubt if you'd find my father's pictures worth the effort…and the sooner Señorita Sanchez rubs that stuff on her leg the better, don't you think?'

'In my experience of minor skiing injuries it's rest not ointment that cures them.' After giving her a thoughtful look he added, 'And I think the gypsy's warning rather than concern for Isa is your main reason for trying to put me off, Miss Browning. Let me relieve your mind. At this stage of our acquaintance I have no intention of…' he paused for a moment, his black eyes glinting with amusement '…trespassing in the locked patio.'

'I never supposed that you had,' she said untruthfully, unable to stop herself blushing under that mocking regard.

'Yes, you did. Why deny it? There's been a strong hint of disapproval in your manner since we arrived. It interests me. I should have thought in your job you'd be used to unmarried people taking holidays together. There's nothing unusual about it. But you seem to have me tabbed as an incorrigible stud who might even make a pass at you, given the smallest encouragement.'

It was disconcertingly close to what she had been thinking about him earlier.

She decided to speak her mind. 'Hotel receptionists— like air stewardesses—do get quite a lot of passes made at them. More on the Everest principle—because they are there—than because of their personal attributes. I don't flatter myself I'm the sort of girl who would normally attract your attention. But you might flatter yourself that, being a *marqués* as well as good-looking, you have only to crook your finger and...' She left the conclusion unspoken.

He laughed. 'Do I really strike you like that? An arrogant rooster who thinks he has only to crow and all the hens will...? Well, as the chickens you eat come to supermarkets via broiler houses, you won't know what hens do when the rooster puffs up his feathers and signals his virility.'

In fact, Cassia had lived in places where domestic fowls scratched the earth for things to eat, laid their eggs where they wished and abased themselves in readiness when the rooster wanted to tread them. But it wasn't an analogy she had ever expected to hear in conversation with a man who was almost a stranger.

Momentarily forgetting that she ought not to reveal staff gossip concerning the guests, she said incautiously, 'I gather Señorita Sanchez isn't the first girlfriend you've brought to the Castillo. There seems to have been quite a string of them...and your grandfather was the same.'

'But he had a wife and I don't. That makes a difference. Or do you belong to a sect which believes all sexual relationships are wrong unless their object is procreation?' he asked.

'No, I don't believe that...but nor do I believe in promiscuity,' she added. 'Anyway, how you behave is none of my business. I'm sorry if I've been impertinent, but it was you who raised the subject.'

'Actually it was the gypsy who brought it up. They're great judges of character. She recognised you as a lamb consorting with a wolf. Has your father been the only man in your life?'

It was a shrewd guess that she would have liked to contradict. In the face of his wide experience she didn't want to admit that her own was negligible. Her father had frightened men off. A jealous and suspicious husband—not without reason, as matters had turned out—he had been a possessive father. In his eyes she had never grown up. He had seen all young men as a threat to his little girl's purity.

It was only after he had been told that his illness was incurable that he had consented to her taking evening classes in secretarial skills, financed by her job as a cleaner. She had never had any real freedom until the day John Browning had died.

'My life has been rather a strange one. But I've liked it that way. What I see of other people's lives doesn't make me feel I've missed out,' she answered. 'Probably you don't have much time for reading. But for me books are better companions than people.'

Yet again he surprised her by saying, 'Up to a point I'd agree with that. But it doesn't do to spend *all* one's time in imaginary worlds, or even in worlds that were real but are now part of history. Books are only one of life's pleasures. There are many others—skiing, for example. Living so near a ski-resort, it's a pity you haven't tried it. Was that a question of expense, or wasn't your father ever well enough to ski?'

'He wasn't always an invalid, but he wasn't interested in sports. Only in art. Have you been in the Albaicín before?'

'Only once, but that was at night and by taxi. We were trying out a recommended restaurant. I come to Granada for the skiing, not for the other attractions.'

'But you have been inside the Alhambra?'

'Yes, and envied my ancestor who saw it as it was when Boabdil, the last sultan, surrendered it to Isabella and Ferdinand five hundred years ago. What the tourists see today is only a pale shadow of the way it was then.'

'But it's still a magical place, especially at night when it's floodlit. Do you know that definition of heaven as eating *pâté de foie gras* to the sound of trumpets? For me, the summit of bliss would be having the Alhambra all to myself for a whole day, early in May.'

Her face lit up at the thought of it. Then with a laugh she added, 'An eventuality as unlikely as...as buying a share in the ticket which wins the big prize in the national lottery. But at least by living in Granada I can get into the Alhambra for less than the tourists pay.'

Speaking of tourists reminded her that many of them found the cobbled lanes and long flights of uneven steps in this ancient neighbourhood a tax on their stamina. But, as she led the way up a succession of ascents which left unfit sightseers red-faced and breathless, the Marqués followed at her heels with the ease of a man conditioned to strenuous exercise.

The house where she lived had nothing about its façade to suggest what lay behind its tall, heavy door and shuttered windows. Unlocked by a heavy, old-fashioned key weighing half a kilo, the door gave into a dark hall with a wide stone staircase which narrowed on the next flight and narrowed again on the third.

'Who else lives here?' asked the Marqués.

'No one at this time of year. In the summer the owner and his family move up from their apartment in the city centre. When the temperature down there hits thirty it's cooler and quieter up here.'

'But as cold as a vault in January,' was his comment.

'On the staircase—yes. But I have a gas heater and I wear woolly tights in the evening. You may find it hard to believe, but one can survive without central heating,' she said, glancing over her shoulder.

'You don't need to tell me that,' he said drily. 'The house where I spent a lot of my early life was heated by *braseros* under the tables. Our shins scorched while our backsides froze.'

She had seen the large shallow containers he was talking about. They fetched high prices in street markets and antiques shops, being used now as decorative objects, not for their original purpose—burning charcoal. But she hadn't expected him to be familiar with their shortcomings as heaters.

'If you heat by *estufa*, how do you get the gas bottles up to this floor?' he asked.

The question was another surprise. Stoves fuelled by butane gas in heavy metal canisters were the heaters in common use among ordinary people. Lorries delivering the brightly painted canisters were a frequent sight. But why should a rich man know that handling them was a problem for women living alone and old people?

'The lorry drops them off at the top of the street and I have a trolley,' she said, unlocking the door to the studio. 'I couldn't carry a full bottle upstairs, but pulling it up isn't difficult.'

'Not for a man, or even a big, beefy woman, but you don't come into that category,' he said as she took off her coat.

His appraisal reminded Cassia that shortly after her father's death a plumber had come to the flat. He had been about the same age as the Marqués. After repairing the washing machine he had continued talking, watching her in a way which had made her increasingly nervous. She had felt seriously at risk and, although nothing had happened, had afterwards vowed that never again would she be alone with anyone she couldn't be certain was trustworthy.

Now she was in that situation again: alone, at the top of an empty house, with a man who had insisted on coming home with her for no better reason than to carry a basket of flowers which weighed less than the average bag of groceries, and to look at paintings she had told him were not for sale.

'I see you have a roof terrace...and a spectacular view,' he said, moving towards the wall of glass installed, with the owner's permission, by an earlier tenant who had also been an artist.

'Yes, the view makes the flat. If it looked out on a blank wall it wouldn't be anything special.'

Cassia opened the door to the terrace and gestured for him to precede her. Not only did the flat have the breathtaking view of the Alhambra and the snowy peaks beyond, it also had, looking down, a bird's-eye view of the many walled gardens called *cármenes* for which the Albaicín was famous.

After admiring both views her visitor turned his attention to the terrace itself. 'Were all these plants here when you moved in?'

'No, they're ours...mine—the nearest I've come to a garden.'

'You obviously have green fingers,' he said, strolling round. 'To have so many flowers out in January is quite an achievement.'

'Some of them are really weeds. This creeper with the yellow flowers wouldn't be allowed in most people's gardens, but I like it and it grows anywhere...as this does.' She touched the glossy dark leaves of the ivy growing up the wall of the house next door which, being higher up the steep street, had its top floor above where they were standing. 'It's hard to believe that as the pigeon flies we're not far from the Gran Vía, isn't it?'

The Marqués nodded. 'If I were your landlord I'd live up here all year round.'

'But where would you put your car? None of the houses in this street has a garage or even a parking space.'

'I should have to walk, as you do.' He returned to the studio and began to study the paintings arrayed on its walls.

In the final months of his life John Browning had destroyed more than half his canvases, leaving only what he considered his finest works. He had also weeded out many of the drawings and sketches in his portfolios. Another artist living in the Albaicín had offered to buy his easels and other painting equipment. They had now gone from the working end of the studio, leaving only the boards on trestles which, with the few bits of furniture, had been there when they'd arrived.

She had done what she could to make the place homely, but it must have seemed a stark and comfortless habitation to anyone accustomed to the luxurious elegance of Simón de Mondragón's various homes. She wondered what he was thinking as he moved slowly from picture to picture.

'Do you like your father's work?' he asked suddenly.

She didn't, but had never said so, and wasn't about to disclose her private reactions now. Her taste was for figurative paintings, not these wild abstracts, the strong, often clashing colours applied with a palette knife or with strokes of her father's thumb, the impression they gave being one of violence and anger.

'I'm not qualified to judge it, but, anyway, time is the only true test of an artist's worth, so I've read.'

From his glance at her Cassia saw that he knew she was being evasive, but he didn't press her for a more definite answer. Nor did he express his own reaction except to say, 'There's a lot of luck involved in an artist being successful in his lifetime. Where did you and your father live before you came to Spain?'

'Lots of places. France...Italy...Greece...Morocco. I liked Greece the best, because we lived on an island and I did a lot of swimming. In the summer Señor

Alvarez lets me use the hotel pool, very early in the morning before the guests are up, but it's not like the sea.'

'Did you learn to speak Greek as well as you speak Spanish?'

'No, we didn't stay there long enough. How do you come to have such idiomatic English?'

'My mother was brought up in England. She has friends there whose children are now friends of mine. I have plenty of opportunities to keep my English updated.'

As he spoke the Spaniard's dark eyes were ranging over the rest of the room. 'You don't have a TV or a telephone?'

'We used to have a rented television. I've given it up. It was company for Father when he hadn't the energy to paint, but there wasn't much I wanted to watch. We didn't need a telephone.'

'When is your day off?'

'I don't have a regular day off now. If I need time off I can have it, but I enjoy my job and I'd rather be working than not working.'

'Don't you have any friends?'

'Only among the hotel staff. My father wasn't very sociable. Creative people often prefer their own company.'

'So they may, but their children need friends.'

'*Your* friend will be wondering where you've got to,' Cassia pointed out.

'Unlike you, Isa laps up TV. She won't notice how long I'm gone if she's watching the latest crisis in one of her favourite soaps. But I can take a hint. You'd rather I pushed off.'

Cassia didn't contradict him. It was growing dusk now, and as they left the studio the stairs and landings were almost in darkness. She switched on the lights, although there were not enough of them to illuminate the staircase properly.

The Marqués went down ahead of her, and again she was struck by the fluid grace of his movements. When they passed under one of the light bulbs, dangling from a long flex, she noticed the healthy gloss of his thick dark hair. She couldn't remember ever being more strongly aware of someone's physical attributes.

At the doorway he turned to shake hands—a normal politeness in all walks of Spanish society, but one often mocked by her father, an undemonstrative man who had never gone in for the kissing, hugging and handshaking indulged in by *granadino* families.

'Goodnight, Cassia.'

She could feel the latent strength in the fingers enclosing hers.

'Goodnight, *señor*. Thank you for carrying the flowers for me.'

'My pleasure. Until tomorrow...'

The following morning, after taking the flowers to the cemetery, Cassia was tempted to call in at the hotel on her way back. She was curious to find out if the Marqués had gone skiing or was keeping Isa company until she recovered. However, she resisted the impulse and spent the rest of her free time window-shopping.

She enjoyed looking at fashionable clothes and shoes, even if she couldn't afford them. But this morning she was more than usually aware that most of the other women doing the same thing were in pairs—mothers and daughters, or sisters, or friends, often walking with arms linked. She felt strangely lonely and restless.

When she returned to the Castillo to take over from her colleague, she found that a drama had taken place in her absence. Apparently Simón de Mondragón had waited for the doctor's second visit, soon after nine o'clock. Shortly after the doctor's departure, the Marqués had come downstairs and asked for a maid to help Señorita Sanchez re-pack her cases. He had also arranged for a car to take her to the station in time to catch the midday train for Madrid.

'You could see she was in a raging temper when she left,' Rosita told Cassia. 'But whether she broke the mirror while the Marqués was with her or in a tantrum after he walked out on her, we can't be certain. It could be that he sent her packing *because* she threw an onyx ashtray at him, which, being fast on his feet, he dodged. Or she could have hurled it at the mirror afterwards, because she was furious at being left on her own.

'Luckily for him it's insured, or he'd have had to pay. It's a valuable antique, with its original glass. Señor Alvarez is very annoyed about it. He won't say so, of course. You know how he bends over backwards for anyone important. But he didn't mince words about Señorita Sanchez when his wife rang up. I was quite surprised at the way he described her. She'd have thrown an ashtray at him if she'd heard him.'

'She was probably spoilt as a child...and we don't know what the Marqués said to provoke her to throw it,' said Cassia. 'I wouldn't mind betting it was aimed at him, not the mirror. They were well matched, if you ask me. She was only interested in having a good time at his expense, and his only interest in her was for sex. Not very nice people, either of them.'

Yet even as she said it she knew that she was being a hypocrite. Somewhere deep down inside her a part of her envied Isa Sanchez. Both for her panache and her escort.

Since Cassia had been on her own, she had often been woken at night by noises peculiar to old buildings, which hadn't disturbed her while her father had been there.

Last night, unable to get back to sleep after a loud creak had woken her, she had imagined herself in Isa's place.

But in the scenario she had visualised the Marqués had come to Granada alone, and Cassia had first set eyes on him in the *rápido*—the fast gondola from Pradollano up to Borreguiles, where chair-lifts and ski-lifts took skiers to the start of the *pistas* suited to their abilities.

In her imagination she had been skiing every weekend since their arrival in Granada. She and the Marqués had been the only two people going almost to the top of Veleta, the peak which, at 3,470 metres, was only a few metres lower than the sierra's highest pinnacle.

They had skied down the Olimpica, a long difficult *pista* eventually connecting with a very difficult stretch on the way back to Borreguiles. There the Marqués had admired her prowess, offered her a lift back to the city and, on the way, invited her to dine with him.

At what point she had fallen asleep, her conscious imaginings causing her subconscious mind to invent a long, vivid dream, Cassia wasn't sure. But she could remember very clearly how, over a candlelit dinner in his suite, the Marqués had invited her to become his mistress, and she had accepted.

The memory of how easily she had succumbed to the inducements he'd offered—a jet-set lifestyle, an unlimited dress allowance, her own car—had shocked her when she'd woken up. Of course it had been only a dream. But, if it was true that under hypnosis people could not be made to perform acts unacceptable to their conscious minds, why had her subconscious allowed her to say yes to him? At the end of the dream she had been in his arms, about to be kissed, soon to be taken to bed.

The kiss had been averted by the ringing of a telephone . . . actually Cassia's alarm clock. Her reaction on waking up had been disappointment that now she would never know what it would be like to feel his firm lips on hers.

Rosita took a more tolerant view of the Marqués and his *amiguita*. 'I don't see any harm in guys and girls getting together, as long as they're not doing it behind other people's backs,' she said. 'If he had a wife or she had a husband I wouldn't hold with it. But Manolo says the Marqués is still single, and I'd be surprised if Sanchez had ever trotted up the aisle and promised to spend the rest of her life having babies and washing dishes.

'You can bet she had an eye to the main chance from the day she started to sprout those spectacular bosoms. If I had her looks I wouldn't be doing this job. I'd be swanning around with a boyfriend like the Marqués... but not chucking ashtrays at him. You only live once. If you've got what it takes to catch the eye of a guy like that, you're a fool not to make the most of it.'

'You say that, but I don't think you mean it, Rosita. If the Marqués came back this evening and invited you to have dinner with him in the Mirador, you wouldn't stand up Tomás. You know you wouldn't.'

Cassia had met Rosita's boyfriend. He worked in a bank and they were planning to marry as soon as he got his next pay rise.

'Sometimes I think I ought to break it off with Tomás,' the other receptionist said worriedly. 'I was in love with him—or thought I was—at the beginning, but now...he's beginning to bore me, Cassia. All he ever talks about is sport, and he's not the world's greatest lover either.'

Lowering her voice to a confidential undertone, she said, 'He never makes me feel the way you're supposed to. He doesn't switch me on at all. He did at first, before I let him go the whole way. But now he doesn't bother with the things I used to enjoy. He only does what he likes.'

To Cassia's relief these unexpected revelations were cut short as Rosita caught sight of the time and realised she would have to run or miss her regular bus. She had only been gone a few minutes when a party of four Americans checked in. They had been to Sevilla and Córdoba, and now wished to make the most of a two-night stay in Granada.

When all the other guests who were skiing had returned from their day on the snowy shoulders of Veleta, with the exception of Simón de Mondragón, Cassia began to wonder if he might have had an accident.

According to Rosita, *he* had not looked in a temper when he'd left the hotel, but he might have been raging inwardly. When people were angry it impaired their concentration, and skiing down *pistas* which were graded 'difficult', and driving a powerful sports car on a busy mountain road, were both activities calling for care and attention.

She was on the point of speaking to the manager about him and suggesting a call to the clinic up at Borreguiles when the Marqués strode in, picking up his key from the porter's desk before turning towards the lifts. The indicators showed that one lift was travelling upwards and the other was on the top floor. Rather than pressing the button to call it to ground level, he chose to go up the stairs, taking them two at a time with a long, lithe stride which suggested that he wasn't as tired as the other skiers had looked when they'd returned.

Cassia was still on duty when, a couple of hours later, he stepped out of the lift and headed for the dining room. He had a book in his hand but she couldn't see its title. He didn't look in her direction. He had probably forgotten her existence.

* * *

Next morning she was working the early shift when he came down the stairs in his black salopette with an apricot-coloured T-shirt—another colour which complemented his tawny skin and black hair and eyebrows.

'Good morning, Cassia.'

On his way out he gave her a friendly smile. For no sensible reason, being noticed lifted her spirits.

She went off duty before he came back, and spent the evening washing her hair, doing her nails and pressing two white blouses left out to dry on the roof terrace. As she mended the start of a run in one foot of a pair of black tights she wondered if the Marqués was dining alone and would remain on his own for the rest of his time here, or if he would find a substitute for Isa Sanchez.

There were plenty of beautiful girls in Granada who would be glad to keep him company—not only the top-level call-girls, but young women of good family and more discriminating habits.

At nine o'clock the next day she was inserting tariffs on separate slips into the Castillo's stylish brochures, before replenishing the perspex stand that displayed them, when he came to the desk.

'Good morning, Cassia. How are you this morning?'

'I'm fine, thank you. And you, *señor*? Did you have a good day yesterday?'

'Very good. Better in the morning than in the afternoon, when the sun makes the snow rather slushy. If you're free this evening, will you have dinner with me?'

She couldn't believe her ears. Why should he want *her*, of all people, to dine with him? She wasn't beautiful. Her figure was nothing outstanding. She wasn't witty and amusing. She certainly wasn't available.

'You did say you could take time off when you wanted it, and I have a proposition to put to you,' he went on. 'The dining room can be noisy when the hotel is full. Let's eat in my suite, where we can talk in peace. I'll expect you at seven-thirty. There's no need to change. Come as you are.'

Before Cassia could recover her wits and her voice, someone else came to the desk. The Marqués stepped politely aside. Taking her acceptance as read, he gave her a smiling, '*Adiós*,' before turning away to give his key to Manolo.

CHAPTER THREE

FOR the rest of the morning Cassia found it an effort to keep her mind on her job and not let her thoughts wander off in futile speculation about what the Marqués might have meant by 'a proposition to put to you'.

When her lunch break came, instead of eating a hot meal in the staff room she asked the assistant chef to make her up a snack to take up the hill to the Generalife gardens.

After paying for a ticket at the gate, she walked up the cypress-lined drive leading to the open-air theatre. A young man with a rucksack beside him was sitting there, writing postcards. He looked up and smiled at her. Cassia smiled back, giving him a friendly '*Hola*!' before walking on to find a secluded seat with a closer view of the Alhambra's towers than the one she saw from her terrace.

It was a peaceful spot in which to ponder why Simón de Mondragón wanted to 'talk in peace' with her. Unwrapping her lunch—a crusty loaf slit lengthwise and filled with lettuce-heart leaves, asparagus and slices of mountain ham—she bit off a mouthful and sat thoughtfully munching.

She knew what Rosita would say if asked to give an opinion on the motive for his behest. She could hear her colleague's response as clearly as if she *had* consulted her. 'There's only one sort of proposition a man like the Marqués makes to girls like us,' Rosita would have answered, with a cynical shrug.

But Rosita, with her full breasts and merry dark eyes, was far more propositionable than Cassia felt herself to be.

She couldn't believe that the Marqués's reading of her character would be so wide of the mark that he'd think she would succumb to his blandishments. Nor, to give the devil his due, did she feel that he was the kind of man who would attempt to seduce an inexperienced girl.

It would have been such a mean thing to do, and somehow she didn't want him to turn out to be an ignoble nobleman. There were many worse vices than being a womaniser, provided that he only made love to women who knew the rules and that no one else was hurt.

But supposing he was less scrupulous? Supposing he *did* make a pass? What was the best way to handle it?

'Do you speak any English?'

In the act of pouring herself a beaker of mineral water, she looked up to find the young man with the rucksack standing near her.

He introduced himself: an American from a small town in New England who was touring Spain on a rented bicycle, at present chained to the entrance gates.

Cassia returned to the Castillo with her dilemma unresolved. Even if she hadn't had to talk to the American, she doubted if she would have decided how to react if the worst came to the worst. She could only hope and pray that it wouldn't.

Most girls of her age would have known how to tackle the situation, because they would have experienced it before. But her father's possessive vigilance during her teens, followed by his dependence while he was ill, had meant that most of her knowledge was theoretical, gleaned from books.

First by choice, and later by circumstance, John Browning had kept her as cloistered as a nun. Only by running away could she have freed herself from his controlling influence. But where could she have run to? Besides, she had loved him, and love was as inescapable as the web a spider bound round a captive fly. Loving someone, you couldn't deliberately hurt them—not even if their way of loving was unintentionally hurting you.

All afternoon she was on a mental treadmill, her thoughts in continuous motion but only going round and round, never reaching a conclusion.

When the skiers began to return she became increasingly tense. Those who had been at the hotel for a few days or longer were sporting deep golden tans, except one or two who had neglected to take the necessary precautions and were now lobster-pink and peeling.

The Marqués had the type of skin which would never burn unless he was lost in a desert. By the end of the week he would be even more deeply bronzed—as dark as the Moorish invaders of long ago, and in some ways as exotic and fearsome as they must have seemed to the indigenous population.

When she saw him entering the lobby, carrying his ski-boots, his thick hair still in some disorder from the hours on the long, fast runs, her heart began to pump uncomfortably fast.

He collected his key and an envelope the porter on duty had already taken from the Mirador suite's pigeon-hole. Cassia knew that the envelope contained a long facsimile transmission to the machine in Señor Alvarez's office. She had been talking to his secretary when it came through and had watched her clip the pages together. Evidently it was something the Marqués had been waiting for. Pocketing his key and slinging his boots, already linked together, over one shoulder, he slit the envelope and started to read the contents.

She watched him crossing the lobby, a slight frown contracting his eyebrows. It seemed that he was too preoccupied to remember his invitation and verify her acceptance.

As he entered the open lift, still reading, she felt angry with herself for spending all day in a state of conjecture while doubtlessly he had dismissed her from his mind when he'd left, and now that he was back was too intent on his fax even to notice and acknowledge her.

The lift did not go to the top floor as she'd expected. It stopped at the first floor. Seconds later the Marqués appeared at the top of the stairs and came down them, looking at her, smiling.

Reaching the desk, he said, 'Some news from Madrid made me forget for a moment that we have a dinner date. Is the time I suggested all right for you? What time are you off duty?'

She found herself saying, 'I finish at seven.'

'In that case, why not come up as soon as you're free? Until seven.'

In fact it was a quarter past seven when she arrived at the door of the Mirador suite, after spending ten minutes in the women's staff washroom, redoing her hair and repairing her make-up.

Today she was wearing a black skirt with an inexpensive white blouse found on the racks at Tienda Corty, the new supermarket-style store which had replaced the city-centre branch of El Corte Inglés, one of Spain's two best known department-store chains. The blouse, an import from India, had cost less than Isa Sanchez probably spent on her tights, and it was no longer as crisp as it had been when the day had started. But there wasn't time to rush back to the Albaicín and put on something more appropriate for dinner in the hotel's most expensive suite.

Not that she owned anything to match the luxurious elegance of the suite.

As she waited for the Marqués to answer the door she wondered what Señor Alvarez and the others would think about her having dinner with Simón de Mondragón. They would soon find out. The waiter who served the meal would be sure to report her presence, and in no time at all the news would be buzzing round the staff grapevine.

The door opened. The Marqués stood looking down at her, his hair freshly washed and smoothly brushed. He was wearing a dark brown linen open-necked shirt and pale grey trousers, with a dark brown braided leather belt slotted through the loops. He wore no jewellery, nor did he smell of the strong cologne favoured by most Spanish men. But his cheeks and chin were a lighter shade than they had been when he'd returned to the hotel, indicating that he had shaved.

He stepped back for her to enter the spacious sitting room. This was the first time that she had been inside one of the top-floor suites, although she had had them described to her by the maids responsible for keeping them immaculate.

Even so, she was unprepared for the exuberant colour and richness of the room, with its three massive sofas grouped round a huge coffee-table made from a slab of darkly veined, rose-coloured marble, on which were stacked old and new books about the history of Spain as well as the current issues of all the Spanish glossies.

'What would you like to drink?' her host asked. 'Shall we share this champagne?' he went on, with a gesture to the bottle in the ice-bucket which must have arrived shortly before she had. 'Or would you prefer a soft drink?'

If his object was seduction, it seemed odd that he should offer the alternative.

'Champagne would be lovely,' she said. 'What a beautiful room. I've never been in here before.'

'It has more character than many hotel rooms,' he agreed. 'Most of my friends who ski here prefer to stay at the *parador* on the Sierra Nevada, to save driving up and down every day. But if I were staying up there I wouldn't have met you—a meeting which could prove opportune for both of us.'

Wondering what he meant by that, Cassia continued to survey her surroundings while he dealt with the champagne. Above a carved and gilded side-table was a painting she had seen being carried through the lobby at mid-morning. It was a temporary replacement, on loan from a local art gallery, for the valuable mirror that Isa Sanchez had broken.

Perhaps, having sent her packing, the Marqués considered it opportune that he had already made the acquaintance of another girl who took his fugitive fancy.

'Was the skiing good today?' she asked, hoping that he couldn't tell how nervous she was.

'Excellent this morning. As usual, less good after lunch. Today I was skiing on the longest *pista*, the Aguila. Here you are.' He came to where she was standing and put a glass in her hand. '*Salud.*'

'*Salud,*' she echoed, before sipping the wine.

'First things first. Come and sit down and decide what you'd like to eat,' he said, with a gesture giving her the choice of the three huge sofas piled with cushions covered in antique velvets and pieces of needlework.

She was far too strung-up to feel like eating anything. She hoped that the champagne would act as a tranquiliser. Seating herself at one end of the sofa facing the massive fireplace in which a clever simulation of a log fire was creating an illusion of leaping flames, she took the folder he handed her before seating himself in the centre of the adjoining sofa.

In the angles formed by the arms, the end-tables held large, silk-shaded lamps and arrangements of flowers.

Each sofa had a fine oriental rug in front of it, laid over a floor of huge terracotta tiles, polished to a soft sheen. The room's real heat came from electric elements embedded in the floor—a form of heating used throughout the hotel during the winter months.

The folder contained details in four languages of all the à la carte dishes that the kitchens offered, preceded by the statement that if what a guest desired was not included in the menu the chef would exert himself to satisfy their wishes.

Eager to learn everything she could about the hotel business, Cassia had long since familiarised herself with everything on the menu. Some dishes she had tried. Some had been explained to her.

She said, 'You must be ravenous after skiing for five or six hours, but I normally have a big lunch and eat lightly in the evening. If you don't mind, I'll just have soup and a salad.'

'As you wish.'

He ordered the meal for eight o'clock, which was when the dining room opened for the benefit of short-stay foreigners accustomed to eating at earlier times than the Spanish. Cassia couldn't help wondering if tonight he was eating early to precipitate the main purpose of the evening—seducing her.

But then, in a businesslike tone, he said, 'Before we dine I want to explain the proposition I mentioned to you. Is your mind fixed on going to England? Or would you be interested in seeing another part of Spain?'

'I might. It depends . . .' she said cautiously.

He rose to top up her glass. She wondered if he was going to sit down beside her.

To her relief he returned to the other sofa. 'A long time ago, when resorts like Marbella and Benidorm were still undiscovered fishing villages, one of my aunts married a man whose family had a beach house near a small seaport called Jávea. It's midway between Valencia and Alicante on what, since tourism started, has been called the Costa Blanca. As a small boy I often stayed there with my cousins. There was also a house in the mountains behind the coast, belonging to my family. It hadn't been used for years but there was an ancient caretaker living in the servants' quarters. Sometimes we picnicked in the garden.'

He paused, his expression abstracted. She wondered what he had looked like when he was a child. Tall for his age, no doubt, and perhaps rather thin and gangly, as big men often were in early childhood.

'I went back there recently,' he continued. 'The whole coast is scarcely recognisable. It's been colonised by retired expats from northern Europe and North America. Even inland it's changed. The mules have gone, replaced by tractors and cultivators. In the villages a few old women still use the communal wash-house, mainly to have a gossip, but the younger ones all have washing machines. Only my house and garden are still in a time-warp. The caretaker I remember was succeeded by his son. Now he wants to give up and live with his married daughter at Callosa de Ensarriá. I have to decide what to do with the place.'

'How large is the house?' asked Cassia.

Surely he couldn't see her as a replacement caretaker? It was so far removed from what she had thought he might have in mind that she had to suppress an upsurge of slightly hysterical amusement.

'It has eight bedrooms, but only one primitive bathroom. It needs drastic modernisation to make it habitable and comfortable, but I don't envisage ever living there myself. On the other hand, it's ideally situated for a project I'm organising. What, if anything, do you know about the so-called Mozarabic trails?'

'Not much. Only that they were a network of tracks and stairways used by mule-trains in previous centuries.'

'Not very much more *is* known,' said the Marqués. 'Their origins are lost in the past. Now that they're no longer the main routes between remote mountain villages and over the passes between valleys, the trails themselves are in danger of being destroyed by neglect. It was actually an American professor who brought them to my attention.'

Having crossed his long legs a few moments earlier, he now drew the ankle of one onto the knee of the other—a relaxed posture which reminded her of her father, who had often sat in the same position.

'The professor and his wife are amateur botanists who spend their holidays mountain-walking,' the Marqués continued. 'While they were staying with his brother—an ex-Navy yachtsman who's chosen the Costa Blanca as his base for sailing the Mediterranean—they discovered and walked some of the old trails. They were concerned to see them in danger of disappearing.'

'But if they're not used any more how can they be preserved? In the past, presumably, the people who used them did running repairs as and when they were necessary.'

'I imagine so. Clearly, now times have changed, they can't all be maintained in good order. But if only a few are kept up it'll be better than letting part of our national heritage be lost. One of Spain's problems is that advances which have taken centuries to evolve in other parts of Europe have happened to us in a few decades. As recently as thirty years ago great tracts of this country were still in the Middle Ages. Some parts are still fairly backward.'

'Even Granada lags behind the times in some ways,' said Cassia. 'Only the other day I heard two Americans discussing the fact that the street sweepers use brooms made of twigs, and that they'd seen a man with three panniered donkeys stopping the traffic in the Gran Vía while he led them across it.'

'That's one of Spain's charms—that it isn't all of a piece. I don't think the next generation will see donkeys in city streets, but we can keep some of the ancient trails and, I hope, combine their preservation with another rescue operation.'

The Marqués's expression was different from any of his that she had seen before as he leaned towards her, saying seriously, 'Our most valuable resource is the youth of this country. At present thousands of teenagers are unemployed. Even those who aren't out of work are exposed to damaging influences, notably drugs. I want to set up a hostel where youths and girls from the cities can spend a few weeks in a totally different environment from the poor *barrios* they come from. It won't be a holiday for them. They'll be expected to work... work very hard.'

'Clearing the trails?'

'Exactly. Doing something useful for the community and in the process, I hope, achieving a self-esteem they may never have experienced before.'

This was so totally at variance with what she had been expecting, and threw such an unexpected and different light on Simón de Mondragón's character, that she was lost for words.

'By a lucky chance, the last time I was in England I happened to hear of a man who seems the ideal person to be an instructor-cum-taskmaster,' he continued. 'Like you, he's British by birth, but has knocked about the world and picked up several languages, including fluent if ungrammatical Spanish. Although he isn't Scottish, the Scots word "dour" is a good description of Jack Locke.

'He grew up in circumstances as tough and disadvantaged as those of the youngsters he'll be dealing with. I suspect it was touch-and-go whether he turned to crime or lived on the right side of the law. So he'll be on their wavelength. I doubt if you'll like him, but you needn't have much to do with him. Your role, if you take the job, will be administration.'

'But I have no experience of that sort of thing.'

'That can be an advantage. Any intelligent person, given a project to tackle, can quickly pick up the necessary expertise. The whole thing is an experiment, which may or may not come off. We'll start small and, I hope, build up.

'Have some more champagne. If you'll excuse me, I have a couple of telephone calls to make. While I'm making them, you can be thinking it over...making a note of questions you want to ask.'

Having replenished her glass and handed her the pad and pencil provided for the sitting-room extension, he then opened a marquetry cabinet containing a large television and cassette player. A few seconds later, orchestral music began. The Marqués closed the cabinet and disappeared into the next room.

He was gone for nearly twenty minutes. In his absence Cassia relaxed for the first time since he had summoned her here.

It was a huge relief to have her misgivings allayed. Now it seemed foolishly alarmist ever to have imagined that he would look lustfully at her.

And with this thought came another, quickly suppressed—a faint flicker of regret that she wasn't the sort of girl for whom he would feel desire.

When he came back, he switched off the music. 'I expect your first question is what salary am I offering. What do you earn at the moment?'

She told him, explaining the hours required for her basic pay, and the overtime rate.

'Right. I'll raise that by fifty per cent, with bed and board provided, and we'll review the situation in six months' time. At this stage it's hard to say what your hours will be. Fairly long, but not always very taxing, I should imagine. Next question.'

'You mentioned administration. Can you be more explicit?'

'You'll be responsible for paying the bills, organising and supervising the cleaners, controlling all household supplies, liaising with contractors. Anything which isn't the cook's responsibility, or the instructor's, will fall on your shoulders.'

'When are you planning to start this operation? I can't leave without giving Señor Alvarez adequate notice.'

'I'll be coming to Granada for more skiing next month. If you've accepted the job and finalised your affairs here, I'll drive you to the village, Castell de los Torres. If you have a lot of belongings you want to take with you, some may have to be sent by carrier. My car has limited luggage space.'

'Perhaps it might be better if I went there by coach. How far is Castell de los Torres from the nearest bus station?'

'About fifteen miles, and the coach trip will take you all day. With me you'll be there in a few hours. But first you must make up your mind if you want the job. You won't see any jet-set people, only peasants and uncouth teenagers.'

'Some jet-set people can be surprisingly uncouth,' she said drily.

'No doubt, but you know what I mean. Life in a mountain village of four hundred people is very different from life in a five-star hotel. When the fish van comes it's a major event.'

'I wonder if your peasants will mind having city teen-agers inflicted on them by an absentee aristocrat.'

A gleam of sardonic mockery came into his shrewd dark eyes.

'You don't like my calling them peasants?'

'Possibly they might not like it.'

'It's not a derogatory description. A peasant is someone who makes his living by agricultural labour. I respect such a man. The people of Castell de los Torres aren't "my" peasants. If they were ever exploited by a large landowner it was a long time ago, and not by one of my forebears. I inherited the house and its garden. Nothing else. The surrounding vineyards and almond groves are smallholdings. I expect you're right—at first they'll be watchful and wary. That's where the skills you've learned here will come in useful. Instead of being charming to hotel guests, you can calm and reassure the village people.'

'Don't they view all outsiders with some suspicion?'

'We aren't an insular race like the British,' he said, with a teasing gleam. 'Spaniards are naturally hospitable. You have till the morning I leave to make up your mind. In the meantime, if there's anything you want to know you have only to ask.'

Soon after they finished dining he drove her home, leaving his car at the top of the street for a few minutes while he saw her to her door.

Already there was no doubt in Cassia's mind that she would take the job. The money was good. She would have more responsibility. It would be interesting to live and work in a different part of Spain. She could go to England next year. A reference from a Spanish *marqués* would be an impressive addition to her CV.

*   *   *

Not unexpectedly, after his morning tour of the hotel the next day the manager called her into his office and told her to close the door.

'What's this I hear about you having dinner in the Mirador suite last night, Cassia?'

'The Marqués has offered me a job, Señor Alvarez.' Anticipating his next question, she explained the nature of the post.

The manager gestured for her to sit down. 'As you have no family to guide you, I regard myself in some measure as *in loco parentis*. What I'm about to say to you is strictly confidential. It's not our place to judge the manners and morals of the guests, but I should have thought your own powers of observation would have told you the Marqués is not—how shall I put it?—a pillar of rectitude.'

'I realise that, but I'm quite sure he hasn't any designs of that nature on me. Once he's set up this project, I don't expect we'll see much of him.'

After questioning her more closely, the manager said, 'In my opinion, you're too young for the job. It needs someone more mature. You're a sensible, conscientious girl, but not old enough to impose discipline on youths and girls who have no respect for authority.'

'They'll be kept in order by the Englishman. He's a tough nut who won't stand any nonsense.'

'Not a congenial companion for someone as refined as yourself,' Señor Alvarez said disapprovingly. 'I advise you to stay here. If you feel some embarrassment about turning down the Marqués's offer, would you like me to speak to him for you?'

'He's given me until he leaves to make up my mind. I haven't done that yet. I appreciate your advice, and your offer, but I shan't be afraid to tell him if I decide to turn the job down,' Cassia said, politely but firmly.

* * *

For the rest of his stay the Marqués acknowledged her presence with friendly courtesy whenever she was in the lobby when he passed through it. But they had no conversation, and the curiosity aroused by her visit to his suite soon died down when it was seen that he was spending his evenings alone or with other skiing guests.

As she had feared, the manager was very put out when, the night before Simón de Mondragón's departure, Cassia gave in her notice.

'I shall have to replace you. You can't expect to come back if things go badly,' he warned her.

'I realise that. If it doesn't work out I'll go to England.'

'A beautiful country with an impossible climate,' said Señor Alvarez. 'As a young man I spent a year in London. I couldn't wait to get back to our better weather. You're throwing away a promising career at the Castillo, Cassia. But young people nowadays will never listen to advice. They think they know it all.'

She spent a restless night, wondering if he was right. A key factor in her decision was the imminent end of her lease of the studio. But for that, she might have played safe and put off leaving Granada. But if she had to leave the Albaicín she might as well leave the city altogether.

The Marqués was leaving earlier than other guests on the list of those checking out the next day. Cassia had scrutinised his bill to make sure that it was in order when he came downstairs after breakfasting in his suite. His luggage and skis would be taken directly to the garage and stowed in his car for him before it was brought to the entrance.

'Good morning, Cassia.'

'Good morning, señor. I hope you've enjoyed your stay with us.'

'Very much, thank you.' He took a wallet from the back pocket of his trousers, extracted a card and placed it on the counter while he cast an eye down the bill.

While Cassia placed his card in the machine he said, 'What have you decided?'

She looked up. Taking a deep breath, she said, 'I'd like to join your project.'

'Good. In that case I'll expect you to be ready to leave at the end of my next visit. In the meantime, if you have any queries you can fax them to this number.' He produced a business card.

It wasn't until after he had gone that she looked at it and found it wasn't his own card but that of his secretary.

The following month was not an easy one. The hotel manager wasn't the only person who thought that she was mad to throw in a good job with prospects for an insecure position somewhere in the backwoods of País Valencia, once the kingdom of Valencia but now, to judge by the way her *granadino* colleagues referred to it, a backward part of the country fit only for *campesinos*—a term they used with a much more scornful inflexion than the Marqués speaking of peasants.

It was not her first experience of the disdain that Spaniards from one part of the country felt for people of other regions, all of them wanting autonomy for their own region. But instead of undermining her confidence their attitude made her more resolute.

She had let her father rule her life, but from now on she was going to make her own decisions, be her own woman.

CHAPTER FOUR

AT FIVE minutes to nine on a sunny February morning, Cassia carried her suitcase to the top of the street to await the arrival of the Marqués at the place where he had left his car after driving her home a month earlier.

She had finished working at the hotel the day before yesterday, spending the previous day leaving the studio far cleaner than it had been when she and her father had moved in. His paintings and a trunk containing some of their other belongings were now in storage. All she had with her were her clothes and a few personal treasures to make her feel at home in her room at Casa Mondragón in Castell de los Torres.

Contrary to the belief that Spaniards had little regard for punctuality, the Marqués arrived as various church clocks in the area were chiming the hour. She had seen little of him during the past few days. This time he had come to Granada alone.

'Good morning,' he said through the open window as he pulled up beside her. 'All ready for your adventure?'

'Good morning. Yes, I'm looking forward to it.'

Before springing out he touched a button inside the car which caused the boot to open. Before she could lift her case he was looming over her, picking it up as easily as if it were empty. Having stowed her cheap case on top of his own expensive one, he opened the passenger door for her.

Apart from the night he had run her home, Cassia had never driven in a luxurious car before. Nor could she herself drive. She bent to sit down and then straightened again, saying anxiously, 'I've just realised that you may be assuming I can drive. Shall I need to? Does the fact that I can't rule me out?'

'It's a disadvantage, but not an insuperable one. You'll have to take driving lessons. If I'd realised you couldn't drive, I would have suggested that you start to learn right away. But it's not essential . . . not at the outset anyway.'

The Albaicín being on the north side of the city, the road to Murcia—the next city on their route—ran close by. Within five minutes of Cassia fastening her seatbelt Granada was lost to view, and they were gliding smoothly up a serpentine hill road, leaving everything familiar behind.

A few kilometres on the Marqués stopped for *gasolina*. While the tank was filling he talked in his easy way to the pump attendant. She wondered if he would chat to her on the way along, or if he would play one of the tapes filling a special storage compartment under the dashboard.

The night they had dined together their conversation had ranged over various topics, and she hadn't found it a strain or felt that he might be bored by someone whose horizons were more limited than his own.

As they were leaving the service area he said, 'Your previous boss isn't pleased with me for filching you from him. This morning, as I was leaving, he dropped the unctuous manner of all hoteliers to tell me, almost severely, that you are a girl of the highest character, deserving scrupulous kindness and consideration.'

'He's a very kind man himself. He takes a paternal interest in all his employees.'

'I am not kind,' said the Marqués. 'Nor have I ever felt fatherly. But Alvarez seemed relieved when I told him the personnel on our project would include a middle-aged cook. No doubt that will ease your mind too,' he added, with an amused sideways glance.

'My mind was never uneasy. Is the cook a local person?'

'No. Her husband was French and she's lived in France for twenty years. She is now a widow and wants to return to Spain. Her name is Laura Boisson. Until she arrives in a few days' time we shall have to manage as best we can.'

She wondered who 'we' referred to, and if it included himself. But instead of asking she said, 'When do you expect the project to become operational?'

'If things go to plan—which in any small village is highly unlikely—we could be ready for action in six weeks.' He selected a tape and slotted it into the player. 'I hope you won't dislike this. My musical taste is the result of early brainwashing by my mother, who might have become a professional pianist if she hadn't married young.'

Cassia said, 'I liked the music you played the night I had dinner with you.'

'I can't remember what it was. This is Rachmaninov.'

Her first glimpse of their journey's end was six hours later when they came to the crest of a hill and, the road being deserted, the Marqués stopped the car to let her take in the vista directly ahead of them—a long, shallow valley sheltered on three sides by mountains and encompassing several small villages, the most distant being their destination.

In the afternoon light of a warm day the long valley presented a pleasant picture of vineyards interspersed with orchards of almond trees, and in places some orange groves.

The modern world had encroached to the extent that one of the villages they passed had a large petrol station on its outskirts, but the valley had so far escaped the incursions of tourism. Here, instead of the colonies of villas to be seen nearer the coast, the lower slopes of the mountains were still either bare or terraced with dry-stone walls, some crumbling from long neglect, others supporting land still in use.

A roadside sign—'Castell de los Torres'—announced that they had arrived at the next addition to the many places where she had lived—so many she had lost count. She wondered how long she would stay here, and if it would be a happy experience or one she would later regret having embarked on.

There were not many people about, and those they saw stared curiously at the car and its occupants. Only one old man raised his hand, but perhaps from habit rather than recognition that although the car had a Madrid registration number its driver was not altogether a stranger here.

'That's the Plaza Mayor—the hub of the village,' said the Marqués, with a gesture at a square with the Spanish flag flying from one of its buildings, and a couple of small dark bars. Even here there were few signs of life.

The Casa Mondragón stood in a smaller square, occupying the whole of one side and towering over its neighbours although they were substantial houses. While they were well kept, with no dust on the wrought-iron *rejas* guarding the windows, and brightly burnished knockers and knobs on their doors, the larger house looked neglected, if not deserted.

'Don't be put off. It won't look like this for much longer,' said the Marqués as he parked the car. 'Luckily this isn't the only way in,' he went on, unlocking the Judas-door in one of the two huge double doors. 'There's a road at the rear, and the builders use that way in.'

Cassia had lived in Spain long enough to know that the fronts of apparently modest Spanish houses often concealed surprisingly roomy interiors. As soon as she stepped inside the Casa Mondragón, she realised that it was even more palatial than its façade suggested. Beyond the wide hall with its stately stairway was a window wall, and beyond it a large patio.

After she had followed the Marqués on his tour of the building to see how the builders were progressing, he said to her, 'We shan't be spending the night here. I've arranged for you to stay at the pharmacist's house, and I'll be at a *hostal* a few miles away where they cater to botanists and walkers. Manners and mores in Castell are some way behind the times. We don't want to raise any eyebrows by sleeping here on our own, without Laura to make it respectable.'

This announcement was a relief to her. With its thick walls and shuttered windows, except where the builders were working, the house was both cold and spooky, and would be more so at night. She wouldn't have fancied sleeping here on her own, but would have been equally uneasy at being alone with him—not because she thought that he might take advantage of the situation, but because she knew how the villagers would view it. It was a point in his favour that although unconventional himself he did sometimes respect other people's sense of propriety.

Madame Boisson returned to her homeland by coach, in the company of a French friend who had an apartment in Benidorm, once a quiet fishing village but now a resort whose skyscraping profile Cassia had glimpsed from the *autopista* on their way to the valley.

Simón had arranged to drive to Benidorm and collect the cook after she had spent a couple of nights with her friend, helping her to put the flat in order for a winter holiday.

As the daily bus service from the valley to and from the city of Alicante passed through Benidorm, many employers would have expected the housekeeper to come to Castell by public transport. It threw an unexpected light on Simón's character that he was prepared to put himself out to fetch her.

'That's Continente, one of the big supermarkets where you'll be buying some supplies,' he said, indicating a large, modern structure flying the flags of many nations on the outskirts of Benidorm. 'Which reminds me—we must fix up some driving lessons for you. Perhaps I'll give you the basic lessons myself.'

'Oh, no...please don't,' she said hurriedly. 'It's kind of you to suggest it, but it would make me nervous to learn in a car like this. I'd hate to damage it.'

'I shouldn't let you,' he said, smiling at her. 'But maybe you're right... Teaching women to drive is notoriously difficult for anyone but a qualified instructor. Perhaps women can teach each other, but when a man attempts it usually it ends with his blood pressure going up ten points and his pupil in tears.'

Suspecting him of teasing her, Cassia said, 'So they say. I'd certainly feel a lot happier learning to drive in a small car belonging to an auto school.' The environs of Benidorm offering an easy change of subject, she went on, 'Did you ever see this place before they put up the high-rise hotels?'

'No, we never used to come here. But these are only baby skyscrapers compared with the ones in New York and Hong Kong and Rio.'

To find the address that Madame Boisson had given him, he had to ask a policeman for directions. The town was teeming with foreigners, most of them grey-haired but with healthy tans and happy faces.

'I wonder if they realise how much nicer it is only a few miles inland,' said Cassia as they drove along a wide boulevard lined with hotels and cafés and shops full of tourist tat.

'They probably wouldn't agree with you. Life in Castell isn't to everyone's taste. You may get bored with it yourself when you've been there a bit longer.'

Two days after Laura's arrival Simón returned to Madrid, saying that he would come and go as his other commitments permitted.

No doubt he was bored with them, thought Cassia after his departure. In spite of his obvious enthusiasm for the project he was setting up, Castell was a very different environment from his natural milieu, and she and Laura were not the sort of women he was accustomed to spending time with.

Small, overweight and vivacious, Laura was a natural chatterbox who had begun the story of her life on the drive back from Benidorm and every day, at every meal, related some more of the details. Cassia didn't mind this. She was interested in other people's lives. What she found mildly tiresome were Laura's frequent criticisms of the way things were done in Spain compared with the superior methods in force in her adopted country. But perhaps the attitude would wear off as she settled down.

One morning, after Cassia had been to the Plaza Mayor to post some letters to Granada, she was on her way back to the house when a vehicle pulled up and the man in it spoke to her.

'I'm looking for the house of Mondragón,' he said, in Spanish.

He was on the other side of the road, leaning out of the offside window of a right-hand-drive, travel-dusty Range Rover. That and his accent told her he was the man they were expecting.

She crossed the street and said in English, 'You must be Jack Locke?'

If he was surprised he didn't show it. 'That's right. Who are you?'

'Cassia Browning...another member of the team. I'm the dogsbody,' she added, smiling.

She got no smile in response, although he did take the hand she offered in a large paw with oil-stained nails and calluses on the palm. Unlike the Marqués he hadn't learned to moderate his grip when shaking hands with women, but she managed not to wince as he ground her knuckles together.

'You'd better hop in,' he said, opening the door for her.

'Turn left at the end of the street, and then first right and second left,' she said as she settled herself beside him. 'How was your journey?'

'OK. When did you get here?'

'Two weeks ago. When the Marqués recruited me I was working in a hotel in Granada. I don't know this part of Spain, but already I'm getting to like it. Where did you stop last night?'

'Dossed down in the back,' he said, jerking a thumb at the space behind them.

'You'll be glad to have a shower and stretch your legs.'

He made no comment, perhaps because he was steering his large, high vehicle between a parked car and a moped propped on the opposite kerb, making the narrow street almost impassable.

While his attention was engaged Cassia made a quick study of him. She had seen at first glance that his hair was cut close to his scalp, giving him the look of a Victorian gaolbird. Usually earrings and even noserings went with that brutal crop, but the man beside her wore no adornment; nor did the sleeves of his shirt, rolled high above his biceps, reveal any tattoos.

All the same, he looked a tough, rough type, who could pass the night by the roadside or in a motorway lorry park without fear of being molested by the pirates-on-wheels who had made random camping unsafe for more vulnerable travellers.

A scruff he was not. The pugnacious jaw had been shaved before he'd set out and his clothes, though cheap and well-worn, were clean. Even his heavy-soled, cross-laced rough-country boots had been polished recently. At the moment she couldn't tell what colour his eyes were. They were hidden by dark glasses with wide side-pieces.

'Left, right and second left...correct?' he said, checking her directions.

'Correct,' she said, equally briskly. Was he always so laconic? She wondered how he would get on with the garrulous Laura.

'Is the *jefe* here?'

It was a term with many meanings, ranging from boss to commanding officer. Concluding that he meant the Marqués, she said, 'He's gone to Madrid for a few days. We're expecting him back tonight or tomorrow.'

'Where's your base in the UK?' he asked.

'I've never lived in the UK. My father was an artist...a nomad. We moved round the Mediterranean as the fancy took him. Where are you from?'

'London...the East End. The wrong end of town,' he said tersely.

Was this the first sign of a chip on his shoulder? she wondered. Chippy people could be a bore, always sniping at those they considered to have unfair advantages.

Moments later they turned the last corner into the street behind their employer's house. After Jack had parked the Range Rover in a corner of the back patio—at present looking more like a builders' yard—Cassia explained about Laura.

'Come and meet her. Then I'll show you your room and leave you to freshen up before lunch.'

Laura, when her plump hand was compressed by his large, rough paw, gave a stifled squeak.

'What a brute!' she said, with a grimace, when Cassia returned to the kitchen after taking him upstairs. 'I hope his table manners are not going to put us off our lunch.'

However, although the new arrival seemed unaware of such niceties as drawing out the women's chairs for them, or waiting until they had everything they needed before starting to eat, at least he didn't do it noisily or with his mouth open.

After he had answered four or five questions with curt monosyllables, Laura gave up trying to draw him out and ignored him, except to offer second helpings.

At the end of the meal he surprised and mollified her by complimenting her on her cooking, albeit in less gracious terms than the Marqués would have used. The Englishman's Spanish, while fluent, was the crude speech of the mean streets rather than the cultured Castilian spoken by Simón.

When he had left them, to unload the equipment he had brought with him, Laura said, 'At least he won't have any trouble keeping the young ones in order. That's something to be thankful for. But as company for us . . .' She finished the sentence with a negative gesture.

Presently, from the kitchen window, as Laura washed and Cassia wiped the dishes, they saw Jack unloading and then, stripped to the waist, hosing down the Range Rover.

'Such muscles!' Laura exclaimed. 'He's built like that creature Rambo.'

She sounded half repelled, half excited by the sight of Jack's brawny torso. Although several inches shorter in the leg than the Marqués, he was equally broad of shoulder, and obviously tuned to a high degree of fitness.

'You'll have to take care of that one,' Laura went on in a warning tone. 'You saw the way he devoured his lunch. He'll be the same with women. You'd better lock your door tonight.'

Cassia couldn't help laughing. 'I don't think he's going to pounce on me without some encouragement, Laura.'

'You don't know as much about men as I do,' said the older woman. 'I can tell you're not as experienced as many girls of your age. Men are not like us, my dear. They have appetites which must be satisfied. When they're in that mood they forget all finer feelings. It's not altogether their fault. It's the way nature made them.'

The statement cast an unflattering light on her late husband, thought Cassia. Aloud she said, 'I expect when Jack's in that mood he'll drive to the coast and find himself a pretty tourist who's looking for a holiday romance. I'm sure there are plenty around.'

'Very likely...but I still wouldn't put it past him to try his luck with you,' said Laura. 'You're very attractive, and to some men every girl they meet is a challenge to their virility.'

'Jack hasn't indicated any interest in me so far,' she said. 'The way he's sprucing the Range Rover, I should think that means more to him than any woman ever could. It wouldn't surprise me if he were a misogynist.'

'Even they feel the lusts of the flesh,' was Laura's comment. 'Sometimes all the more powerful for being repressed,' she added darkly, her eyes on the strapping figure in the courtyard.

Cassia was on the roof, enjoying a magnificent sunset over the mountains to the west, when she heard the toot-toot of a horn and looked over the parapet to see Simón's car gliding into the rear courtyard.

She watched him climb out, stretch himself, and then go to close the tall gates, left open for him after the builders had finished for the day. In the heat of summer they probably took a longer lunch break and would have been working later. At this time of year they spent an hour at the village bar before resuming operations.

While the Marqués was locking the gates Jack came out of the house. As they shook hands she was struck by the contrast between them—the tall, elegant, self-assured Spanish aristocrat and the stockier, plebeian Englishman, with his own brand of assurance but very few social graces.

It was he who, while they were talking, suddenly seemed to sense that they were being observed and, looking up, saw her peering down.

She had noticed at lunch that his eyes were a good shade of grey. What colour his hair might be if grown to a normal length was hard to guess, except that around his ears the stubble was noticeably silvery.

When Simón also looked up she waved to them both and withdrew. She had come to the roof to retrieve some underwear hung out to dry on a line strung between the chimney stacks. There was also a weather-bleached cane chair and table on the roof, suggesting that the last caretaker had sometimes sat up here.

Provided the timbers would stand the additional weight of plant pots, it could be made into a roof garden, Cassia thought. One which, unless a helicopter or a microlight passed overhead, was as private as the main patio. There were many flat roofs in the village, but all on a lower level. Even the bell tower of the church didn't overlook the roof of the Casa Mondragón.

At supper that evening, discussing the project which had brought him to Castell de los Torres, Jack showed that he could be talkative on a subject of interest to him. In spite of their disparate lives and backgrounds, he and Simón seemed to have more in common than Cassia had expected.

It turned out that the Marqués was not only a skier but a climber and scuba-diver. He had also tried paragliding and free-fall parachute jumping—a sport which made Laura shudder with horror at the thought of it.

After declining coffee, saying that he never drank it, Jack leaned back in his chair and gave a hippopotamus-sized yawn, only remembering to hide a healthy set of teeth with his hand when he noticed the housekeeper's disapproving expression.

'Why don't you turn in, my friend?' said the Marqués in Spanish—the language they had been speaking throughout the meal. 'Tomorrow I'll show you some of the terrain around here. We'll take a packed lunch and spend the day "on the hill" as the Scots say.'

The remark reminded Cassia of his description of Jack the first time he'd mentioned him to her. She was beginning to feel that Jack might not be dour by nature. It could be merely a façade he put up in the company of people with whom he wasn't at ease, such as women like Laura and herself.

'I'll do that.' The feet of his chair scraped on the worn clay tiles as he rose to his feet. 'Goodnight all.'

'Perhaps you'd be good enough to prepare substantial packed lunches for us, Laura,' said the Marqués as Jack was leaving the room. 'The bakery here makes excellent *barras negras* which I prefer to their white bread, especially for picnics.'

'I'll fetch them for you, Laura,' Cassia offered. 'I love the smell of new bread in the bakery when they take the first batch of loaves out of the oven.' She turned to the Marqués. 'But I find it very frustrating to listen to people talking in the shops and not understand what they're saying. They speak Castilian to me, but only Valenciano among themselves. It's like being in another country.'

'I'm sure you'll soon pick it up, but whether you'll find their conversations worth listening to is another matter,' he said drily. 'Most of the locals have very narrow horizons. Television could open their minds...if they watched the better programmes and there were more of them. Mostly they watch the soaps, imported and home-grown.'

This prompted Laura, who was missing the French soap operas, to ask if he'd mind if she had an aerial erected for a TV in her room.

'Not as long as you don't allow any of our guests to watch it. While they're here the emphasis will be on active rather than passive entertainments.'

'I shall keep my room locked once they arrive,' she assured him.

After drinking his coffee, Simón said, 'I'm going to stroll up to the *mirador* by the cemetery. Will you join me, Cassia?'

Although expressed as a suggestion, she had a feeling the question might be a directive.

'I'll get my jacket.'

The days since her arrival had been mild and, at midday in the sun, warm. But once darkness fell the temperature took a sharp drop.

They left the house by the imposing main door, the Marqués wearing a quilted gilet over his sweater with a canary-yellow scarf wound round his neck, and Cassia in her old anorak.

They walked in silence as far as the *plaza* in front of the church. As they began to climb the steep, sloping way to the cemetery, bordered on one side by tall cypresses and the whitewashed pillars representing the first stations of the Cross, he said, 'Would you like to come with us tomorrow? We shan't be doing any serious climbing. I'm sure you can cope with some easy rock scrambling.'

Although she suspected that Jack wouldn't be pleased to have her with them, she said, 'I'd like to come.'

'Now you've met him, what do you make of Jack Locke?'

'It's too soon to say. He was much less forthcoming at lunch than he was at supper. I don't think he's too keen on Laura, or she on him.'

'They're opposite poles,' he agreed. 'How are you getting on with her?'

'From my point of view, very well. I hope from hers too.'

'Her outlook could be more flexible. I hope she's going to be good with the youngsters. From what I've read, most of the teenagers we'll be dealing with have very little sense of self-worth. They won't respond to disapproval. What they need is encouragement to develop their best qualities... and praise when they succeed.'

'I'm sure when Laura actually meets them they'll appeal to her motherly instincts. She's been very nice to me,' said Cassia.

'Being nice to you isn't difficult. Are you warm enough?' He surprised her by taking her hand. Finding her fingers cold, he said, 'No, you aren't. Here, have this. I don't need it.'

Pulling off his scarf, he curled it into a loose roll and tucked her hands inside it, as if it were a muff. It was very soft—perhaps cashmere—and warm from being round his neck.

At the top of the slope, where a hairpin bend led up to a hilltop Calvary, they came to the wrought-iron gates of the enclosure where the village dead were interred in rows of vaults which were built into the white walls and sealed with slabs of marble engraved with the occupants' names, and in most cases accompanied by a photograph.

'Perhaps I shouldn't have brought you here. It must remind you of your father,' Simón said quietly.

'Yes, but I like this place. I've been up here before,' she answered. 'I don't find it sad or depressing. It seems part of the natural cycle of birth, life and death. I think this is the way people are meant to live—in small communities where everyone knows each other and their forebears' graves are close by.'

'You wouldn't think that if you'd lived here since you were born. You'd be itching to spread your wings and escape all the watchful eyes and the tattling tongues. It's because you've never had a permanent home that you envy these people their more restricted existence. We all tend to want something different from whatever life has assigned to us.'

They were standing beside the low wall surrounding the *mirador*, looking out at the moonlit valley, ringed by the mountains whose names she had yet to learn.

'I shouldn't think you do...do you?' she asked, glancing up at him.

Behind him the high lime-washed wall of the cemetery made his dark hair look even darker. The moonlight accentuated the forceful structure of his face.

'I used to when I was your age. I wanted to be free to go where I pleased and do as I chose.'

'But surely you *are* free...far more than most people. You're rich, you're educated, you're a grandee of Spain, you're—'

She had been about to add 'very good-looking' but stopped short, substituting, 'You have it all, as they say.'

'You may not realise it, but being a *marqués* has its downside,' he told her drily. 'When I was twenty it felt like a strait-jacket. The price of privilege is responsibility, and young men don't want to be lumbered with a load of baggage handed down from their ancestors. My inheritance was a burden—half a dozen houses, some of them falling apart, numerous dependent relations and even more numerous retainers...'

The broad shoulders shrugged, the hard mouth twisted sardonically. 'I wanted to pack a rollbag and get the hell out of all that. Sometimes I did... and do. But only for short spells—like my visits to Granada.'

Something impelled her to say, 'How is Señorita Sanchez? Completely recovered, I hope?'

'I believe so. I saw her dancing at a party in Madrid last week. We are not on close terms any more. She has found other fish to fry.'

'Only because you ditched her, I should imagine.' As soon as the words were out Cassia regretted speaking her thought aloud.

Tensely, her eyes on the moonlit rooftops below them, she waited for his reaction.

CHAPTER FIVE

'AM I to conclude from that combative statement that you think I treat women badly?' Simón asked, with an edge in his voice.

'I spoke out of turn,' said Cassia. 'Your relationships with other people are none of my business. I'm sorry I said that. It was impertinent of me.'

'Having said it, you can't retrieve it. I'd like to know your reasoning. Is it based on something you heard from other members of the staff?'

As he wasn't going to let her off the hook, she said, 'The thing which caused talk was the damage to the antique mirror. Naturally everyone thought you and Señorita Sanchez had a major row before she walked out or you sent her packing. What other conclusion would they draw? The staff at the hotel are very discreet. It would cost them their jobs if they weren't. But you can't expect them not to gossip among themselves when something unusual happens.'

'What was the consensus?'

'I don't think there was one. Everyone saw it differently.'

'*Your* sympathies being with Isa?'

'I'm not in sympathy with anyone damaging other people's property—particularly something irreplaceable—in a fit of temper. But some people aren't brought up to control their emotions, and I don't know what provoked her to hurl something at you. You may have driven her to it. I should think you could, if you felt like it,' she added, with impulsive candour.

In a *corral* somewhere below them three or four Spanish hunting dogs began barking in unison, perhaps because one of the village cats had walked along the wall of their enclosure. A lot of the men in Castell kept a pair or a pack of the large ginger dogs. Friendly enough when not hunting, they were as lean as greyhounds but with larger ears, like the dogs of the ancient Egyptians. In her first few nights in the village Cassia had found their occasional outbursts—and the half-hourly chiming from the bell-tower—disturbing. But already she was used to both noises and no longer woke up.

Simón waited for the barks to subside before he said, 'Could I provoke you into letting your emotions off the leash? Or are they so tightly controlled that you never lose your temper?'

'I don't know. I never have so far. But I suppose everyone has a breaking-point. I can imagine getting pretty angry if someone ill-treated a child or an animal in front of me.'

'What about if someone kissed you—someone you didn't approve of?'

A long time ago with her father Cassia had flown on a cheap flight to the Canary Islands, where John Browning had thought that he might settle in preference to mainland Spain. Part of the flight had been alarmingly bumpy.

The sensations she was feeling now—expecting that at any moment the man beside her would kiss her—were remarkably similar to the inner turmoil experienced in those scary moments at thirty-nine thousand feet.

But instead of doing what she expected, Simón answered the question for her.

'No, I don't think that would be enough provocation,' he said reflectively. 'My guess is that you'd handle the situation with outward hauteur but be inwardly seething . . . even if you had liked it.'

While the aircraft had been bouncing its way through ten minutes of strong air turbulence, and other passengers had shown varying degrees of alarm, Cassia had managed to continue reading her book, while inwardly longing for a reassuring smile and pat on the hand from her father.

Now, although her heart was behaving like a yo-yo and she was aware of other disturbing reactions, she said with assumed self-possession, 'I think I'll be able to cope if any of the boys who come here try getting out of line. But why should they bother with me when they'll have girls of their own age to make passes at?'

'Under the macho posturing, teenage boys are often a lot less confident than they appear, and teenage girls can dish out some nasty put-downs. The skills you used to keep the hotel guests happy could be balm to these boys' fragile egos—an aphrodisiac balm,' he added, in an amused tone. 'If you haven't had much to do with adolescent males, I should warn you they live in an almost permanent state of arousal. It doesn't take a lot to start them snorting and pawing as excitably as young bulls.'

Seeing a chance to change the subject, she seized it. 'Are you an aficionado of bullfighting?'

'I admire the courage of the matadors. I don't go to the corrida. I'm not keen on any spectator sports. Have you been to a bullfight?'

She shook her head. 'I know I shouldn't enjoy it. I've seen bits of fights on television at the hotel, but watching a man risk his life doesn't excite me, and I felt the horses must be terrified, even with protective padding.' The church clock chimed the half-hour. 'I think it's time I turned in.'

'As you wish.'

Near the house she returned his scarf. 'Thank you.'

'My pleasure. I'm not used to country hours so I'll go for a walk. I'll see you at breakfast tomorrow. Sleep well.'

Taking her by surprise, he took one of her hands and brushed a kiss on the knuckles before turning to cross the *plaza* and disappear round the corner.

Cassia was almost at the door of her room when she changed her mind and went up to the roof. Simón had turned in a direction which led to the lanes through the vineyards. A few minutes later, as she stood in the shadow of the chimmey-stack, she saw him come into view, and would have recognised him even if she hadn't been expecting to see him.

She could still feel the fleeting pressure of his lips on her knuckles, and her thoughts and emotions were in a confusion induced by their conversation up at the *mirador* as well as by the unexpected caress.

A kiss on the hand at meeting or parting was a courtesy normally reserved for married women. On one or two occasions she had seen Señor Alvarez greet the wives of regular guests with the old-fashioned salutation, 'At your feet, *señora*.'

It seemed a shame that the expression had fallen into disuse. From what she had seen at the hotel, young Spaniards rarely kissed women's hands—not even those of girls they appeared to be in love with.

What had prompted Simón to kiss hers she couldn't imagine. Unless, in the absence of any better entertainment, it amused him to see how she would respond to his flirting with her.

She watched him until he was lost to view, envying him the freedom to go where he pleased at night. Not that the lanes through the vineyards held the hazards of city streets, but it wouldn't have occurred to her to go for a walk at this hour.

*   *   *

Jack looked displeased when, next morning, he learned that Cassia was going with them.

'Have you got boots?' he asked.

She shook her head. 'Won't trainers do?'

'Not in the mountains.'

'She can buy some boots on the way,' said the Marqués. 'Not as good as yours and mine, but adequate for the easy terrain we'll be covering.'

Both men had come down to breakfast in sweatshirts with shorts and wool socks but the Spaniard's long legs were tanned and Jack's thicker legs were white under a heavy furring of curly hair.

Cassia was wearing jeans and one of her father's shirts, with a patchwork waistcoat bought from an arts and crafts shop in an alley at the foot of the Albaicín.

'You'll need a sweater and a waterproof,' Jack told her.

'But it's going to be another hot day. There isn't a cloud in sight.'

'Not now. There could be later. No one who knows what they're doing ever goes mountain-walking without the gear they'll need if the weather changes. If you haven't got a cagoule, I'll lend you one.'

He also lent her a knapsack in which to carry her lunch and a litre of water.

'One would think you were going to walk to the other side of Spain. What do you have in there?' asked Laura, voicing Cassia's curiosity about the contents of Jack's much larger pack.

'First-aid stuff, flares, emergency rations, a survival bag. People who go off the beaten track can get lost or have an accident which might involve staying out overnight,' he told her. 'It isn't likely that will happen today, but I never take chances. If you're always prepared you never get caught out.'

The Marqués also had a pack, although not as large as Jack's. After they had stowed their gear in the back of the Range Rover, he opened the front passenger door but, instead of climbing in, waited for Cassia to take the seat next to the driver's.

'She can go in the back. I'll need you in front to direct me,' Jack said abruptly.

With a slight movement of one eyebrow, Simón opened the rear door for her.

The small town where they stopped *en route* had a shop selling all the equipment used by hunters, from shotguns to cartridge jackets. The proprietor produced a pair of boots in a boy's size which Cassia found comfortable and Jack considered adequate if not ideal. They were not expensive, and she had brought some money with her, but the Marqués insisted on paying.

'They're not something you'd have bought if you hadn't come to work for me,' he said. 'I'll cover any expenses to do with the job.'

'I didn't realise you spoke Valenciano,' she said as they left the shop.

'The gift of tongues is a family characteristic. One of my uncles was a diplomat, and I also spent a few years in our foreign service.'

'How many languages do you speak?'

'Half a dozen,' he said casually. 'If those boots start to feel uncomfortable you must tell us. Ideally they need to be used for several short periods before being worn on a long walk.'

'At the moment they feel very comfortable.'

'They're to light for serious walking,' Jack said critically.

She felt that he was still annoyed at having her with them.

*   *   *

The village where they left the Range Rover to continue on foot was even smaller than Castell de los Torres. Only one old woman was using the *lavadero*—a long, waist-high tank of running water, roofed but open on three sides—when they passed it. She gave them a friendly greeting, her small, black-clad figure making Cassia aware of the vast gulf between her own life and opportunities and those of the Spanish widow—the growth of her generation stunted by malnutrition, the pattern of her life determined by lack of education.

The Marqués was leading the way, with Jack behind him and Cassia at the rear. As the path wound downhill between plots of vegetables and small orchards of fruit trees with their blossom season approaching, she noticed how differently the two ahead of her moved, and wondered if a man's gait was a reflection of his character.

The Marqués was light on his feet, even in thick-soled boots. Jack walked with a heavier tread. In summer, when snakes might be sunning themselves on the less used parts of the mountain tracks, they would feel the reverberations of those clumping footsteps in plenty of time to glide out of sight.

Jack's smile at the granny in the washhouse had been the first sign that he could smile. For a moment it had changed him into someone different from the man whose manner so far had been anything but friendly.

Presently they came to a spot where Simón stopped to point out a zigzag line on the hillside on the far side of the valley below them.

'That's one of the ancient trails.'

He had a small pair of field-glasses hanging from a strap round his neck. Lifting it over his head, he handed the glasses to her. As their fingers touched she felt the same unnerving tingle induced by his caress last night—like a very slight electric shock.

They walked for an hour, then stopped for a five-minute break and a drink from their water bottles.

'In April this will be a botanist's paradise,' said Simón, with a gesture at the scrubby vegetation around them.

Cassia took the opportunity to apply some more sun-cream to her nose, eyelids and hairline. She debated offering the tube to Jack, but decided that he had probably applied some protection of his own before coming out.

When they set off again he took the lead, setting a pace which presently made Simón glance round to ask her, 'Are you OK with this?'

'I'm fine, thanks.'

Even if she had not been happy with their present rate of knots, she wouldn't have admitted it. She was determined to keep up, not to confirm Jack's evident feeling that her presence was a liability.

All morning the temperature rose. This still being wintertime, it wasn't hard to understand why only the hardiest plants survived the scorching heat of the summer months on these almost treeless mountainsides.

They had lunch where an overhanging rock created a patch of shade. The backs of the men's shirts when they took off their packs were soaked with sweat where the packs had rested. Both stripped to the waist, spreading their shirts in the sun to dry. Cassia had already removed her waistcoat, and wished that she had had the forethought to put on a bathing top instead of a bra. The one she was wearing was too transparent for her to sit shirtless.

'Where did you come by your tan?' Jack asked Simón as they unwrapped their food.

His own torso was pale, like his legs, but Simón's shoulders and chest were as brown as his face and legs.

'I spent Christmas in the Seychelles. A friend of mine lives there. His island, Praslin, is a great place for sailing and fishing, but there isn't much else to do there unless you're a painter, as my friend is.'

'I don't go for the Tropics myself. I don't like the humidity,' said Jack. 'I was in Canada at Christmas. A pal of mine in the Legion asked me over. He's in security now...a married man with a family. It was nice and warm in his house, but outside it was cold enough to freeze the—'

'Jack served in the French Foreign Legion,' Simón cut in. 'For how long? Five years, wasn't it?'

'Ten,' the other man said tersely, and bit off a mouthful of roll.

'Spain also has a legion, but it no longer accepts foreign recruits,' Simón continued smoothly. 'There were never as many foreigners in our Legión Extranjera as in the French one.'

Cassia wondered if he had intervened to prevent her hearing an expression he thought would embarrass her, or to spare Jack embarrassment. In her view, the Englishman was much too plain-spoken to care if his barrack-room language offended people like Laura and herself.

She could see that Simón's upbringing would make him aware that women of Laura's age and older were put off by coarseness, but she doubted if his own girl-friends would have minded the expression Jack would have used if he hadn't been interrupted. Her impression of Isa Sanchez had been that plenty of four-letter words would have been screeched at Simón before he'd dodged the ashtray that Isa had hurled at the mirror.

'Your friend was a French Canadian, presumably?' said the Marqués.

The other man nodded. 'He spoke the lingo from day one. I had to pick it up. I reckon now I speak it better than the teachers who thought I hadn't the brains to learn it at school.'

It was after the lunch stop, when they had set off again, that Cassia became aware that her right boot was starting to rub the back of her heel. She was wondering whether to ask Jack if his first-aid equipment included a plaster which, applied now, would prevent the slight soreness from becoming a blister, when Simón called, 'Hold it, Jack!'

The Englishman stopped and looked round. 'What's up?'

'I thought I heard bells.'

As they listened a muffled tinkling could be heard from somewhere nearby.

'There must be sheep grazing near here,' said Jack.

'I doubt it. Not at this height. The shepherds stay lower down. I think we're about to meet some much larger animals.'

'Bulls, do you mean?' asked Cassia rather apprehensively.

'Either bulls or their mothers and sisters...who also need to be treated respectfully. Don't worry—they'll be with a herdsman. I'll go ahead and have a word with him.'

Passing Jack, Simón went ahead towards a gap between two large crags forming a gateway into the adjoining valley.

'Rather him than me,' Jack remarked to Cassia as she closed the gap between them. 'The cows can be more dangerous than the bulls from what I've heard.'

She had heard the same thing, but in Jack's place would have held her tongue. She had a feeling that he wasn't worried himself but expected her to be afraid and was testing her nerve.

'I've never heard of any walkers being attacked by Spanish cattle,' she said calmly.

'You wouldn't, would you? They keep that sort of news out of the papers. Gorings aren't good for the tourist trade,' he said, with a wicked grin.

He was obviously trying to alarm her. She felt the best way to handle him was with a succinct comment used by her father to dismiss something as nonsense.

Having said it, she didn't pause to see his reaction but moved quickly past him to follow Simón between the crags.

The valley through which they had to pass as part of a circular route back to their starting point presented a peaceful scene—except that the beasts grazing in it were not dairy cattle but the fighting bulls bred not only for the *corrida* but also for running through the streets and being challenged in small rings by youths during the many town and village fiestas.

Only one animal was belled—a large cow who stood out from the others, not only because her movements caused the bell on her leather collar to make a clanking sound, but also because she was a brown and white piebald, while the rest, apart from a couple of brown cows and calves, were black.

They were spread out across the valley. There was no way of avoiding them. Among them, clearly their leader, was one very large bull who seemed to be gazing directly at her. At the thought of walking past him, expecting at every moment that massive head to swing low before a charge, Cassia felt her stomach clench.

But Simón had been right. There *was* a herdsman, and he and Simón were walking towards each other, the bulls' guardian with the assurance that his charges wouldn't harm him, and Simón with an air of confidence which Cassia wouldn't have felt had she been in his place.

After some conversation the two Spaniards came over to where she and Jack were waiting and Simón introduced the herdsman.

'He's going to escort us through,' he told them. 'These cattle aren't usually aggressive when they're grazing, but they're not used to seeing anyone but him when they're up here.'

Even in the herdsman's charge, and with a stalwart man on either side of her, passing through the herd was not an experience that Cassia wished to repeat. Every step of the way she was conscious of the large bull turning his head to follow their progress. It made her respect more than ever the courage of men who duelled with such formidable animals.

The herdsman seemed pleased to have someone to chat to, and they were delayed for some time while he and Simón talked. Then, with thanks and more handshakes, they resumed their walk.

By half a mile further on, the chafing inside Cassia's boot was becoming increasingly uncomfortable. But she thought that they would probably stop to drink water again before long, and then, on the pretext of going behind a bush, she could take a quick look at her heel. It might be that a wad of tissue would serve better than a plaster. If she could avoid it she didn't want to let on that she had a problem.

Unfortunately her plan was thwarted, because neither of the men seemed to want another stop. Instead of keeping an eye on her, as he had during the morning, Simón now took it for granted that at least on this route anything they could do, she could do.

With Jack in the lead and Simón close on his heels they were talking about cars, and, on the downhill sections, moving very fast, their thick soles designed for these rocky tracks.

Cassia found that she had to concentrate hard to avoid losing her balance on pockets of loose stone or rocks worn and weathered to a slippery smoothness. As well as the pain in her heel, the fronts of her thighs were beginning to ache from several hours' unaccustomed exercise. But she gritted her teeth and pressed on, determined not to let them know that, for her, the day's outing was turning into an ordeal.

By the time they got back to the village the pain was intense, like a red-hot wire lancing her heel at every step. Somehow she managed neither to limp nor to wince. But when Jack suggested having coffee in the bar she almost groaned aloud at the thought of having to walk past the Range Rover in search of some smoky bar full of men with loud voices and a television going full-blast.

'I think Cassia might prefer a long, iced drink in the patio at home,' said Simón. 'You look tired,' he told her.

'I enjoyed it,' she said, half-truthfully. 'But I am looking forward to a shower and taking these boots off. They feel much heavier than the loafers and sandals I mainly wear.'

'I wear boots most of the time. I'm more comfortable in them,' said Jack, unlocking his vehicle.

Simón said, 'You have the front seat on the way back, Cassia.'

It was bliss to sit down. Her blistered heel was still painful, but less agonising than when she had been walking on it.

An hour later, in the privacy of her room, Cassia took off her left boot and then, with gritted teeth, the right one. On Jack's advice she was wearing two pairs of socks—an inner pair of white cotton and an outer pair of brown wool. Both were sticking to the back of her foot, and what the white sock revealed as she peeled it away from her heel made her grimace with dismay. She had had small blisters before but never one this big. It had blown up and burst, and now the raw flesh was bleeding.

Hours too late, she regretted not asking Jack for a plaster as soon as it had started to hurt. Now it was long past the stage when a plaster would cover the damage and protect it from infection.

After a few moments' thought she decided that the first thing to do was to have a refreshing shower. Then, wearing her flip-flops, she would slip out to the pharmacy and hope to buy dressings large enough to cover the site of the blister while it healed.

After the day's exertions it was good to stand in the shower and feel her energy reviving as the hot water streamed down her body. Probably Simón and Jack had already had their showers and would soon be having a beer together in the patio. She would have to sneak out the back way, and cut through the alley connecting the road at the rear with the street leading to the chemist's shop with its distinctive green cross.

As far back as she could remember, her father had always sought advice from chemists rather than doctors. In his view they knew as much as many GPs, and their advice was free. Thinking of her father, she sighed. He had been a difficult man, but there were times when she missed him with an almost physical ache, and this was one of them. The painful smarting of her heel reminded her of all the times in her childhood when he had patched her up after some minor injury.

There was still a small scar on her wrist where another child had accidentally jabbed her with one blade of a pair of scissors. The mother of the child had panicked and wanted to rush Cassia to hospital, but John Browning had told her to calm down. He had pressed the lips of the cut together and fastened them with a butterfly suture made from a strip of plaster. A week later it had healed, leaving only the small pearly mark now hidden by her watch strap.

There being no one about when she left the first-floor shower room a few doors away from her bedroom, she allowed herself to limp. Simón and Jack had rooms on the floor above and, the main staircase being on the other side of the building, had no reason to come past her room whether going down or up.

So it was a shock when a voice behind her said, 'What the hell have you done to your heel, girl?'

Cassia gasped and whirled round. 'What are you doing—sneaking up on me?'

'I was coming to get your boots. New boots need going over with dubbin.' Jack had on a clean white T-shirt and a pair of black jeans. The reason she hadn't heard him coming was that he was barefoot.

'What's dubbin?'

'It's a leather dressing. Makes boots waterproof and softens them. How long were you walking on that bloody great blister?'

'It looks worse than it is. It's nothing to make a fuss about.'

'Are you kidding? It looks like raw steak. If that isn't dealt with properly it could go septic on you. You'd better come up to my room and let me sort it out for you.'

'If you'll lend me your first-aid stuff, I can do it myself.'

'I'll do it better. I've had some training in first aid. Have you?'

'No, but it's just common sense.'

'If you had any of that you wouldn't have walked all the skin off your heel,' he informed her. 'But you've plenty of guts, I'll say that for you. Most girls would have been in tears long before it had got that bad.'

Again taking her by surprise, he stepped forward and scooped her off her feet.

'I don't need to be carried!' she protested.

'The way you were walking, you do.' He settled her against his chest. 'Put your arm round my neck.'

She was wearing a clean pair of briefs under her thin cotton robe, but her clean bra was in her room, where the underwear she had put on that morning was soaking in the hand basin. Fortunately her toilet bag had a wrist-loop at one end of the zipper. She was able to put her left arm round Jack's solid shoulders while holding the front of her robe securely together with her other hand.

'If you'd been in my company in the Legion, I'd have put you on a charge,' said Jack.

'Do they have women soldiers even in the French Legion now?' she asked incredulously. 'I'd have thought it was the last bastion of masculine solidarity.'

'It is...and it always will be,' Jack said with grim satisfaction. 'Women are useless as soldiers. The army's a man's world.'

'There are quite a few armies which do recruit women,' she said.

'You wouldn't catch me serving in them. Fighting is a man's life. Women should stick to nursing and jobs like that.'

Cassia had already decided that among male chauvinists Jack was a fundamentalist. She wasn't planning to try to open his mind to less reactionary ideas. There might be some committed feminists among the girls coming in who would attempt to convert him. She doubted if they would succeed. It was a waste of breath to reason with people like him. They had a fixed view of the world, and no amount of argument would budge them from their beliefs.

'I thought in the Legion a soldier would be expected to ignore a minor flesh-wound,' she said as they reached the stairs to the floor above.

'Depends on the circumstances. In action he might have to. What you did was plain bloody stupid.'

She said in French, 'Watch your language, please, Captain. I'm not one of your soldiers. You can't have it both ways. If you want us to be ladylike, you have to remember to behave like gentlemen towards us.'

He took the reproof in good part. 'I didn't know you spoke French. Where did you learn it—at school?'

'Like you, I picked it up out of necessity. My father was an artist. We spent a few years in France, mostly at Collioure near the border with Spain.'

Taking the stairs two at a time, Jack reached the top of the flight with no obvious sign of exertion. Considering she weighed a hundred and twenty-five pounds, it was not something any man could do. But she had the feeling that he had been showing off a little. She wondered who, if he and Simón had to fight each other, would win the contest. Jack was more heavily built, and presumably trained in all forms of hand-to-hand combat, but Simón was a powerful man with a more subtle mind. At least, that was her impression. He would think faster than Jack and perhaps beat him that way.

At the door of his room Jack said, 'Open it, will you?'

Cassia let go of her robe and reached down to turn the doorknob.

He set her down by his bed. 'Lie on your face so I can get at you heel.'

She stepped out of her flip-flops and, after a moment's hesitation, did as he told her, raising herself on her elbows to watch him going to the cupboard for a large plastic box of the kind sold in DIY stores for storing nails and screws.

He put this on the foot of the bed and then crossed the room to the washbasin. On the way there he swung the door closed.

This made Cassia slightly uneasy. Why did the door need to be closed if all he had in mind was to attend to her heel?

CHAPTER SIX

TELLING herself not to be foolish, while being at the same time aware that they were a long way away from the two other people in the house, or any workmen who might still be about, Cassia noticed that this room of Jack's was much the same as hers in size and appointments.

But while she had tried to personalise her room—draping a Spanish shawl over the bed and tucking picture postcards and snapshots under the frame of the large mirror over the writing-cum-dressing table—this room had no individual touches. Only his toothbrush and shaving kit on the glass shelf over the washbasin, and a magazine, a book and a rubber-clad torch on the bedside table showed that someone was sleeping here. All his other possessions were in the cupboards and drawers.

She angled her head to read the title of the book—*Climbing in Patagonia*. The magazine underneath was called *High* and subtitled *Mountain Sports*.

Jack finished washing his hands, which must have been clean already. While he had been carrying her she had smelt the aroma of soap or shower gel on him. If his hair had been longer it would still have been damp, as hers was.

Jack grasped the back of the upright chair at the table and moved it to the foot of the bed.

'Move further down, will you? So your foot's sticking over the edge.'

She obeyed, rucking up her robe above the backs of her knees. She was not showing any more leg than if she had been wearing a short skirt, but somehow, in these circumstances, she felt over-exposed. But to try to pull her robe down would only draw attention to it.

'I'm going to swab this with antiseptic,' he told her.

'OK. Whatever you say.'

Considering the size of his hands, he was surprisingly deft and gentle. Presently he said, 'You could do with a pair of clogs to wear until this has healed. D'you know the things I mean? Thick soles and no backs to 'em.'

'Mules,' said Cassia. 'Hospital nurses wear them, but I don't know where I'd get a pair around here. Anyway, it wouldn't be worth buying them for the short time my heel will be sore.'

'You were stupid to get in this state... but I'll give you credit for pluck. Stamina too. You kept up with us better than I expected. You don't look what I'd call sturdy, but I reckon you are.' For the first time he sounded friendly.

'My word, that *is* a compliment,' she said, with a teasing glance over her shoulder.

Jack gave her one of his rare smiles. 'Don't let it go to your head, kid.'

Suddenly she felt certain that he wasn't the type to try anything unwelcome.

At that moment someone knocked on the door.

'Come in,' Jack called.

The door opened and Simón stood on the threshold, one black eyebrow shooting up when he saw Cassia lying on the bed.

'Would you look at what this silly girl's done to herself?' said Jack.

He seemed oblivious of a change in the atmosphere, but she was instantly aware that although it wasn't apparent in his manner their employer was seriously displeased at finding her there. To her, the glacial vibes were so strong that they were almost palpable.

Simón moved forward to inspect the damage. 'You don't get a blister this size in five minutes, Cassia. Why didn't you say you were in trouble?'

'I didn't realise it was as bad as it is.'

'An air-head, but she gets ten for grit,' said Jack.

'Not from me,' Simón said curtly. 'I've no sympathy for self-inflicted injuries. It's going to take at least a week for that to heal.'

Apparently forgetting the reason he had come to Jack's room, he walked out, leaving the door open behind him.

Jack said nothing, and neither did Cassia. He gave her a pat on the back of her calf. 'You can get up now. I'll take another look tomorrow.'

'Thanks very much.' Being careful not to let her robe gape open, she rolled over and swung her feet to the floor. The whole of her heel was now neatly sealed by a large, ventilated dressing.

'Any time.' Jack was replacing the things he had used in the well-stocked box. 'We'd better find out what the facilities are, in case the kids need professional medical attention. I'll check that out in the morning.'

Cassia returned to her room. Before dressing, she blow-dried her hair. She had a feeling that Simón's terse comment in Jack's bedroom wouldn't be his last word on the subject.

When she went downstairs to help Laura with the supper, the housekeeper said it had been put back an hour because 'Excellency' had had to go out. Referring to Simón in the official style seemed to give her a buzz. She didn't approve of the others using his first name. She herself always called him Don Simón.

While all Spain's *duques* were grandees, she had explained to Cassia, not all the *marquéses* were. Because he was so informal himself, it was easy to forget that Excellency's title was very old and illustrious, she had added, glancing at Jack, whose manner towards their employer she didn't consider sufficiently respectful.

The first part of the house to be modernised had been the old-fashioned kitchen and the adjoining refectory. This didn't yet have its tables and benches installed but did have some easy chairs grouped round the corner fireplace. Jack had fetched in some logs cut from an old olive tree from the woodstack left by the caretaker, and had a cheerful blaze going by the time Simón returned.

The others were sitting round it having a glass of wine, and there was a savoury smell emanating from a large pan on top of the kitchen stove when Excellency returned.

'You look very cosy,' he said. 'It's much colder out now. I'm told there's often a spell of bad weather at this time of year. But it doesn't usually last more than three or four days.'

'A glass of wine for you, *jefe*?' Jack asked him. 'Or something stronger?'

'Wine will be fine.'

After taking off his leather jacket Simón opened a carrier and took out what looked like a shoe box. He handed it to Cassia.

'What's this?' she asked, puzzled.

'If you open it, you'll see.' There was an edge in his tone which might not have been audible to the others but was to her. She knew that he was still annoyed with her.

She opened the box, turned back a fold of coarse tissue and uncovered a pair of dark blue leather mules of the kind suitable for street wear.

'You can't go about in those flimsy rubber things at this time of year.' Evidently he had noticed her flip-flops on the floor by Jack's bed.

'You didn't go out specially to get these, did you?' she asked.

He shrugged. 'I also needed some stationery. You told the man at the boot shop you normally wore size thirty-seven, so those ought to fit you. Try them on.'

This evening Cassia was wearing a pair of red and pink carpet slippers with the backs folded down. She slipped them off and replaced them with the cork-soled mules.

'They fit perfectly. It was very good of you to go out and get them for me.' She didn't ask him what she owed him. The price would be on the box. She would put the money in an envelope and slip it under his door.

He dismissed her thanks with the customary '*De nada*' and turned away to talk to Jack.

Laura had bought *cocas* from the village baker. They resembled small pizzas, usually topped with slices of tomato and red pepper, or perhaps snippets of tinned anchovy or whatever else the baker had to hand. Laura had embellished them with some additions of her own, and the discs of hot dough with their savoury toppings made an appetising start to the meal.

The *cocas* were followed by a French dish of pork with potatoes and mushrooms in a rich garlicky gravy.

While they ate Simón made pleasant conversation, but addressing himself to the others, never to Cassia. His behaviour baffled her. To make a special trip to the nearest town to buy footwear which would enable her to move about comfortably while her heel healed, and yet now to ignore her seemed strangely inconsistent.

During the afternoon two dishwashers had been delivered and plumbed in. When the meal was over Simón said, 'If you'd help Laura load the machine, Jack, I want to speak to Cassia in private. We'll talk in the office, Cassia.'

She followed him from the room, telling herself that it was absurd to feel like a miscreant schoolgirl about to be given a carpeting by a severe headmaster. She had done nothing wrong.

It was cold in the rest of the house. In the office Simón switched on an electric radiator before waving her to a chair and lifting one long, hard thigh onto the front edge of the desk, with his other leg stretched out straight.

It was a characteristic posture. When he was talking to the workmen, she had noticed, he often stood with his fingers thrust into the back pockets of his jeans. Unlike most Spaniards, he didn't usually gesticulate when he was talking. Only rarely did he illustrate a point with a graphic gesture. Now he sat with one hand in his pocket and the other resting on his thigh.

'The day I brought you away from Granada I told you that Señor Alvarez had charged me with being responsible for your welfare,' he began. 'He said you had been more sheltered than most of your peers and had no experience of discos or boyfriends. You knew the theory of sex, he said, from reading and listening to your colleagues. But he didn't think you had any practical knowledge. After finding you in Jack's bedroom this evening, I wonder if you know the theory as well as you should.'

Sitting very straight, with her chin up, Cassia said, 'Jack took me to his room to attend to my heel. Perhaps *you* can't envisage having a girl in *your* room without making a pass at her. I don't think it occurred to him.'

'It occurred to him,' Simón said sardonically. 'That he did nothing about it only shows he has more sense than you have. But if I hadn't come in he might have done something about it. When a girl lies down on a bed, in a flimsy dressing-gown, she's putting a lot of strain on a man's self-control—especially a guy like Jack who's in peak condition and may not have had a roll in the hay for some time.'

Cassia sprang to her feet. 'That's how you think of us, isn't it? Rolls in the hay...on a par with a meal or a drink. If the world was run to suit you, we'd all be slaves and concubines.'

Simón said coldly, 'You're losing your temper over nothing. I didn't set out to provoke a tirade on equality and all the rest of that claptrap. I was merely explaining what you appear not to know—that most single men spend a lot of time starving for sex. Therefore it's neither fair nor sensible to excite needs you aren't going to satisfy. Your mother would have explained that to you. Perhaps your father didn't discuss such matters.'

'My father set an example of how decent men treat women...with respect and consideration...not as playthings,' Cassia retorted.

'In general men give women the treatment they invite,' he answered. 'If they walk down the street showing their cleavage and wearing a tight miniskirt, they get whistles and lewd remarks. If they dress in a more modest style but have very good figures, they may still get the whistles without the coarse commentary. Going to Jack's room in your dressing-gown was giving a misleading signal. You should have got dressed first.'

'I didn't *go* to his room. As a matter of fact I was going to consult the chemist. Jack saw me leaving the shower. I was limping and he insisted on carrying me. I didn't have a lot of option.'

Simón's dark eyes narrowed slightly. 'Was that exciting?' he asked her.

'It saved me a lot of discomfort climbing the stairs.'

'That doesn't answer my question. Did it excite you?'

'The question doesn't make sense to me. Where does excitement come in when someone has a painful foot?'

'You didn't have a broken leg. I wouldn't have thought your heel was sufficiently painful to make you indifferent to being swept off your feet by Jack in caveman mode,' Simón said drily.

'He wasn't. He was just being kind...as you were when you went into town to get me those mules,' she added, suddenly remembering that he was her employer and she shouldn't have flared at him.

If the hotel manager had read her a homily, she wouldn't have answered back. She had momentarily forgotten that Simón was paying her wages.

'Sit down and listen to me,' he said quietly. 'Jack has changed his mind about you. This morning you were an encumbrance. He would have preferred to leave you behind. Perhaps you knew that.'

She nodded.

'Today, although you behaved like what he calls "an air-head",' he went on, 'you also showed you had grit— the quality he admires above everything else. That could create problems.'

'Surely it's better for your staff to be on good terms with each other?'

'Good terms—yes. But not too close. I know more about Jack than you do. Nothing to his discredit, but he was brought up in a children's home and he's led a tough, lonely life. I'm telling you this to make you realise that under his rugged exterior he may be extremely vulnerable. I don't want him falling in love with you, which he might very easily do.'

Cassia was taken aback. After a pause, she said, 'I think that's most unlikely. I'm not his type.'

'What is his type?'

'I don't know, but certainly not me.'

'I agree...but that won't stop it happening. Men frequently fall in love with women who aren't right for them. Women do the same. If you haven't experienced it yet, love is like a squall at sea. It sweeps people off their right course and can do a lot of damage.'

'Are you speaking from experience?'

'No, from observation only. I have friends who are happily married and other friends with a trail of disasters behind them. There's one big difference between them. The ones who—' He was interrupted by the telephone. 'Excuse me a moment.' He picked up the receiver. '*Diga*!'

After a pause he asked the caller to wait and, putting his hand over the mouthpiece, said to Cassia, 'This call will take some time. We'll continue our talk tomorrow. You've had a long, stressful day. Go to bed now. Goodnight.'

As she was leaving the room he started speaking Italian. It was a language with many similarities to Spanish, and she thought what he said was, 'No, you're not interrupting anything important. You know I am always delighted to hear your voice.'

'What did Don Simón have to say to you last night?' Laura enquired when Cassia went down to the breakfast.

As she didn't want to take Laura into her confidence, Cassia said, 'He gave me a ticking off for not saying I had a blister as soon as it started.'

'Yes, it was very silly of you,' the housekeeper agreed. 'But you've come out of it with a nice new pair of shoes.'

'They weren't a present. I've paid him for them.'

'Did he ask you to pay?'

'No. I put the money in an envelope and slipped it under his door before I went to bed.'

'If he didn't ask, I should have taken them as a gift. He can afford a few *mil* better than we can,' said Laura. 'He's rolling in money. If you ask me, this set-up here is probably some kind of tax dodge. Do you believe he's really interested in young drop-outs and delinquents? I don't. Why should he be? If I had been born in a fine cradle like he was—' she was using the Spanish equivalent of a silver spoon in the mouth '—I wouldn't worry about the rest of the world. I'd concentrate on enjoying myself.'

'Why did you take this job if the project doesn't interest you?'

'I didn't say *I* wasn't interested. But is he?' Laura shrugged her plump shoulders. 'Perhaps . . . for a while. Then he'll lose interest. When rich people take up causes, it's usually to suit themselves. There's a lot of corruption in high places in this country,' she added darkly.

Later, thinking over her remarks, Cassia had to admit that her own first impression of Simón as a playboy and womaniser didn't tie in with the role of a caring philanthropist. But had he arrived at the hotel without Isa Sanchez in tow, she would not have had that impression.

She remembered what he had said to her in the office the night before. 'Most single men spend a lot of time starving for sex.' Perhaps he was speaking from experience. He, like Jack, was in peak condition. Perhaps his libido drove him to have affairs with girls like Isa, apparently prepared to sleep with anyone who gave them a good time in luxurious surroundings. Cassia's father hadn't been a philandering man, but from time to time his libido had driven him into relationships which had differed from Simón's affairs only in being longer-lasting.

She found her thoughts about Simón deeply puzzling and unsettling. Also, she was intensely curious to know what he had been going to say about the difference between the happy and unhappy marriages of his friends. When the right moment arose she would remind him.

But the right moment didn't arise that day, or the next, and the day after that the Marqués announced at breakfast that he was off to Madrid.

Before he left they did have a few moments together. 'Remember what I told you. Don't get too friendly with Jack. Don't let your curiosity lead you down the wrong road. That's all it would be if you let him start something with you. That's the irresistible urge which gets most girls into bed the first time. Not because they need or want sex. Not even because they're in love. But because they can't wait to find out what it's all about.'

He had written out lists of tasks he expected them each to accomplish in his absence. She had not expected advice on her personal conduct.

'And a big disappointment it is, in most cases,' he added. 'So don't be tempted to let Jack initiate you.'

Retaining her self-possession with difficulty, she said, 'I don't need this lecture . . . Excellency. I'm not just out of a convent, although you seem to think so. Compared with other people of my age, I've been around more than most.'

'Geographically, yes. Not emotionally. It wouldn't surprise me if you've never been kissed,' he said, smiling.

'Of course I've been kissed!' she exploded indignantly.

'Like this?' He cupped her chin and her cheek in the warm curve of his palm and, tilting her face up, put his lips lightly on hers. For a moment, while her heart bungee jumped, his mouth remained on hers, motionless. Then, softly and slowly, it moved in a kiss so gentle yet so subtly arousing that her response astonished and horrified her.

Simón raised his head and looked down at her, knowing—she could see it in his eyes—precisely how she was feeling—how he had made her feel.

'Not like that,' he said mockingly. '*Adiós, chica.*'

The effect of his kiss stayed with her all the time he was gone. She went to sleep thinking about it, dreamed about him, and woke up wondering if today he would come back.

She knew that she had fallen in love with him. Madly, deeply, foolishly. Unutterably foolishly. For the chance of his loving her was infinitesimal.

In his absence, her heel made good progress. Every morning Jack brought his first-aid case down to breakfast and replaced the dressing with a fresh one. Within a week of the walk the place didn't need to be covered, although it was still somewhat tender and he felt a plaster would protect it from an accidental knock.

The following Saturday night Jack went out for the evening. Before he left he said that if the weather stayed fine the next day he might have a swim.

'At this time of year! You must be mad,' exclaimed Laura.

'I met an old guy—a German—in the village this morning who swims all year round. He's seventy-something. If he can do it, I reckon I can. Would you like to come, Cass?'

The thought of a day by the sea was very tempting. It was a long time since she'd seen it. She couldn't resist saying, 'Yes, please. But I don't promise to swim if the water's cold.'

'No use asking you to join us, I suppose?' he said to Laura.

With a vehement shake of the head, she said, 'My friend from Benidorm is coming to spend the day with me. She rents a little car while she's here. We may go out for a drive. Do you wish to take a packed lunch, or will you eat out?'

'We'll find somewhere to eat—if that's all right with you, Cassia?'

She took this as a hint that they would be going Dutch. 'Fine,' she agreed.

*   *   *

They set out just before nine the next morning, by which time the misty vapour lying over the vineyards had cleared and it promised to be a hot day.

'Brought your swimsuit?' Jack asked as they left the village behind.

'Yes, but it's falling to bits. I shall have to buy another for the summer. I used to love swimming when we lived on a boat. But that was a long time ago. Did you grow up near the sea?'

He shook his head. 'Never saw it when I was a kid. I learnt to swim in a big indoor pool with the water stinking of chlorine, making your eyes sting. But with us lot all peeing in it I reckon it would have smelt worse without the chemicals.'

Cassia laughed. 'Children aren't the only ones who do that. I've seen grown-ups get up from their beach chairs, wander into the sea for a few minutes and then come out again. It was perfectly obvious what they were doing.'

'That doesn't bother me,' said Jack. 'It's the bad pollution I watch out for. But I've heard the beaches on this coast are cleaner than most. Anyway, the old fellow who recommended the one we're going to says he's swum there for years, and he looks as fit as a flea.'

Their route took them over a pass into the neighbouring valley and then by the bed of a river which, although dry at the moment—perhaps because its main source had been dammed higher up—had at some time swept its way through the rocky terrain, scouring away the red earth which around it nurtured *almendros*, their branches now bursting with blossom.

Some groves were pink, others white. Soon, Cassia knew, the ephemeral beauty of the blossom would be replaced by green leaves and furry cases already almost as large as when the embryos inside had grown to full-size almonds. But today, as they would for a week or two more, the trees gave the arid landscape its most beautiful aspect—long before spring would break in more northerly Europe.

'Where did you learn to swim?' asked Jack.

'I can't remember. Probably somewhere in Greece. My father said I could swim before I could walk. Babies living on boats have to be drownproofed as soon as possible.'

'You're on your own now, is that right?'

'If my grandparents are alive, I don't know where they are.'

Jack said, 'I suppose I've got grandparents somewhere. It's not likely they'll all be dead yet. Me, I don't even know who my parents were.' After a pause he added, 'I used not to like having no family when I was a kid. Now it doesn't bother me. Families aren't always that close. Sometimes they hate each other.'

'Families in Spain seem closer than families in some other countries,' said Cassia. 'I always feel envious when I see them on Sunday picnics—the grannies dandling the babies and all the sons and sons-in-law attending to the paella while their wives have a rest and a gossip and the older children run about.'

Jack didn't answer, perhaps because there was a blind bend ahead and the road there was barely wide enough for two vehicles to pass each other. After a winding stretch the view opened out, traversed by the east-coast *autopista*—a broad ribbon of speeding traffic supported, where the land dipped, on massive pillars of concrete. Far from being an eyesore, its sweeping curves were beautiful.

It reminded Cassia of the journey from Granada. She wondered if Simón would disapprove of her accepting Jack's invitation. But if she hadn't she would have been at a loose end today. Laura and her French friend wouldn't have wanted her with them.

The beach that Jack had been told about was a small, stony cove at the foot of rust-coloured cliffs. It was at one end of a large bay near the town called Jávea, which stood a kilometre inland but had spread to form a resort of a quieter type than Benidorm. At the back of the cove was a terrace belonging to a café-bar, but at present the bar wasn't open and they had the cove to themselves.

'I expect most people are having a lie-in,' said Jack. 'It's early yet. Give it an hour. The sea looks pretty good, don't you think?'

'It *looks* most inviting,' she agreed, admiring the sparkling blue-green water lapping the sea-shiny cobbles.

'I'll check it out,' said Jack.

This morning, in place of boots, he was wearing thick rubber soles attached to his feet by Velcro-fastened straps. He walked down to the water's edge, bending to roll up his trouser legs before letting the sea wash over his sandalled feet.

'It's not too bad,' he reported. 'I won't say it's warm, but it should feel pretty good...once you're in.'

'Maybe I'll go in later. We're going to be here all morning, aren't we?'

'I thought we'd have lunch here,' said Jack, returning to where he had dumped his knapsack. 'In summer, so the old guy says, there's a place at the other end of the bay where they serve *paella* out of doors under a split-cane awning. But it isn't open at this time of year.'

As he spoke he unzipped his trousers. He was already wearing a brief black slip. In a matter of moments he was ready to bathe.

'Right...here we go, then!' Still wearing the sandals, he strode into the sea, and when it was up to his thighs flung up his arms for a plunge dive.

He was under the water for some seconds, surfacing with a characteristically masculine shake of the head—

a reflex, perhaps, from the days when he had had longer hair.

His scalp, almost bald when she'd first met him, was looking a little less shorn, she noticed as he started an energetic crawl in the direction of some red floats lying on the surface two or three hundred yards out.

Predictably Jack was a powerful swimmer, but he made a lot of splash. Cassia had the feeling that Simón would also swim well, but in a more stylish manner.

Suddenly changing her mind, she unzipped her holdall and pulled out a towel and a black Lycra one-piece dating back to her mid-teens. Since the last time she had worn it, her vital statistics had changed, her waist now being slimmer than at sixteen, her bust and hips fuller.

She was wearing a white T-shirt under a loose blue denim pinafore with a dropped waist and side-seam pockets. There still being no one about, she pulled off her briefs and stepped into the swimsuit, drawing it over her hips before stripping down to her bra and reaching behind her to unfasten the clip.

As she did so Jack stopped swimming. He rolled over and, treading water, waved to her at the same moment as Cassia removed her bra and felt the warmth of the sun caressing her bare breasts.

Although she had never exposed her breasts in public, as many women did at the beach, he was too far away for her to feel any embarrassment. She waved back and pulled up her swimsuit, then applied a waterproof suncream to her shoulders and back. Her face and arms she had sunproofed before coming out.

Having no plastic beach shoes, she found the stony beach made walking very uncomfortable. Nor was getting in painless. Unable to stride in and plunge, she had to endure the ordeal of the water creeping up her legs as she felt her way forward on slippery footholds. When she did throw herself forward the shock of immersing her warm flesh in the cold sea made her stifle a howl of agony.

'It's great . . . once you're in, isn't it?' said Jack when they met a hundred yards out. 'I'm told there's a nice little beach over there.' He jerked a thumb at the cliffs between the cove and the end of the headland. 'Let's go and investigate, shall we?'

The beach, hidden from the cove, was sandy. As they landed on it Jack said, 'Old Fritz—or whatever his name is—comes out here to strip off and tan his backside. Don't worry, I'm not going to do that,' he added with a grin, sitting down and leaning back on his elbows.

Cassia sat down beside him and surveyed the view from this different perspective. Halfway across the bay, on a low promontory, was a grove of palm trees.

Pointing them out to Jack, she said, 'I wonder what they're doing there. It seems a funny place for palm trees to be growing.'

'That's where the main beach is. The palms were brought in for the garden of a modern *parador*. Fritz said we can drive back that way, cutting across those low hills at the back,' he said, pointing to a wooded hinterland dotted with white villas. 'You're not cold now, are you?' Jerking into a sitting position, he laid the flat of his hand on the bare skin between her shoulder blades.

She had an intuitive feeling that he wanted to kiss her.

CHAPTER SEVEN

EITHER Cassia's instinct was wrong or Jack chose not to act on the impulse.

Answering the question himself, he said, 'No, you feel warm as toast.' Then, taking his palm away to lock both hands behind his head and stretch himself at full length, he went on, 'I should have brought a mask and fins. Have you done any snorkelling?'

Relieved that she'd been mistaken, Cassia said, 'As a child, yes. Not for a long time.' She was struck by a worrying thought. 'Do you think it's all right to leave our gear unattended? When I followed you in I didn't think I'd be coming out of sight. Maybe I should go back in case someone grabs the chance to make off with our valuables.'

'By God . . . you're right!' he exclaimed, jackknifing to his feet. 'My credit card's in my wallet. If that gets nicked I'll have to ring the UK, and I don't know the bloody number. It'll mean going back to the house.'

Seconds later he was in the water, thrashing up foam as he tore back the way they had come.

Swimming flat out, Cassia was not far behind him when a shout made her pause.

'Panic over,' Jack called.

Treading water, she saw that the bar had opened and now an elderly couple were sitting at a table on the terrace. But the beach was still empty.

They swam the rest of the way breast-stroking alongside each other. Where the water came up to his chest, Jack stood up. 'I've got sea shoes. You haven't. I'll give you a lift over the stones.'

This time being picked up and carried was less surprising, but in a way more disturbing. It was her first close contact with a naked male torso.

Beside their things, he set her on her feet.

'Thanks,' she said casually, bending to pluck her towel from the rock where she'd left it after unintentionally catching sight of the evidence that he too had been affected by the intimate contact.

Jack wrapped his towel round his hips and sat down. 'Have you ever smoked?' he asked.

Starting to towel her hair, Cassia paused to shake her head. 'I tried one once. I didn't like it.'

'People don't...not the first few. Then they get hooked. I gave it up five years ago. Sometimes—like after a swim—I feel the old urge to light up. But I never will. I've more respect for my body than I had then. Most soldiers smoke and drink. You'll find the odd one who doesn't, but not many.'

'Tell me about your time in the French Foreign Legion.'

'Légion Étrangère,' he corrected her. 'Well, I served two five-year contracts. It's a great outfit. I went in a bumptious kid with a chip on my shoulder, and they made a man of me.'

'If you liked it, why did you leave?'

'I liked it and I miss it,' he said, staring at the horizon. 'But there's more to life than being a fighter, which is what the Légion is about. They're crack fighting men— France's best—but it's like being a monk—except that a *légionnaire* doesn't swear to give up women,' he added, with a fleeting grin.

'Are they allowed to marry?' Cassia asked.

'They're allowed to, and some do. But they can be away from their families for months on end. It's better for a *légionnaire* to be single and screw around,' he went on bluntly. 'There's no shortage of willing birds for any guy wearing the *képi blanc*.' Suddenly turning his head to look directly at her, he said quietly, 'That's OK in your early twenties, but after a while it's not what you want any more. You want a woman of your own. Someone to love...to love you.'

Cassia found this statement, coming from such a tough-looking man, profoundly touching. It brought a lump to her throat.

'Everyone wants that, I guess,' she said, hunting for a comb to sort out her tangled hair. 'How old were you when you joined the Légion, Jack?'

'Seventeen, but I looked older. I've been out four years. I'm thirty-one. How old are you?'

'Twenty-two.'

'At times you seem younger...other times older,' he told her. 'I guess that's because you're quiet. Most young girls make a lot of noise. I don't like all that giggling and chattering. Shall we go up and have a coffee?'

It was late afternoon when they returned to the village. Laura and her friend were still out.

'Would you like a cup of tea?' Cassia asked.

'Good thinking. While you're making it I'll rinse the salt out of our beach stuff and hang it out to dry.'

Handing over her rolled-up towel, she cautioned, 'My swimsuit won't stand a lot of vigorous wringing. It needs to drip dry.'

While they were drinking tea, and Jack was eating a wedge of Manchego cheese in a chunk of *barra negra* to keep him going until suppertime, he said, 'Would you like to see my photo gallery of the guys I was with in *sauteurs ops*?'

Thinking he meant to bring down a photograph album, she said, 'Yes, please.'

'They're taped to the door of my cupboard. Let's take a refill up with us,' he said, reaching for the teapot.

Mindful of Simón's warning, she searched for a tactful pretext for changing her mind, but couldn't think of one. Anyway, she was sure that Jack had no ulterior motive for inviting her up to his room. Or was she being foolishly naïve? They were alone in the house.

'What does *sauteurs ops* mean?' she asked on the way upstairs. 'Something to do with parachuting?'

'It's a special operations force—the equivalent of the Special Air Service in the UK. At the end of my basic training I went on to do parachute training.'

In his room he opened the wardrobe, revealing that both doors were covered with mementoes of his service life.

'That's a picture of Capitaine Danjou's wooden hand,' he explained, pointing to a photograph of an articulated hand lying on top of an elaborate, glass-sided casket. 'It's the Légion's most revered relic.'

While she peered at the finely carved and polished hand, Jack brought a chair for her to sit on and named and described some of his brothers-in-arms. As he talked she began to understand the strength of their camaraderie and to sense how much he missed it.

She was about to ask him if he could re-enlist if he wished, when they heard a sound from below.

'That'll be Laura coming back.' Jack swallowed a mouthful of cooling tea.

'Was that your everyday headgear?' Cassia asked, looking at the green beret hanging near the top of the door.

He took it down from its hook. 'Yes, the *képi blanc* is for walking out and parades. We wear these pulled down to the left, not to the right like the British.' Suddenly he put it on, moulding it to his head, his expression remote, as if the feel of it took him back to the world he had left and still missed.

'You've been swimming, I see,' said a voice from the doorway, making Cassia jump. It wasn't Laura who had come up to join them.

It was Simón.

Jack whipped off the beret, as if he felt foolish to have been caught wearing it. Cassia rose to her feet, also feeling uncomfortable. Suddenly the atmosphere was full of tension.

'Ah, Capitaine Danjou's famous hand,' Simón said, his eyes on the photograph.

'You know about him?' Jack sounded surprised.

'Of course,' said Simón. 'The stand at Camerone is one of the most famous incidents in modern military history. Sixty men against two thousand...and, when the Mexican commander demanded the last three *légionnaires* surrender to him, although they were wounded they would only give up on condition that they kept their arms and were allowed to look after their comrades with worse wounds. He's on record as saying, "One can refuse nothing to men like you".'

As he spoke Cassia saw the reason they hadn't heard him coming was that he was wearing tennis clothes and rubber-soled shoes, suggesting the decision to return to Castell today had been an impulse.

'We weren't expecting you,' she said. 'Laura's still out with her friend. As we've all had lunch out today, it's going to be a cold supper...if that's all right with you?'

She was thinking that if he hadn't had his main meal at lunchtime she had better start preparing something hot for him. It was possible that Laura might not get back until late if, after their drive, the two women had gone to Benidorm.

'Fine with me,' he answered, giving her the briefest of glances before returning his attention to the array of mementoes.

'The founder and hero of Spain's Foreign Legion was Colonel Millan Astray,' he told Jack. 'He was wounded five times and lost a leg and an eye. His battle cry was *"Viva la muerte!"* Long live death. He borrowed a lot of ideas from the French Legion.'

Cassia knew that he was angry with her. It would not be apparent to Jack, but she knew it was so—even though it must be clear to Simón that nothing had been going on except a demonstration of the other man's on-going allegiance to the army which had, in his own words, made a man of him.

In a gap in the men's conversation she excused herself and slipped away. It had not needed Simón's return to remind her of his parting kiss. It had been at the back of her mind every hour of every day since he'd left. Why he had kissed her goodbye she was still not sure. To tease her, seemed the most likely answer.

In her room, tidying herself for the evening, she remembered the feel of his palm against her cheek and the pressure of his lips on hers. Not technically her first kiss, because when she was fourteen a boy of fifteen had planted an inexpert kiss on her startled mouth while they'd gathered shellfish together. And there had been a couple of one-off kisses since then. But Simón's kiss had been the first to make her long for more.

She had changed her T-shirt for a butter-coloured cotton sweater, replacing the pinafore over it and adding a twisted scarf to the neck of the sweater, when there was a knock on her door.

Unless Laura had returned, it could be Jack or it could be Simón. She couldn't see any reason for Jack to come to her room, which meant that it was probably Simón. She debated calling out that she wasn't decent at the moment, but she knew that would only postpone the reprimand she was expecting. She went to the door and opened it.

Simón was still in his tennis kit, but the cable-knit sweater which earlier had been thrown over his shoulders with the sleeves loosely tied at the front was now pulled on over his white shirt.

His expression unrevealing, he said, 'How have things been going?'

'Pretty well.' She took a step back. 'Come in.'

He walked into her room, looking round it, taking in the changes she'd made—the shawl and cushions on the bed, the books on the chest of drawers, the other personal touches.

'Won't you sit down?' She gestured towards the basket chair by the window, seating herself on the upright chair by the table. 'I think I know what you're going to say.'

The other chair creaked as he settled himself, crossing his long brown legs, their colour emphasised by the whiteness of his shorts and socks.

'What am I going to say?'

'My guess is you're going to repeat what you said before...about my being in Jack's room.'

'Actually, no...it would be wasting my breath. I told you what I thought. You chose to ignore it. That's that,' he said astringently.

'I didn't *ignore* what you said. I did think about it. When Jack offered to show me his Legion photos I didn't realise where he kept them. I thought they'd be in an album he meant to bring down to the kitchen. When I found out they weren't, how could I refuse to go upstairs with him? It would have been hurtful and insulting.'

'If Jack were half as au fait with the outcome of recent battles in the sex war as he is with successful actions carried out by the Légion Étrangère, he might have been wary of asking you to his room,' he said coldly. 'These days a woman has only to claim sexual harassment and a man is in serious trouble.'

'Jack knows I wouldn't do that.'

'You might, if something happened you couldn't cope with and you panicked. According to my mother, a lot of the things defined as "harassment" now were, in her day, considered the natural hazards of being an attractive female.'

'I thought Spanish girls of your mother's generation always had a duenna keeping an eye on them.'

'Most of them did, but my mother happens to be English. She had to cope on her own . . . and, judging by what she's told me, did it with great aplomb.'

'You mentioned that your mother was brought up in England, but I didn't realise she *was* English,' said Cassia. 'You look totally Spanish.'

'The de Mondragóns are mongrels. We have Moorish genes, Genoese genes—all kinds of genes in our bloodline. Fifty-seven varieties. Being mostly diplomats or soldiers, the majority of my ancestors found their wives outside Spain, although my grandfather married a girl who gave us a transfusion of undiluted Spanish blood.'

His eye fell on the photographs on her dressing table. 'Are those your parents?'

'Yes.'

Simón rose, crossed the room and picked up the picture of her father—a snap she had taken herself while John Browning had been at work on a painting.

'A very distinguished-looking man,' he said as he replaced it.

The photograph of her mother was a print of a studio portrait that Cassia had found between the pages of a book. Fearing that her father might order her to destroy it, she had said nothing about it, and had not bought a frame for it until after his death.

'Very pretty,' observed Simón, studying the oval face and then turning his head to compare it with Cassia's. 'Much prettier than her daughter,' he said, with deflating frankness. 'But you, as your father could have told you but probably didn't, have the makings of a beauty.'

'Me . . . a beauty?' she said, staggered.

'Certainly . . . in a few years. Even now you're . . . very taking.' He replaced the photo beside that of her father and cast his eye over the other things on the dressing table, which luckily she had dusted and tidied that morning. They included the silver hoop earrings that she had been going to put on when his rap on the door had deflected her. He picked them up. 'Are you wearing these tonight?'

She nodded, intensely aware of his nearness. Being close to him like this disturbed her more, she discovered, than lying against Jack's bare chest.

Simón removed the butterfly fastener from the pin of one of the hoops. Holding it between his finger and thumb, he put the tip of his longest finger behind the lobe of her ear and inserted the pin in the hole, then made it secure with the butterfly. The touch of his hand against her cheek, and the intimacy of the service he was performing, made her heart lose its normal rhythm and beat in palpitating thumps. He did the same with the other hoop.

'Spanish girls have their ears pierced as babies. When were yours done?'

'When I was sixteen.'

'Was it very painful?'

'Only for a few seconds.' She had fixed her eyes on the V of the neck of his tennis sweater, unable to meet his gaze at such close quarters. 'The jeweller did something to deaden the pain. He was very quick and expert.'

'Take care to choose someone equally expert to perform that other, not dissimilar rite of passage in a woman's life,' he said, resting his hands on her shoulders.

As she grasped what he meant she flashed a quick, upward glance and saw his dark eyes glinting with wicked amusement.

On an uneven breath, she said, 'What makes you think someone already hasn't?'

'If they had, you wouldn't be blushing so deliciously. You may have been kissed before, but you haven't had a lover, have you?'

'No, I haven't,' she admitted. 'I suppose in your world that makes me some kind of freak.'

'It makes you a rarity,' he said drily. 'Do you understand the term "sport" in its botanical sense?'

She shook her head.

'I picked it up from my mother, an enthusiastic gardener. A sport is a plant that differs from others of the same species in some significant way. That can make it very desirable.' His hands shifted slightly, his forefingers gently caressing the sides of her neck.

She knew that he was making love to her and she didn't know how to deal with it, so she did nothing, submitting in pulse-racing silence to his touch and his look, waiting for what he would do next, which she was almost certain would be to kiss her again.

It was one of those moments in life when time seemed to come to a stop.

'Cassia . . . Cassia . . . telephone . . .'

Laura's urgent voice, coming up from somewhere below, made the world start spinning again.

Simón took his hands from her shoulders and Cassia pulled herself together. 'It can't be for me. I don't know anyone who would telephone me. It must be for you.'

'Perhaps it's Alvarez, calling to find out how you're getting on,' he suggested.

'I did write to him last week, but he wouldn't ring me on a Sunday. He'll be at home with his family,' she said as, with Simón moving more leisurely at her heels, she hurried downstairs.

'Ah, there you are!' exclaimed Laura, starting to come up the stairs as they came quickly down.

'Who is it, Laura? Did they say?'

'A girl . . . she didn't give her name. I had only come in a few moments before the telephone started ringing. When did you get back, Don Simón? I didn't see your car outside.'

On her way to the telephone, Cassia heard him say, 'I came in a friend's private plane and he dropped me off in his car.'

The call was from Rosita, wanting to know how Cassia was getting on. 'Señor Alvarez said he'd heard from you, but he didn't pass on any details. How's it working out?'

'Very well up to now. We haven't really got going yet. How are things with you?'

'The same as they were when you left. I could do with some excitement in my life, I can tell you,' Rosita said, with a loud sigh. 'So how are things going with your new boss? Has he made a pass at you yet?'

Cassia said firmly, '*Absolutamente*!' in the negative sense of 'Absolutely not!'

But even as she said it she was wondering if what had happened upstairs had been the beginning of a pass that Simón would have followed through if her ex-colleague hadn't chosen this moment to call.

Whether he would do that later was the thought paramount in her mind while she helped Laura prepare some tapas, and listened to the housekeeper describing her lunch out with her French friend.

When the men joined them conversation became general. Jack had heard that the king of Spain, Don Juan Carlos, was the owner of a Harley-Davidson motorbike on which, his identity concealed by his crash helmet, he had been known occasionally to give a lift to one of his subjects.

Simón confirmed that this was so, and was then asked by Laura if he had met the king and Doña Sophia, the popular queen of Spain.

'Only in formal circumstances—receptions and so on,' he told her, clearly not as interested in the life of his country's royal family as Laura.

Cassia was still digesting the surprising fact that his mother was an Englishwoman.

After supper Jack said that he was going to stroll down to the bar for a *tercio*, which she knew was a third of a litre of beer, and Simón said that he would join him.

'There's no side about him, is there?' said Laura when they had gone. 'I know people much lower down the scale than Excellency, who would turn up their noses at that scruffy little bar.'

Cassia suspected that going to the bar was a deliberate PR exercise on Simón's part. In small doses he might find the company of the men of the village interesting. But she doubted if he liked the noise level in the bar.

The two men were still out when she and Laura retired to their rooms. Cassia spent ten minutes resewing a couple of buttons which had been coming adrift on the shirt she would be wearing tomorrow.

As she stitched them on more securely she wondered what would have happened if Rosita hadn't rung up. Had Simón been toying with the idea of initiating her so far non-existent love-life? He certainly had the expertise, if indeed a long list of experienced ex-girlfriends was a qualification for teaching a girl with no experience.

She had always hoped that when, at long last, her
curiosity was satisfied it would be with someone she
loved, who loved her. Perhaps, if she hadn't met Simón,
she could have fallen in love with Jack. They had a lot
in common. With Simón she had nothing in common,
except that he seemed to fancy her and she was irresistibly drawn to him.

The next day, her heel having healed, she accompanied
the men on another day in the mountains.

They were looking for a place where Jack could teach
abseiling and climbing on a bluff of sound rock. There
were many spectacular bluffs within a few miles' radius
of the village, but not all were stable. They looked at
one where several huge chunks of rock, each weighing
many tons, had fallen away from the face. It looked as
if it might jettison others before long.

After some more exploring they arrived at a cliff which
looked more promising. This was half an hour before
their planned lunch break. Leaving Cassia to relax after
the strenuous walk from where they had left the Range
Rover, the two men set out to climb the cliff and, if
successful, to abseil down it.

To her it looked unclimbable. But, starting in different places, each man found his own route up it, and
she couldn't help wondering if there was a competitive
element in the way they tackled the ascent, perhaps both
hoping to reach the top first. Or perhaps not, for
although his relations with women might suggest the re-
verse she didn't think Simón was an irresponsible man
in the other areas of his life. He didn't drive recklessly,
and she didn't think he would take chances on a rockface
in order to beat Jack to the top.

Shading her eyes to watch their slow but steady upward
progress, she wondered if she could do it. Perhaps when
Simón had gone back to Madrid she would ask Jack to

give her a lesson. With him, she wouldn't mind finding out that she had no aptitude or even a poor head for heights.

Women did climb, and climb well. She remembered reading a feature in a French magazine left behind by one of the guests at the Castillo about the woman who was one of France's most daring and expert rock climbers. Cassia didn't aspire to reach that level, but suddenly, watching the technique the men were using to climb the escarpment above her, she wished she were up there with them instead of being left behind.

But the first time she tried it she didn't want Simón to be there, in case she chickened out. Not that she thought he would despise her or mock her—he wasn't that sort of person—it was just that she wanted him to respect and admire her, to take her more seriously than any of his other women. Not that she was in that category, and she had no intention of joining it.

But it was one thing to tell herself that while she was down here, with her feet firmly on the ground, and he was up there with his mind focused on scaling a rockface. Later today he might find an opportunity to focus his attention on *her*. If and when he did, she knew it would be much harder to stick to her resolution not to succumb to the almost overwhelming magnetism he could exert— had exerted on her last night.

She hadn't forgotten the feel of his hands on her shoulders, his fingers moving against her neck. She had no illusions about her own vulnerability if he was determined to have her.

CHAPTER EIGHT

AFTER spending some time out of sight, presumably admiring the views from their higher vantage point, the men came down the escarpment in a fraction of the time it had taken them to haul themselves arduously up it.

Abseiling also looked fun, thought Cassia, watching Jack descend in a series of swoops, on a line attached to a harness round his hips, his feet keeping him clear of the rockface.

During lunch, as they discussed other climbs that they had done in other places, their conversation was peppered with words—arête, traverse, slabby rake, flake—which had little meaning for her. She felt that in some way the climb had put them on a new footing, their shared enthusiasm for the sport making other differences irrelevant.

'This must be boring for Cassia,' said Simón, suddenly turning to her.

'She might like to try it,' said Jack. 'I've met some first-rate women climbers.'

'Have you?' Her eyes lit up with interest. 'Where did you meet them?'

Before he could answer, Simón said, 'Some women do climb well, but the ones I've met have been very tough and not very feminine. Would you agree with that, Jack? I'm not saying they looked aggressively masculine—except for having more muscle to call on than most women—but they had different mind-sets from other women.'

'I couldn't say about that. I've seen them climbing but I haven't had a lot of direct contact.' Jack turned to Cassia. 'Climbing goes on everywhere, but the public don't see much of it because they're not usually near the places where it happens. You don't see it on TV often, because of the technical problems and because it's either a loner's sport or co-operative, not competitive. I've climbed in France and Corsica, where I was based as a para. I've also—' He broke off to look through binoculars at something which had caught his eye on a shoulder of hillside further along the valley.

A few moments later he said, 'Seems like someone's in trouble.'

Simón put aside his bread roll to have a look through his glasses. With the naked eye Cassia could only see a number of people moving slowly downhill.

'A party of walkers...one of them injured by the look of it. Perhaps we'd better get down there and see if they need any help,' he said, scrambling to his feet and beginning to gather his belongings together.

Jack followed suit. 'At the rate they're going down, it'll take them a month of Sundays to get up that steeper track on the other side of the valley...assuming they set out where we did.'

'There's nowhere else they could have started from in the area,' said Simón. 'Ready, Cassia? Right—let's get going.'

With him setting a cracking pace, it took them about twenty minutes to catch up with the four elderly people who had stopped for a rest when his party joined them.

The others turned out to be Belgians. One of the two women had tripped and fallen off the path, which at that point had skirted a drop of two or three feet. She was not only badly shaken but had a gash on her forehead and couldn't walk on her right foot. The two men—one tall, but overweight and unhealthily florid, and the other much shorter—had been carrying her down, but with difficulty. She was now in tears, being fussed over by the other wife.

'Would you look at their shoes, for heaven's sake?' Jack murmured to Cassia. 'This lot belong on the esplanade at Benidorm. What the hell are they doing out here, got up like that?'

She gave a nod of agreement. It seemed an act of madness for two women, both in open-toed town shoes and tights, to be where they were. Looking at the two men, both of whom had been sweating heavily in the midday heat, she thought it wouldn't be long before they became dehydrated.

Between them, Simón and Jack attended to the hurt woman's cut and the worst of her scratches and gave her a painkiller. Then they took turns to carry her on their backs, the one who wasn't transporting her carrying both their packs.

Cassia, left in charge of escorting the other three up, found it an anxious assignment. They went up the steep track like snails on what at the outset, she learned, had begun as a leisurely ramble before lunching on leg of lamb at a restaurant in the village.

As she gave her hand to the second woman and heaved her up the steepest sections while keeping an eye on the two men, she was worried that one of them might collapse before reaching the top.

Earlier, Jack had been saying how quickly mishaps could escalate into disasters when people were badly equipped or mentally unequal to coping with the unexpected. What had befallen these four townies seemed a good example of that.

Presently Simón reappeared. 'We assumed they had come by car,' he said to her. 'Unfortunately not. They came in a taxi which is coming back to pick them up—but not until four.'

By this time Cassia had discovered that both couples lived on one of the many *urbanizaciónes* near the coast—enclaves of holiday and retirement houses built to accommodate the droves of sun-seeking foreigners who had been colonising Spain since before she was born.

'They can't hang about until then,' she said. 'Can't we contact the taxi driver and get him to come back immediately?'

'Jack has a better idea. He can squeeze them into the Range Rover and take them to the nearest hospital for the other old girl to have her foot X-rayed. You and I can either wait for the taxi or try to hitch a lift back.'

'Before they go anywhere these three need something to drink, or they're going to flake out with heat exhaustion.'

'Yes, they're all in bad shape,' he agreed. 'Couch potatoes trying, in a moment of madness, to be mountain goats.' His smiling glance lingered on her slimmer contours.

The look took her back to the evening before, in her bedroom.

Half an hour later, rehydrated with water supplied by the village bar, and with ham rolls to eat on the way, Jack's charges left for the coast—the injured woman in front with him, the other three squeezed in the back.

'Better expect me when you see me,' he said, leaning out of the window. 'As they don't have a word of Spanish, I can't dump them at the hospital and leave them to it. I'll have to hang around. *Dios!*'

With a wave of the hand, he drove off.

'Let's have some coffee, shall we?' said Simón as the vehicle disappeared round a bend in the narrow village street. 'I'll bring it out.' He went back inside the bar, leaving Cassia to sink gratefully into a chair at one of the two metal tables on the pavement outside.

The morning's brisk walking hadn't tired her. It was the laggardly drag up the hill with the elderly Belgians which had been fatiguing. She felt hot and sticky, and longed for a cooling wash, but a brief visit to the bar's loo had discouraged her from attempting to freshen up there. In her experience it was unusual in Spain for the washrooms in bars to be squalid. But they were at this establishment.

When Simón came out with the coffee he said, 'I'm told there's a path we can take that cuts across country, connecting with a road going in the general direction of Castell. If you feel equal to walking a few more kilometres, we stand more chance of picking up a lift from there.'

'It sounds a better idea than hanging about for nearly an hour and a half for the Belgians' taxi to come back.'

'That's what I think.' He stretched his long legs. 'The driver won't be pleased when he finds he's come back for nothing and has to chase up his fare.'

'It's a long way to come by taxi from where they live. It seems strange they don't have their own cars.'

'Perhaps they don't often leave their urbanisation,' he suggested. 'It has its own supermarket and shopping arcade, so our piggy-back passenger was telling us. Most of the residents have their own pools, so they don't need to go to the beach. It's a world of its own. *In* Spain, but not *of* Spain.'

'You've certainly done your good deed for the day, lugging the one who hurt herself up that steep bit. She'd be where we found them still if you and Jack hadn't turned up.'

'I'd rather have carried you the day you blistered your heel. Are you sure it's not hurting today?'

'No, no... it's fine,' she assured him.

After they'd left the bar their way led them past a *lavadero* similar to the one they had passed on the first walk, except that this wasn't in use.

'I'd like to wash my face and hands,' said Cassia.

'A good idea,' he agreed. 'I could do with a clean-up myself.'

To her surprise, while she washed her face and hands with a small piece of soap from her pack, and dried them with a cotton kerchief, Simón stripped off his shirt to sluice his chest and arms as well as his face and neck. Then, after drying himself with his discarded shirt, he produced a clean white T-shirt.

'That feels better.' He raked back his wetted hair which, being thick, clean and well cut, seemed not to need a comb to make it look presentable.

They moved on, their pace more leisurely than earlier in the day. Where the path was too narrow for them to walk abreast, Simón drew back to let her go ahead of him.

That morning they had passed a mountain which took its name from a legend going back to Moorish times. Now they talked again about the Moors—a subject on which he was unexpectedly well-informed, although she was less surprised by that now than she would have been in the early days of their acquaintance. Then it had seemed unlikely that he would have any seriously intellectual interests.

Talking, they reached the road much sooner than she expected. She felt a twinge of regret that this enjoyable interlude—the easy path with its peaceful views, an interesting conversation free from personal undercurrents—had ended so quickly.

'Shall we wait, or continue walking until something comes along?' Simón asked.

'Which would you rather do?'

He glanced up and down the road. 'In the absence of anywhere to sit, I think we may as well stroll on. Unless you've had enough of St Ferdinand's car, as my nurse used to call going on foot.'

'No, I don't mind walking,' said Cassia. 'Did you see much of your parents when you were small? Or were you mostly with your nurse?'

'Unfortunately my father was an invalid. A riding accident had damaged his brain. It was very hard on my mother and says a great deal for her character that she stayed with him and never allowed herself to become over-possessive with me. She's remarried now, and lives in America, but we see quite a lot of each other. She's an extraordinarily strong, fine person.'

This was a different version of the story that Cassia had heard, and she would have liked to hear more about his mother. But Simón changed the subject. Perhaps he felt that the conversation had become too personal.

The first car to come along was a large Mercedes. Although the back seat was empty it swept past them, with the driver and his passenger averting their eyes from the two would-be hitchhikers.

'As they've probably both got gold watches and wallets stuffed with five *mil* notes, maybe they're right not to pick up strangers,' said Simón, watching the opulent car glide round the bend ahead of them.

'Here comes another,' said Cassia, a few minutes later.

This time the car was a small blue saloon. As they saw when it pulled up in response to his signal, it had only one seat to spare, the back being occupied by the elderly mother of either the portly Spanish driver or his buxom wife.

'Where are you going, my friend?' the driver enquired.

'To Castell de los Torres. But I can see you haven't room for us. It was good of you to stop,' said Simón.

'We're going near Castell. We can fit you in, if you don't mind a bit of a squeeze. You're a big fellow, but the young lady isn't. She can sit between you and my mother.'

The invitation was seconded by the driver's wife and parent with smiles and beckoning gestures.

In view of Simón's height, it would have made sense for him to sit in front with the three women sharing the back seat. However, as this wasn't suggested, after Cassia climbed in, making polite remarks about their kindness, he followed her.

Instructed by her husband, the driver's wife did adjust her seat to give Simón a few more inches to accommodate his long legs. But, as her mother-in-law weighed at least a stone more than she did, there was very little room for Cassia, squashed between the billows of female flesh on her left and the less yielding male physique on her right.

As the driver let in his clutch Simón lifted the arm pressing against hers and, shifting sideways, laid it along the shelf behind the backrest, a manoeuvre that made better use of the space available but left her less comfortable inwardly, because now she was tucked against him in a far more intimate way than merely shoulder to shoulder.

The Spaniards were curious to know who their passengers were, where they had come from and why they were going to Castell. Cassia left it to Simón to answer their questions, and to fire back several of his own, so that soon the others were telling him their life stories without gleaning more than the bare essentials from him.

Presently they came to a succession of bends which made the driver's mother grasp the handgrip above the window and caused Cassia, with nothing to hold, to sway from side to side until Simón again moved his arm, this time to hold her against him.

Turning her face towards the offside window, in the hope that he wouldn't see her heightened colour, she met a beady look from the old lady.

'You are *novios*—yes?' she asked.

Cassia shook her head.

The old lady clicked her tongue. 'It's different from my young days. I wouldn't have been allowed to go for a walk in the country with a man, not even if we were engaged to be married.'

'That was fifty-five years ago, Madre. The world has changed,' said the driver.

'You're telling me! And not for the better,' his mother said tartly. She laid her hand on Cassia's arm. 'I was younger than you when I married his father, and we stayed married until his heart attack, two years ago. Life was never easy for us, but we managed. I still miss him. He was a good husband and father.' With her other hand, she fumbled in the pocket of her grey and black print dress for a handkerchief and mopped her eyes.

Cassia patted the hand still resting on her arm. 'I'm sure you were a very good wife to him, *señora*.'

Unembarrassed by her tears, the old lady said, 'What part of the country do you come from? Not from round here, by your accent.'

'I'm a foreigner.'

'You're not an American, are you? My eldest brother Alfonso went to America. He liked it there and did well for himself.'

By this time the road was running fairly straight again, but Simón didn't take his arm away. All the time that the old lady was talking about her brother's decision to try his luck on the other side of the Atlantic, his fingers were moving lightly over Cassia's outer arm, several fingers slipping gently under her rolled-up shirt sleeve— not far, but far enough to send a slow quiver through her.

She tried to pay attention to Alfonso's experiences, to ignore the sensations engendered by having her back heat-sealed to Simón's chest.

The driver's wife rolled down her window, increasing the current of air fanning the interior of the car and ruffling Cassia's hair. A strand must have blown across Simón's face. He removed it and tucked it behind her ear, his fingertips lingering on her neck.

She wondered how much further they had to go—how much further *he* would go before they were dropped off. There wasn't much more that he could do without the old lady noticing. But what he was doing now was enough to stir dangerous longings in her.

It wasn't solely out of gratitude to these kind people that, when they were back in the familiar landscape of the valley surrounding Castell de los Torres, Cassia said in English, 'Would they like to be invited in for a drink or coffee, do you think?'

She couldn't see Simón's expression without twisting her neck to look up at him, but the pause before he replied made her wonder if he'd guessed that she had an ulterior motive for the suggestion—to put off being alone with him. It was doubtful if Jack would be back yet, and Laura had an appointment with the hairdresser in the next village immediately after the afternoon closing hours.

His response, when it came, was to ask the driver if he and the two ladies had the time to take some refreshment before continuing their journey.

The outcome was that the Lopez family were still at Casa Mondragón when Laura returned with her hair done in a style which, she told Cassia later, was not at all to her liking.

'Next time I shall go to Babette's hairdresser in Benidorm. The girl who did my hair today is useless,' she said crossly.

In Cassia's private opinion, the softer style was actually more becoming than the way Laura's hair had been before. But she kept that thought to herself, saying only, 'The pharmacist has her hair nicely done. I wonder where she goes. Why not ask her? It would be more convenient to have yours done locally than go all the way to Benidorm.'

Preparations for supper were under way when Jack returned. There had been a long wait at the hospital, and after the X-ray the Belgian woman's foot had had to be put in plaster.

'I should think you could do with a stiff drink,' said Simón, when Jack had finished explaining why he had been so long.

'Several!' Jack said, with feeling. 'But I guess it was useful to locate the hospital's casualty department in case I ever have to take one of our lot there. How did you two get on, getting back here?'

'No problems... apart from the fact that the people who gave us a lift outstayed their welcome when we invited them in,' Simón told him, glancing at Cassia with a look suggesting that he knew she had been glad they had.

'Although they didn't find out that their host was a *marqués*, they were very impressed by the house. They'd never been in such a large one,' she told Jack.

'Who did they think he was, then?' he asked her when, a few minutes later, Simón was answering the telephone.

'I don't know. He told them his first name but glossed over his identity. I suppose they assumed he was an employee, like me. Did you tell the Belgians who he was?'

Jack shook his head. 'Those four weren't the sort to be interested in anyone except TV personalities.'

Simón came back with the news that the friend on whose plane he had come had had an unexpected change of plan and was returning to Madrid the following day instead of next weekend.

'I'll have to go back with him, if you wouldn't mind running me to the airstrip early tomorrow, Jack?'

'Sure. What time d'you want to leave?'

'He wants to take off at nine, so we'd better leave here at eight.'

Disappointed that he wasn't going to be with them for the rest of the week, Cassia wondered when they would see him again.

After supper, at Jack's suggestion, the men went out to the bar. Laura, complaining that the tightness of the rollers and the excessive heat of the drier at the hairdresser's had given her a headache, retired to her room.

Left on her own, Cassia put on a jacket and went up to the roof. It was a mild, clear night, and she stood with her elbows resting on the parapet and her head tilted back to gaze at the starry sky. She had often done this on the terrace of the house in the Albaicín. In some ways she longed to be back there, still working as a receptionist, her senses undisturbed by the turmoil aroused by being pressed close to Simón in the car this afternoon.

She had not been there long when she heard the door to the staircase creak on its hinges, and the next moment saw him stepping onto the roof.

She tensed. 'You're back soon.'

'I wasn't in the mood for the noise down there.' He came towards her, his expression unreadable in the pale half-light of a crescent moon and innumerable stars. 'I kept thinking about you—how you felt against me in the car...the scent of your hair...the enticing glimpse of your breasts...'

He put both arms round her and drew her against him and kissed her.

When the long kiss ended, it was like coming up for air after her first deep dive into the amazing world under the surface of the sea.

This too was a revelation of wonders that she had read about, seen at the cinema and elsewhere, but had never fully understood. Like diving, it had to be experienced. Reading about it, even watching other people do it wasn't the same as living it, feeling the strength of his arms, the compelling warmth of his mouth.

'It's a nuisance I have to leave tomorrow,' he murmured against her cheek. 'But anyway not having my car here is an inconvenience. I'll be back very soon. Meanwhile...'

He kissed her again, sending a long shudder through her. She found herself pressing against him, sliding her arms around his neck, touching the thick black hair with its own distinctive texture—crisper than cats' fur, springier than her own hair.

When he kissed her eyelids, she felt the slight roughness of his chin rasping her cheek. But his lips were gentle on the delicate skin of her closed eyes.

A few moments later he swung her up in his arms, carrying her to the old chair, sitting down with her on his lap, kissing her again, less gently.

For Cassia this belated experience of passion, until now only imagined, was even more exciting and wonderful than she had thought it would be. Intoxicated by it, she returned his kisses with all the pent-up longing of her innermost nature.

As he cradled her close to him, each kiss a little more demanding, she felt herself coming alive in a completely new way. Her responses were instinctive—as involuntary as laughter or a lump in the throat. There was no other way she could react except with this wordless expression of love and tenderness.

When his hand slid under her jacket, and she felt him unbuttoning her shirt, desire overwhelmed her. It was like being swept off her feet by a powerful wave, but in a warm summer sea so that she felt no alarm, only a willing surrender to an imperative force.

His exploring hand was gentle. She was scarcely aware of the strap being slipped off her shoulder and the cup of her bra being peeled away, replaced by the warmth of his palm. It felt as if all her life she had been waiting to experience these delicious sensations, and now, at long last, they were happening with the man she had always known would materialise some day—the only man she would ever want as a lover.

'You feel as soft as a dove,' he murmured, stroking her.

When he kissed her neck, it made her gasp with pleasure. If she felt like this now, at the beginning...

A few minutes later he said, 'The air's turning cold. Let's go down.'

Replacing her bra, closing the front of her shirt, he rose and set her on her feet. With her hand in his, he led her towards the staircase.

They were on the way to his room when, from below, the reverberating bang of the main outer door being closed broke the stillness of the huge house. It was Jack coming back from the bar.

The sound didn't cause Simón to pause. Leading her swiftly along the glassed-in gallery between the main stairs and his room, he appeared not to notice it.

But for Cassia the muffled thump brought an abrupt awakening from the daze of sensual delight induced by his caresses.

What am I doing? she asked herself. How am I going to feel about this in the morning?

Simón felt her hanging back and misread the reason for it. 'He's gone to the kitchen,' he said quietly. 'He isn't coming up here.'

'I know, but...' She slipped her hand free, her thoughts in a whirl of confusion. It was another deep instinct which made her say awkwardly, 'I'm sorry... I know I led you on... but... this isn't what I want.'

She expected him to be angry. To her surprise, he smiled. Taking her face in his hands, he said, 'I think I was doing the leading, not you, my sweet girl. Don't worry, I'll take care of you.'

The light kiss he dropped on her mouth was irresistibly tender and seductive. But somehow she did resist it, pushing him away and forcing herself to say firmly, 'I'm sorry, Simón... truly sorry... but I can't go to bed with you.'

And then, because she couldn't trust herself to go on resisting him, or to fight down the traitorous feelings undermining that resistance, she turned and fled.

The following morning, Cassia was tempted to stay in her room until after Simón and Jack had left from the airstrip where Simón's friend kept his plane. But, apart from the fact that Laura and Jack would think she had overslept, and Laura would bustle upstairs to bang on her door, not to go down would be cowardly. It would also leave her not knowing how Simón was going to react to her chickening out last night.

Unaccustomed to being rejected, would he now be in a rage with her? What man wouldn't? From what she had heard and read, the one thing calculated to exasperate the entire male sex was being turned on and then turned down. Especially now, when it didn't happen as often as it had in the past. Now, if women were going to say no, they took care not to get to the stage where yes or no became an issue.

Looking at her reflection as she brushed her teeth, wondering if the others would notice the signs that she hadn't slept much, Cassia wondered if it wasn't only men but also most of her own sex who would think her last-moment panic incredibly stupid.

It hadn't been the fear of getting pregnant which had made her back off. Nor had she any doubt that a night in Simón's bed would have been a gloriously sensual experience.

But not the best experience. That was the one she wanted. And for that you had to have love—on both sides. Anything less was bound to be a let-down—something she would have regretted had she woken in his room instead of her own.

The men were already at the table when she entered the kitchen. As he always did, Simón half rose from his chair. Jack stayed seated. Both said 'Good morning'.

'Good morning.' With the briefest of glances in their direction, she went to the hotplate to pour herself a cup of coffee. Then Laura came out from the pantry with a bag of sugar in her hand.

'Is your headache better?' Cassia asked.

'Much better, thank you, dear. But you look a bit heavy-eyed. I suppose you were reading till all hours? Ruins your eyes, reading in bed.'

Cassia said nothing. Many of Laura's ideas had no basis in fact, but it was pointless to argue. She believed them, and her mind was set.

'So when d'you think you'll be back?' Jack asked, spreading butter on a hunk of bread.

The men were eating French omelettes with grilled tomatoes.

'I'm not sure. I have other commitments as well as this project. If, for some reason, I couldn't come back for several weeks, you could manage without me,' said

Simón. 'All the basic arrangements are set up. From here on, it's up to you.'

As he spoke he looked down the table at Cassia. It was impossible to tell what he was thinking. The possibility that it might be weeks before she saw him again made her spirits sink. How could she live with the uncertainty of not knowing what he thought about her, if he had written her off as an uptight puritan whom he wouldn't waste any more time on?

She wondered if he would find a way to speak to her privately before he left the house. Or if he would go without even shaking her hand.

CHAPTER NINE

JACK looked at his watch. 'If you've nothing more urgent to do this morning, Cass, how about coming to the air-field with us? On the way back I'll give you a driving lesson.'

'All right . . . if Simón doesn't mind?'

Without looking up from his breakfast, he said, 'Whatever suits you.'

A few minutes later both men rose from the table, leaving Cassia to finish her coffee. She had her sun-glasses with her, and was ready to go without returning to her room.

'He's not in a good mood this morning,' Laura mur-mured, looking sage.

'Who? Jack or Simón?'

'Don Simón. I'm very sensitive to atmosphere. I knew he wasn't pleased about something as soon as he said good morning to me. Perhaps he's annoyed at having to go back sooner than he intended. He's a man who doesn't like having his arrangements altered, except by his own wish. It's important to him always to be in control. I'm a student of human nature. I can sum people up very quickly.'

In Cassia's opinion Laura's judgement of character was elementary compared with Señor Alvarez's pen-etrating assessments. But even he would have been un-likely to attribute the Marqués's mood to its true cause—the failure of an attempted conquest. One which, on the face of it, should have been easier than most.

143

She was waiting beside the Range Rover when the two men came out of the house.

Simón slung his grip in the back and then, with his usual courtesy, opened the front passenger door for her.

'No, no...you sit with Jack. I'll go in the back.'

As she moved to open the rear door he did the same. Their hands reached the handle simultaneously. Her re-action—to recoil as if from an accidental contact with a razor-sharp blade—made Simón raise his eyebrows and give her a sardonic look.

'There's no need to be nervous,' he said quietly, so that Jack, who had opened the bonnet, wouldn't hear. 'You made yourself clear last night. We'll go back to square one...and stay there.'

During the half-hour drive to the airfield the men dis-cussed Jack's vehicle and various cars that Simón and his forebears had owned. Jack had bought his third-hand, his dream being to own a new model.

Cassia would have preferred to learn to drive on one of the small runabouts used by the driving schools, but enquiries had revealed long waiting-lists. While the grandparent generation still thought nothing of walking to neighbouring villages and distant parcels of land, all her contemporaries—of both sexes—wanted wheels.

While the men were discussing emission controls and automotive gas turbines, she was preoccupied with Simón's last remark to her. How could they go back to square one after the passionate embrace on the roof last night? To put back the clock was impossible. Perhaps he, having slept with so many girls, could forget what had happened quite easily. She never could.

Looking at the broad shoulders rising from the seat in front of her, remembering how strong and solid they had felt against her hands, she knew that she would have total recall of every moment in his arms for the rest of her life. And would always be plagued by doubts about her decision not to trust herself to him.

'Don't worry, I'll take care of you.'

If only that statement had meant 'for ever'. But she knew it hadn't. All he had meant was that she needn't be afraid of getting pregnant.

No doubt with most of his girlfriends there was no risk of that happening. They were too experienced and worldly-wise not to be armed against such eventualities.

Playgirls like Isa didn't have accidental babies. It was girls like herself who did that—unwise virgins, usually much younger than she, who let themselves be swept away on a tide of reckless emotions, only to be left high and dry when their lovers opted out of the consequences.

At least she wasn't going to find herself in *that* situation. The most marvellous night of love in the history of the world couldn't be worth the ordeal of having a baby on one's own—especially in her circumstances, with no family to help her. Even with a supportive family it couldn't be easy to be a single parent. And children needed two parents. She knew that better than most.

She wondered how Simón would react in the unlikely circumstance that someone he made love to did become pregnant. Somehow she couldn't see him walking away from the responsibility. If he were that sort of man, he wouldn't have bothered to set up this project. His only concern would be to enjoy life, and to hell with everyone else.

On the other hand it wasn't responsible to make love to a girl with no sexual track record, who might easily take the affair far too seriously.

At the entrance to the airfield, Simón said to Jack, 'If any problems come up, my secretary always knows where to contact me. In any case, keep me informed. I'd like a situation report twice a week.'

They dropped him off near the building topped by a small control tower. Jack got out to unlock the tailgate and when Simón had retrieved his grip the two men exchanged powerful handshakes.

Out of politeness Cassia had turned sideways to respond to Simón's goodbye. His good manners were too deeply ingrained for him to ignore her, even if he might feel like it.

For a moment he looked straight at her, his expression at its most unreadable, except that the shape of his face and the tautness of his brown skin made it easy to see the sudden tightening of his jaw.

But his voice, when he spoke, didn't confirm the impression that inwardly he was displeased. 'Goodbye, Cassia. The next time I come down you may be able to drive this thing.' Turning to Jack, he added, 'When she makes a mistake, remember she's a girl—not one of your paras.'

Jack grinned. 'I'll go easy on her.'

Simón clapped him on the shoulder. '*Hasta luego.*'

Then he walked away, Jack closed the tailgate and Cassia turned to face forward, blinking back foolish tears.

'You're picking it up a lot faster than I expected. We'd better find out how soon you can take a test,' said Jack, at the end of Cassia's third driving lesson.

They had found a stretch of a new, wide road through the mountains, which eventually would carry a lot of traffic from the coast to the inland part of the province. At present virtually deserted, it was an ideal place for her to become thoroughly familiar with gear changes, three-point turns and the other basics of driving before attempting to drive in traffic.

Under Spanish law, novice drivers had not only to prove their capabilities at the wheel, they also had to have some knowledge of how a vehicle functioned. Jack taught her about the Range Rover's internal workings in what he called 'the backyard'—actually a large, walled garden where, next year, if the project proved successful, Simón was considering building a swimming pool.

'You're a very good teacher, Jack,' she said, after the latest of his mechanical tutorials. 'I thought you might be impatient if I didn't get the hang of it right away.'

'I like showing people how to do things...if they're interested. It's the bolshie, couldn't-care-less attitude that gets up my nose. You may hear some blasts of barrack-room language if I see any signs of that among the riff-raff,' he said in a grim tone.

He had taken to using this term to refer to the young people that they were expecting. Sometimes he called them 'the rabble'. Cassia suspected that this was partly to annoy Laura. She also thought that at rock bottom it was the housekeeper, with her deeply embedded, genteel middle-class values, who would view the teenagers with suspicion and distrust while Jack, outwardly a ruthless disciplinarian, would be the one who understood and cared for them.

'Time I had a haircut,' he said, passing a hand over his head. They were sitting on an old stone bench, he drinking beer, Cassia eating a *mandarina*.

'Must you? You look much nicer with it as it is now.'

In the time she had known him the original convict-crop had grown to a GI crew cut, and now was beginning to show signs that, left to itself, it might be luxuriantly curly. Even at its present length it made him look much less brutal than her initial impression of him. He would never be a handsome man, but neither was he as *bruto* as he had seemed at first sight. In a sisterly way, she was becoming very fond of him.

'Why not let it grow a bit more?' she suggested. 'One day you may go bald, and then you'll wish you'd enjoyed your hair while you had it.'

'Maybe I should have a perm like Manuel,' Jack said sarcastically.

The builders had only a few minor jobs left to do. Manuel was the youngest and least skilled, his heart set on becoming a pop star like the idol whose long, tangled hairstyle he had copied. In a few days the men would be gone, and the house would no longer resound with shouted exchanges in Valenciano, and bursts of heavy metal from Manuel's ghetto-blaster.

Cassia laughed. 'I can't see you with a perm or a pony-tail, but in a different way a shaved head is just as way-out. It makes you look threatening.'

'That could be a good way to look when the riff-raff arrive,' was Jack's comment. 'That reminds me—we'd better fax another sit. rep. tonight. We haven't done one since Monday, and we'll have the *jefe* on our backs if we don't keep him up to date. Don't let his friendliness fool you. He may not stand on ceremony, but when that guy says do something, he means it. I've met officers like him in the Légion. They don't throw their weight about. They don't have to. They're tough on themselves and even tougher on anyone who doesn't match their standards.'

'I wouldn't describe the Marqués as tough on himself,' said Cassia.

Since his departure, she had taken to referring to Simón by his title rather than by his first name. Probably there was some fancy psychological term for her reason for this, but she wasn't into self-analysis at present. She felt that the cure for her condition—if there was a cure— was keeping busy, not thinking.

However, as Jack had raised the subject, she couldn't help saying, 'Some people would consider his lifestyle was the acme of self-indulgence.'

Jack shook his head. 'No way. OK, he's got plenty of loot, and a title as long as your arm. But if you forget what you know about him, and look at the guy himself, what do you see?'

In her mind's eye Cassia saw various images. The Marqués coming down the stairs at the hotel in his black salopette and coral-coloured T-shirt, his arms as brown as a gypsy's. At the wheel of his car on the drive from Granada. Vigorously washing himself in the cold spring water flowing through the *lavadero* a few hours before he had changed the world for her.

'I don't know. What do you see?'

'Someone who in a rough-house I'd sooner have with me than against me.' Jack drained his bottle of beer. 'He may go to glitzy parties and know lots of VIPs, but he wouldn't be in good shape if his life was all wine and women. Come on—let's get that fax done. This time next week we won't be taking it easy. We'll have the first batch of rabble here.'

The first intake of teenage 'rabble' arrived on a coach from Madrid. Watching them disembark, Cassia was torn between foreboding and pity. Some looked trouble-makers. Others looked apprehensive. But, having not always had it easy in her own life, she guessed that even the most loutish were inwardly somewhat nervous at being taken far from their sleazy but familiar *barrios* and dumped down in an alien environment.

'*Gracias a Dios por Juanito*!' was Laura's heartfelt exclamation as she looked at a youth with tattoos on the backs of his hands and a safety pin in his ear.

Jack didn't like it when she called him by the Spanish equivalent of his name, and it was a measure of her reaction to the coachload that she should thank God for his presence. Their mutual antipathy was, if anything, growing more pronounced.

Although he had not yet had his head shorn, this afternoon he was wearing military-green combat clothes, with a strip of Velcro over the right breast pocket where the tape with his name had been worn when he was in the Légion. As he checked off the youngsters' identities on the list on his clipboard, and gave them each a fierce stare, he looked more than capable of keeping them in order.

Although Jack had made several caustic remarks about social workers *en masse*, the two people in charge of the coach party looked a sensible pair. The man introduced himself as Roberto and his colleague as Maria-José. He looked to be about forty, she in her middle thirties. Their friendly but no-nonsense manner towards their charges led Cassia to hope that they would turn out to be very different from Jack's estimation of the profession as a whole. Having never come into contact with social workers before, she was reserving judgement.

While Jack took Roberto and the boys to their quarters, Cassia showed Maria-José and the girls to theirs. The girls would be sleeping in a dormitory, their supervisor in a room nearby.

'This is very nice,' said Maria-José as she looked round her accommodation.

By the standards of the Castillo del Sultán, its appointments were adequate but basic. But, compared with those in lower-rated hotels, the bed was probably more comfortable, the furnishings in better taste. All it lacked were some personal touches, and Cassia had done what she could to remedy this by hanging a chart of Spanish wild flowers on the wall, putting some second-hand paperbacks from a swap-shop on the bedside table and buying a pottery vase at a car-boot sale. This, filled with pale carnations, stood on the window ledge with a hand-written card—'Welcome to Casa Mondragón. We hope you'll enjoy your stay here'—propped against it.

'The meal times, the fire drill and so on are pinned up inside the wardrobe door,' Cassia explained. 'If you haven't enough hangers, or if there's anything else you need, please let me know.'

'Thank you. I'm sure we're all going to have a wonderful time. I've never been to this part of the country before. This is a beautiful valley,' said the older woman, looking out of the window at the mountains.

'I'm a newcomer here too. I came from Granada.'

They exchanged the basic facts of their lives before Cassia said, 'I'll leave you to settle in.'

On her way downstairs she was astonished to hear a distinctive male voice speaking to someone below. Her heart turned over. Simón was back.

He had finished his conversation and was on his way up the staircase when they met.

'I...we weren't expecting you today,' she said, suddenly breathless.

He gave her a sweeping appraisal. 'Am I a pleasant surprise?'

'Of course.' For something to say, she added, 'I—I've just been chatting to Maria-José—Señorita Moreno, the girls' supervisor. Have you met her?'

'Many times. She was once a social butterfly. Then her *novio* was killed in a microlight accident. It made her rethink her life. She's now committed to helping other people. Considering her background, she has an extraordinary rapport with girls from the roughest *barrios* in the city...and Madrid has some very bad quarters, where many girls see prostitution as their only option.'

He moved on up the stairs and Cassia continued down, wondering what Maria-José would say about him, if questioned. It would be interesting to know how someone who had her origins in his milieu but was now dedicated to helping the underprivileged would see him.

Of course, from Maria-José's point of view he was a benefactor. But how would she reconcile that aspect of his character with the downside? If she had been a butterfly in the upper echelons of Madrid society, she would be bound to know about Simón's reputation. She might even have attracted his attention. Ten years ago, fashionably dressed and coiffed, she must have been strikingly attractive. Even now, in a sweatshirt and jeans, with her hair cut close to her head and no make-up, she might not turn heads but she wouldn't be ignored.

Maria-José sat next to the Marqués during the evening meal. On his other side was a girl whose make-up and clothes suggested that she might already have taken the option he had referred to. None of the girls was more than sixteen, but this one appeared to be eighteen or nineteen, until one looked closely and saw the signs of adolescence lurking under the veneer of mean-street sophistication.

Later that evening, the six adults met for a drink and discussion in a room reserved for them to relax in.

Warned that they would be called very early the following morning, most of the girls had already gone to their dormitory. The boys were still in the games room, playing pool and table tennis. Most of them were accustomed to staying up, watching TV or hanging about in the streets until midnight or later.

'But this time tomorrow night I'll have them all so flaked out they'll be hitting the sack as soon as they've swallowed supper,' Jack said with grim humour.

'There was a lot of waste after tonight's meal,' Laura said crossly. 'They hardly touched the salads.'

'These young people aren't used to good food, *señora*,' said Maria-José. 'In general we eat a healthy diet in this country. But now, in the cities, the junk-food culture of other countries is taking hold. I'm sure, after a few days here, in this wonderful fresh air and with plenty of physical activity, they'll be eating their meals with as much enjoyment as Roberto and I did tonight.'

Her tact earned her an approving look from Simón, Cassia noticed. For supper the girls' supervisor had changed into a white shirt and black skirt. Even in flat-heeled black shoes, gun-metal-coloured tights and a conservative mid-calf-length skirt, her legs were noticeably good. Except that her head was uncovered, she could have belonged to a religious order.

Cassia wondered if it might be her presence which had brought Simón back, and if he found Maria-José's nun-like appearance a challenge.

The next day when, except for Laura, they all went out on the first trail-clearing exercise, it became clear to Cassia that whether or not the Marqués was challenged by Maria-José, he would be wasting his time. She was interested in her colleague, and he in her. The warmth of their feelings for each other might not have been obvious to anyone else, but Cassia, in love herself, was more than ordinarily attuned to the nuances of other people's behaviour. She quickly picked up the small but significant signs of a more than professional rapport between the two supervisors.

By mid-afternoon most of the youngsters were as tired as Jack had predicted they would be. Their day had begun with a pre-breakfast march along the lanes through the vineyards. He wouldn't tolerate lagging on the return to the village at the end of the first day's work. He had taught them a simple marching song and moved back and forth along the double line, making them pick

up their feet, straighten their backs and swing their arms.
No one rebelled. In the combat fatigues he was wearing
he looked awesomely tough. Even the youth with the pin
in his ear didn't have the nerve to test Jack's authority.

A kilometre from the village, Simón fell into step with
Cassia.

'Tired?' he asked, in English.

'Do I look it?'

'No, but you're good at hiding your feelings and may
feel it's incumbent on you to set the girls an example.
Maria-José tells me there were flowers and a welcome
note in her room and in the girls' dormitory. Was that
your idea or Laura's?'

'Mine, but I expect Laura would have suggested it if
I hadn't.'

'I doubt it. I'm not sure Laura fits in as well as I'd
hoped. What do you think?'

It surprised her that he should discuss the housekeeper with her. 'She seems very capable to me, and she
gets on well with the cleaners.'

'Yes, but she disapproves of this lot...and is also
nervous of them,' he said, indicating the double file
ahead. 'If they're insolent, I don't think she'll know how
to handle it.'

'I'm not sure I shall,' said Cassia.

'They're less likely to test your mettle. Laura's an obvious target for cheeky backchat. They'll see you as an
icon.'

'Me? An icon? You're joking!'

'On the contrary. You're only a few years older. You've
got your act together as far as appearance goes.' After
a slight pause, he added, 'If they knew about it, they
might even envy you your virginity. It's a safe bet they've
all lost theirs. Sex starts early in the *barrios* they come
from. According to Maria-José, it's one of the factors
that keeps girls like these trapped. Only a few will break

out. The rest, unless they get help, will end up as worn-out slatterns, like their mothers and grandmothers.'

At this point one of the girls who had been walking ahead of them suddenly turned round and clouted the boy behind her. When he attempted to hit back another girl jumped to her friend's defence. The incipient scuffle was nipped in the bud by Simón striding forward to grab the boy by the scruff of his tracktop and fend off the two irate girls. All three were quickly subdued, more by his innate air of command than by his physical strength, Cassia thought, watching.

The Marqués didn't come back to her, but walked the rest of the way with the now pacified combatants, leaving Cassia to mull over his conversation with her. It didn't throw much light on his current state of mind in relation to what had happened the night before his last departure.

When she got back to her room, she looked at herself in the mirror and wondered if he'd been serious with that remark about her being seen as an icon.

It was rewarding to see how quickly and positively most of the teenagers adapted to their new environment. Given a longer stay, they would soon become as healthy and hopeful as the children born and bred in the valley, thought Cassia.

One morning Jack announced that, instead of trail-clearing, they were going to be taught to abseil. No one with a poor head for heights would be forced to take part, but he hoped that everyone, including the girls, would give it a try.

Cassia was still having breakfast when Simón stopped by her chair. 'I'd like you to come with me this morning, if you will.' As she would have risen, his hand on her shoulder restrained her. 'Not yet. In half an hour. Meet me at the office.'

She could still feel the pressure of his hand when she rose from the table and, wondering what he wanted to see her about, went to the downstairs washroom to touch up her lipstick.

Simón was at his desk, with the door open, when she arrived at the office. He signalled her to sit down, said, 'I shan't be long,' and went on tapping the keyboard of a notebook computer.

Even though he was concentrating on the screen, she didn't risk staring at him in case he suddenly looked up and something in her expression gave her away. At the moment he couldn't possibly know how she felt about him. Her near-surrender proved nothing. You didn't have to be in love with a man to respond to his physical magnetism.

She had left the door as she'd found it—admitting the sound of young voices, laughter and running feet. In a few minutes they would be gone, swinging off down the back lane, with Jack shouting good-humoured orders to straighten up and speed up.

By the time Simón switched off the screen and closed the notebook the cheerful noises were dying down. He put the computer in a drawer and locked it with a key clipped, with others, to a chain attached to his belt. Replacing the keys in the pocket of his jeans, he said, 'Jack tells me you'll soon be ready for a driving test, but the testers are even busier than the professional instructors. I may be able to pull some strings for you. But before I do that I want to see how you're getting on. I brought some L-plates with me. You can have a go at driving my car.'

'Is that a good idea?' she asked nervously. 'I mean, your car is very expensive. I'd hate to damage it.'

'There's not much fear of that. I'll drive to the place where Jack gives you lessons. You can take over there.'

Cassia wasn't happy about handling his luxurious car, even on a deserted road. Recognising her dubiety, he said sardonically, 'This is not, I assure you, a scheme to lure you to an isolated spot and force my attentions on you.'

A deep flush swept up from her neck. 'I didn't think it was!'

He lifted a sceptical eyebrow. 'You tense every time I come near you, Cassia,' he said drily. 'It may not be obvious to the others. It is to me.'

She didn't know what to say. She couldn't deny it. Her nerves had been as tight as bowstrings since she had first heard his voice in the hall. Merely knowing that he was in the house made her feel deeply uneasy. Being with him like this, alone, was even more stressful. To look at him was to remember how it had felt in his arms, to be torn between regret for what she had missed and dread that he might try again—and she wouldn't have the strength to resist him a second time.

The Marqués rose from his chair. 'Most people feel strung-up whey they're taking their test. Driving with me will be a useful learning experience—how to keep calm while being inwardly *muy nervioso*.' As he came round the desk his dark eyes gleamed with malicious amusement.

She had the unnerving feeling that she was going to be punished for being the first in a long history of conquests to repulse him.

In the car, she forced herself to watch and memorise everything he did. It wasn't easy. He drove the way he made love—with a light but sure touch. Even Jack, who called his vehicle 'she' and paid more attention to the Range Rover than some men gave to their wives, did not stroke through the gears the way Simón did. The movements of his long fingers reminded Cassia how they had felt caressing her neck, her bare shoulder, her uncovered breast.

It was one of Spain's golden mornings, when the mountains were sharply outlined against a pale blue sky, every crag and cleft clearly visible as far as the eye could see.

Simón pointed out a kestrel hovering in the bright air, scanning the vineyard below it for the movement of some small prey. Some weeks ago the vines had been pruned, the rust-red clay soil rotary-ploughed. Seen from her bedroom window, the grotesquely shaped vines had looked like rows of black cross-stitch. Now the first new leaves and clusters of minuscule grapes were appearing.

In Granada she had often seen men driving aggressively, pounding their horns at the slightest delay. The Marqués's manners didn't deteriorate when he was at the wheel. When they passed through the neighbouring village he slowed down to a crawl, smiling and raising his hand to housewives who, chatting in the narrow streets on their way to and from the shops, drew aside to let the car pass.

Cassia saw by their faces that they'd got a momentary lift from eye-contact with the good-looking driver of the opulent car with a Madrid number plate. Perhaps, if they'd noticed her beside him, they'd envied her for being young and free and out with a man whose charisma was as powerful as his car.

Leaving the village, he said, 'Apropos what we were talking about yesterday—'

Did he mean her virginity? She hoped not.

'Although I have doubts about Laura, I have none about Jack... not as far as his relations with the kids are concerned. He's the man for the job. There's no question about that.'

Ignoring the implication that there were other aspects of Jack that he was less happy with, she said, 'It turns

out that Roberto did his *mili* in the Spanish Foreign
Legion, so he and Jack have a lot in common. Did you
do military service?'

'Of course. Everyone does...or did, when I was con-
scripted. I was in the Navy.'

'Did you enjoy it?'

'Very much. I was based at Mahon in the Islas
Baleares. Menorca's an interesting island. For a time it
belonged to the British, and one of my mother's
ancestors commanded the garrison in Admiral Lord
Nelson's time. So I felt I had links with the place.'

Cassia had never been to the Balearics herself,
although her father had spent time on Mallorca before
she was born. She visualised Simón in uniform—not,
perhaps, as unnervingly sure of himself as he was now,
but still devastatingly attractive, especially to girls
sequestered on a small island like Menorca which, so she
had heard, had never been as 'swinging' as Ibiza, a mecca
for drop-outs.

She wondered how many Menorcan hearts he had
broken, and if most of the girls he had dated still had
wistful or painful memories—memories such as she
would have ten years from now.

'Why are you frowning?' he asked. 'What are you
thinking about?'

'I—I was thinking about my father.'

'Sorry...I should have guessed.' He took his right hand
off the wheel, reaching for her left hand and giving it a
quick squeeze. 'You must often miss him.'

The sympathetic tone and gesture were immeasurably
warming. She wanted to take his hand and hold it against
her cheek. She wanted so much to love him and show
her love. But that wasn't what *he* wanted. If and when
he embarked on a long-term relationship, it wouldn't be
with someone like her. She wasn't the stuff *marquesas*

were made from. She might seem classy to the girls from Madrid, but she wouldn't pass muster with his mother.

Simón took his hand away. Glancing at him, she saw a tight knot of muscle showing at the angle of his jaw—usually a sign of impatience or annoyance.

Then, the road being clear, he began to point out the dials and buttons on the dashboard. There was no irritation in his voice. Perhaps she had imagined his displeasure.

When the time came for her to take the wheel she fixed her mind firmly on proving Jack a good teacher and herself a good pupil.

Half an hour later Simón directed her in and out of a small town which didn't have any hazardously narrow streets but where it was market day and there was a policeman on duty at a central roundabout.

Cassia kept her head, and acquitted herself well enough for Simón to say, 'Your road sense is excellent. I'm impressed, and I'll see what I can do to get you tested as soon as possible. I've no influence myself, but some of my friends have. Unless, of course, you have strong moral objections to queue-jumping?'

Being still at the wheel, she kept her eyes on the road, but knew by the tone of his voice that he was teasing her. She said, 'I might . . . in other circumstances. I wouldn't feel comfortable taking the place of someone waiting for medical treatment. But it would make life easier for Jack if he didn't have to do all the driving.'

'Your wish is my command, *señorita*.'

If only it were, she thought longingly. To have Simón at her feet—even metaphorically—was a fantasy she had forbidden herself to indulge in.

Presently they changed places, and she took it for granted that they were heading back to Castell de los

Torres until, with the surrounding countryside still totally unfamiliar, she realised that they were travelling west, which must be taking them further inland.

CHAPTER TEN

'WHERE are we going?'

'I thought we'd have lunch out,' Simón said casually. 'There's a restaurant on the way to Albacete, recommended by my friend with the aeroplane. I called them this morning to make sure they were open today. You're not in any hurry to get back to the house, are you?'

'There are things I ought to be doing, but nothing which can't wait, I suppose,' said Cassia. 'Did you tell Laura we'd be out?'

'Naturally. If we weren't back when she expected us, she might think we'd had an accident.'

As it was not yet mid-morning, and an inland restaurant would be unlikely to start serving lunch before half past one at the earliest, Cassia wondered how he was planning to spend the interval.

When they stopped at a village bar for coffee, it turned out that their destination was near a large, lake-like reservoir which Simón intended to walk round. 'We shan't need boots. There's a road. I gather it's a popular picnic area at weekends and on *fiestas*.'

Later, as they strolled in the sun along a lane near the water's edge, passing one or two anglers but otherwise having the lovely place to themselves, she wondered why she was here with him. She couldn't fathom his motive for bringing her, unless, after lunch, he meant to make another pass. But he had specifically said that that wasn't his intention, and he wasn't behaving like a man with seduction in view.

162

Today, judging by their conversation, it seemed to be her mind, not her body that he was interested in—her favourite painters and authors, even her political opinions. He seemed to be taking her seriously and that, she discovered, could be as seductive as being flirted with. She felt herself warming, weakening, becoming dangerously happy when it turned out that they shared an enthusiasm or a dislike.

Their lunch was served at a table in the corner of a terrace. The rest of the restaurant's clientele, who all looked like travelling salesmen, ate inside in the busy dining room, which soon became noisy and, at the coffee stage, smoky.

The Marqués and Cassia could see the smokers lighting up through the window overlooking the terrace but were spared the noise, which would have made their own quiet tête-à-tête impossible.

'Not great cuisine, but very well cooked, don't you think?' he said, peeling a pear while she dipped her spoon into a crunchy topping on a home-made *flan*.

Cassia savoured the contrast between the caramelised sugar and the creamy smoothness of the custard before saying, 'I've enjoyed every mouthful. Thank you for bringing me.'

'Would you have come if you'd had the chance to opt out?'

'I don't know. Possibly not.'

'Why not?'

When she didn't speak, he answered for her. 'Because of what happened the last time I was down here.' It was a statement, not a question.

She put down the spoon, her enjoyment evaporating.

'Why did you have to bring that up?' she said in a low voice, looking towards the lake.

'Would you rather we ignored it?'

'I—I hoped we were on a different footing now. Friends.'

There was a long silence. When she flicked a glance at him, he was looking at the mountains on the far side of the water. His face gave nothing away.

Eventually he said, 'Very well, if that's the way you want it. Coffee?'

On the drive back they listened to a tape of what Simón called 'mountain music'—classical orchestral pieces.

Sitting beside him, Cassia was aware that somehow the day had gone wrong, and their pre-lunch rapport had been lost. They weren't friends. They could never be friends. It was a textbook case of a man wanting one thing and one thing only from a woman—something she wanted too, but not on the same terms.

When they got back, Laura greeted the Marqués with the news that soon after he'd left a lady had called from Madrid to say that she was paying him a visit and would arrive in time for dinner. Her name was Antonia Bretano. Laura had already prepared a bedroom for her.

Less than an hour later a loud tattoo on a horn drew Cassia to a window overlooking the *plaza* in time to see Simón coming out of the front door and opening his arms to the driver of a silver sports car.

When they finished hugging each other, his visitor drew back to reveal herself as a tall, thin redhead in her late twenties, obviously on close terms with him.

Evidently she was an artist. As Cassia watched she unlocked the boot and unloaded an aluminium easel, a collection of boards strapped together, and a motley assortment of bags—including two airline bags, three shopping carriers and a Greek-island bag.

Feeling another pair of hands might be needed, as well as being curious to meet her, Cassia ran downstairs to help.

By the time she'd emerged from the house Simón had his visitor's belongings slung over his shoulders, tucked under his arms and held in his hands.

To Cassia's surprise, he introduced them in English. 'Toni, this is Cassia Browning, whose father was an artist. Toni is also a professional painter.'

'How do you do? May I help you with your things?'

'That's kind of you. *Gracias*. I came *impulsivamente*, and packed in a hurry,' said the redhead, her English having an American accent. She was not a beauty, but she had beautiful eyes as golden as *níspero* honey.

'Tell me about your father. What sort of painter was he?' she asked, handing over a rolled mohair rug, a canvas satchel and a plastic bag full of shoes.

After Cassia had told her, Toni said, 'I paint windows...old windows. I'm obsessed by them. Don't ask me why.' She paused to look up at the façade of the Casa Mondragón. 'I expect I'll paint some of these...if I'm not going to be in the way?'

'You're never in the way,' the Marqués assured her, his voice warm, his eyes affectionate.

Suddenly Cassia had the feeling that this lanky woman, with her almost flat chest, boyish behind and wild mane of dark red hair, might be the only member of her sex, apart from his mother, for whom he felt any real warmth.

Toni flashed him a smile. Although she had none of the attributes flaunted by Isa Sanchez, she had a lot of sex appeal. In Spanish she said, 'Thank you, darling. I only wish everyone felt the same way. I always love staying with you. You let me be myself...unlike the aunts.' Turning to Cassia, she explained, 'I was brought up by two bossy aunts...both of them "ladies who lunch". They want me to join that club, but shopping and socialising bore me. How about you?'

'Cassia's life has been dominated by her father,' Simón answered for her. 'She might enjoy all the things you reject.'

'Are you being bullied by this sexist beast?' Toni asked, with a grin. 'Simón has some attitudes to women that would get him lynched by the fundamental feminists. But he isn't *all* bad.'

Considering she was talking to one of his employees, Cassia expected him to look rather put out by this disrespectful comment. But he said, 'Toni has been a thorn in my side since before she could walk. I remember her lurching into a nuclear reactor I was constructing on the Arenal beach during one of our holidays at the Jávea beach house. She's been making a nuisance of herself ever since.'

That evening Antonia Bretano came down for supper in a pair of supple suede trousers, a silver-studded belt, a tie-dyed shirt and a mirror-glass Indian waistcoat—an outfit that brought all the teenagers' eyes out on stalks. Especially as her accessories included dramatic earrings, abundant rings and bracelets all unusual and interesting—and a velvet peaked cap, worn back to front with a brooch pinned above her forehead.

Whatever her paintings might be like, it was soon clear that she had a genius for making friends with people, regardless of their ages and backgrounds.

After the meal Laura beckoned Cassia to her, saying in an excited undertone, 'I knew her face was familiar. It's suddenly come to me where I've seen her before.'

'Where?'

'In *Hola!* magazine, that's where. My friend has a stack in her flat going back four or five years. I was leafing through some of the old ones, before she threw them out, and who should I see but her... Antonia Bretano.'

'Are you sure? I thought all the people in *Hola!* were showbiz stars or royalty.'

'Most of them are. She's the daughter of a count,' said Laura. 'It's all coming back to me now. Her parents were married about the same time I was. Her father, the Conde de Bretano, was one of the richest men in Spain at the time he inherited the title. But he was a compulsive gambler. After his wife died in childbirth he gambled the whole lot away. Then he took to the bottle until his liver gave out.'

'What a dreadful thing. Are you sure?'

'I'm certain. You ask Don Simón.'

'I think he'd tell me to mind my own business,' said Cassia. 'I do know that he and Señorita Bretano have been friends since they were children.'

'Condesa de Bretano,' Laura corrected her. 'She's inherited the title.'

Cassia said, 'I shouldn't mention this to anyone else, Laura. If Toni's social status was important to her, Simón would have introduced her more formally. First and foremost, she's an artist.'

'They showed one of her paintings in *Hola!* I wouldn't have wanted to buy it. A shabby old *persiana enrollable*, some of its slats broken, hanging over a balcony. Who would want that on their wall?' said the housekeeper.

Cassia liked the old-fashioned exterior Venetian blinds, still to be seen at the windows of older houses, but rapidly being replaced by more modern aluminium blinds in new buildings. There was something typically and intriguingly Spanish about a weathered *persiana* draped over the rail of a balustrade to keep out the summer sun but admit any breath of air to the shadowy interior within.

'Those old *persianas* will have disappeared before long.'

'High time too,' said Laura. 'They might look picturesque, but you try keeping them clean!'

The next day Simón took Toni to revisit the beach where they had played as children.

Cassia accompanied the others on a trail-clearing outing. By now the wild flowers were out, and Roberto, a keen botanist, did his best to fire his charges with some of his own enthusiasm.

Although it would have been impossible not to enjoy the sunny day and the wild beauty of the scenery, Cassia's thoughts were often elsewhere.

She felt sure that Toni's visit wasn't merely a sudden whim to recapture the mood of carefree holidays at the seaside. She had come with a purpose, and Cassia thought that purpose might be to bring Simón to the point of proposing to her. It seemed likely that a marriage between them had always been on the cards. People in their walk of life chose their partners for different reasons than those whose known family history went back no further than two or three generations.

Like thoroughbred horses, Spanish grandees had bloodlines going back centuries—in Simón's case at least five centuries. The men might occasionally marry a less well-bred heiress if the family coffers were empty, but mainly they married their own kind. When they had known each other all their lives, as Simón and Toni had, and a strong affection existed, as clearly it did between them, it must work out quite well. Better, perhaps, than a passionate love match.

During the afternoon, while fooling about on some rocks, showing off to the girls, one of the boys missed his footing and fell, hitting the back of his head. For some moments he lay stunned and then staggered up, bleeding profusely.

Jack and Roberto dealt with him, while Maria-José and Cassia calmed several girls whom the sight of blood made hysterical. Others took a ghoulish interest, and had to be dissuaded from crowding round.

Cassia knew that head wounds always bled alarmingly, and she also knew that anyone who had lost consciousness, even if not for long, might be seriously concussed. She wasn't surprised when Roberto insisted on taking the boy back to the nearest village, there to telephone for a taxi to take them to the nearest hospital.

Jack drew her aside. 'Might be a good idea for you to go with them, Cass... if you don't mind?'

'Of course not. I'll see you later.'

He changed his mind. 'No, hang on. I think we'll all start back. It's a half-hour walk to the village. If that kid should start feeling woozy, he could need to be carried. I can rig up a stretcher. Roberto won't know what to do. If he'd been doing his job properly, this wouldn't have happened. Instead of watching the lads, he was chatting up Maria-José.'

'It's impossible to keep an eye on them all every second,' said Cassia.

At the time of the mishap Jack had disappeared for a few minutes. Had he been present when the showing off had started, if he had thought it risky, he would have stopped it. Both he and Simón had the ability to bring the boys to heel very quickly. Roberto was a nice man, but he lacked the steely authority of the other two.

At the village a taxi was sent for, and Jack decided that he and Cassia would escort the boy to hospital while the rest of the party returned to base on foot.

'We may as well go for a coffee,' he said about an hour later in the hospital, when the boy had been taken away to be X-rayed.

It was just as well that he had taken over from Roberto. They had arrived to find the casualty department crowded with people suffering from minor injuries. Having been there before, with the Belgian woman, Jack knew the drill. Even so it had taken a fierce altercation with the bureaucrat at the reception desk to get the boy seen immediately, instead of taking his turn.

'I doubt if Roberto would have put his foot down as forcefully as you did,' said Cassia, on the way to the hospital's cafeteria.

'I'm damn sure he wouldn't,' said Jack. 'But you can't afford to hang about when there might be internal bleeding.'

'I wish they had let one of us stay with him. He was rather obnoxious before, but now he looks really scared. I can't help feeling sorry for him.'

Jack put a hand on her shoulder, the one furthest from him. 'You're too soft-hearted, my love. He's been a bloody nuisance. For all you know, those expensive trainers he's wearing may have been paid for by mugging little old ladies.'

'I feel sorry for all of them,' she said. 'If my father had died when I was thirteen or fourteen, I might have taken to stealing or worse.'

'Never! You're not that kind. You've too much sense to get into that sort of trouble. Nobody with a brain in their head needs to go down that road. If these girls we've got with us now end up as whores, it won't be because they have to. Nobody *has* to make a mess of their lives. Not these days, not with do-good outfits and helplines springing up like mushrooms everywhere you look.'

Privately Cassia thought Jack's own gritty strength of character made it difficult for him to grasp how much weaker most people were. But she didn't argue with him.

The cafeteria having no *tapas* that appealed to them, Jack bought two bags of crisps to eat with their cups of coffee. The place was not full, and he carried the tray to a corner where the tables were unoccupied.

'It'll take at least half an hour for them to X-ray him and stitch up that gash on his head. Maybe longer. Suits me all right. It makes a change to have you to myself,' he said, breaking the seal on both bags and handing one to her.

'Thank you.' Cassia's concern for the injured boy gave place to a different disquiet. Why should Jack want to have her to himself?

'Do you like the job? D'you think you'll stay?' he asked, unwrapping two cubes of sugar and dropping them into his cup.

'I *need* the job, Jack,' she said drily. 'I liked my last one, but the hotel didn't have room for staff to live in and my landlord wanted the flat where I'd lived with my father. But yes, I do like this job. Don't you?'

'Sure. It suits me fine. I could do without Laura, but then she's not crazy about me,' he said, with a shrug. 'I don't think she'll stay long anyway. Women like her are more comfortable living in towns...trawling the shops...showing off new outfits at the evening *paseo*.' He stirred his coffee. 'You've looked a bit unhappy lately. Not so that most people would notice, but I've been watching you.'

This increased her unease. She said, 'If I looked down in the dumps, I expect I was thinking about my father.'

He stopped stirring his coffee to look intently at her. 'I don't think you had him on your mind. You've fallen for the *jefe*, haven't you?'

His astuteness came as a shock. She had tried so hard not to show her innermost feelings and thought she had succeeded.

Before she could make up her mind whether to admit or deny it, Jack said, 'You can tell me to mind my own business . . . but I can't do that. You're the first woman I've known who mattered to me, Cass. I don't know if the way I feel about you is what people call being in love.' He reached across the table and put his hand on her wrist. 'All I know is I want to take care of you and make life easy for you.'

'Oh, Jack . . .' she murmured in dismay. Instinct had warned her that something like this might be coming, and she wasn't sure how to handle it.

'Listen to me,' he said earnestly. 'Before you tell me it's no go, let me tell you the way I see it.'

'All right—how do you see it?'

Jack looked at his broad-knuckled hand curled over her lightly tanned wrist. His thumb moved in a light caress and then his eyes met hers again. 'I don't see any future for you with Simón, and I don't think you do either. That's what's making you miserable. You're a lovely girl. Intelligent. Educated. A real sweetie. But you're not Spanish and you don't have the right connections.'

'His mother is English,' she said. It seemed pointless now to deny that she was in love with Simón. Jack wouldn't believe her if she did.

'She is? You surprise me. He looks completely Spanish. OK, his mum's a foreigner. But I bet she had plenty of money behind her . . . and a title too, I shouldn't wonder.'

'I don't know about that. You could be right.'

'I'd bet money on it,' he said. 'Those people all marry each other. It's like a private club—non-members not welcome. If you're dreaming about him making you his *marquesa*, forget it, Cass. He fancies you, yes. Anyone can see that. But, unless you're willing to be his *amiguita*, there's no future in it.'

'You don't need to tell me. I know it. In fact, I think there's a good chance Toni will be his *marquesa*. They're obviously fond of each other. They'll make a good pair.'

'She's OK... too skinny for my taste. Doesn't hold a candle to you. You're...' he searched for the right word '... magic. I get a high just looking at you.' He reached for her other hand. 'You're beautiful, Cass... just beautiful.'

It was the first time in her life that she had known herself to be loved. Her mother had deserted her. Her father had never been more than moderately fond of her. Now she saw in Jack's eyes and heard in his voice the love that she had always longed for. But she couldn't return it. She could give him affection and respect, but that wouldn't be enough. He wanted her to feel the way he did. The way she did. But not about him.

She broke the silence. 'It's funny... the first time we met, we didn't take to each other. I could see you weren't keen on me, and I was wary of you.'

'I'd had a few bad experiences with girls in the UK. When I was in the Légion, unless you were an officer, nice girls didn't want to know you. The only friendly ones were tarts. Then, when I went back to England after ten years away... my God! What a difference.'

'I've never been to England. What had changed?'

'Women had changed. Suddenly men were in the dog-house. I'm not saying we didn't deserve some comeuppance. But not that much. I expected you to be like that. Aggressive. Hostile. I'd had enough of it.'

'I had some misconceptions about you,' she said, steering him back to the point she had started to make. 'But now I like you very much, Jack. Only not in the way you want. I'm sorry; I wish I did. We have a lot in common.'

'Maybe you won't always feel the way you do now... about him,' he said. 'He's a good-looking guy...

He's a *marqués*... He has all the polish, the charm...but he isn't available—not on the basis you want. You'll get over him, Cass. You'll have to. You can't waste your life on a daydream.'

'I know. But it could take years. I really do love him. It's not just infatuation. He's a fine person...worth loving.'

'Yeah...I know he is, dammit! I like him too. If he hadn't been who he is, he'd have made a good officer—the kind you know you can depend on when things get tough.'

As he finished speaking there was a tap on the nearby wall of plate glass. Looking towards the sound, they were surprised to see Simón himself standing there. Toni was with him. It was she who had tapped on the glass and now was smiling and waving at them.

'What the hell are they doing here?' Jack muttered crossly. But he didn't show his irritation facially, just made gestures for the others to join them.

When they did, it was Toni who explained their arrival at the hospital.

'We telephoned Laura to say we would be out for dinner and she told us what had happened. So we thought we'd come to the hospital. How is the boy? Any news?' she asked in Spanish, her English not being as fluent as Simón's.

'Not yet. Can I get you a cup of something?' Jack offered.

She asked for *café solo*. Simón said he would have the same. Jack went to the counter, leaving Toni to sit down next to Cassia while Simón took the chair diagonally opposite her.

'I'm afraid our arrival is inopportune. We've intruded on what would appear to be an important tête-à-tête,' he said, at his most sardonic.

'Not at all,' she said awkwardly, wondering what construction he had put on Jack holding her hand and wrist. Gazing into each other's eyes, they must have looked like lovers. If only they were! If Jack held her heart there would be no problem.

'If you'll excuse me, I'll go back to the desk and ask what's happening,' she said.

She thought she had escaped and gained a few moments to collect herself from the double shock of Jack's declaration and Simón's arrival. But in the long walkway connecting the cafeteria with the other parts of the hospital she heard footsteps behind her, and glanced over her shoulder.

'I'll come with you,' Simón said, catching her up.

'What about your coffee?'

He dismissed it with a shrug. 'Why was Jack holding your hand?'

'I don't think that's your business.'

They were a few metres from a corner. As soon as they turned it, and were out of sight of the cafeteria, he clamped a hand on her shoulder and forced her to a standstill.

'Is there something between you? How long has this been going on?'

'Are you crazy?' Cassia exclaimed. 'You have no right to interrogate me like this.'

'You gave me the right,' he said harshly. 'On the roof. Last time I was here.'

'I don't know what you mean.'

'I'll refresh your memory.'

His arms went round her. He jerked her roughly against him. The swoop of his head was as swift and deadly as a kestrel dropping out of the sky to snatch up its frantic prey. None of his previous kisses had prepared her for the merciless onslaught of this kiss.

CHAPTER ELEVEN

'Now do you see?' Simón said thickly, releasing her mouth but keeping her pinioned to his chest. 'You're mine. You belong to me. It's why I brought you to Castell. It's why you came.'

In her heart, she couldn't deny it. She *was* his. She always would be. But pride wouldn't let her admit it.

Then the fierce light went out of his eyes and he eased his hold on her slightly.

'My mother, who knows me very well, seems to have guessed what's been happening. She asked Toni to come down and suss out the situation. Toni also knows me very well. She spotted at once that I'd met my Waterloo, but she couldn't make out how you felt. I've spent most of the day pouring my heart out to her and being told it would be more to the point to confide my feelings to you. But yesterday you made me feel I could have been mistaken—they might not be reciprocated.'

He took one arm from around her to trace, with a gentle finger, the lips he had bruised moments earlier.

'I'm asking you to marry me, Cassia. I was going to wait...give you more time...but I have to know now. I love you. I need you. I can't get through life without you.'

'Oh, Simón...if you only knew! I've been in agony too. I love you so much it's been killing me.' The joyous relief of hearing him say that he loved her made her burst into tears.

A group of hospital cleaning staff came out of a door further along the corridor but paid little attention to the

176

tall man giving his handkerchief and speaking sooth-
ingly in a foreign language to the weeping girl in his arms.
Grief and attempts to comfort it were a common sight
in the hospital.

By the time the cleaners had turned the corner Cassia
was recovering herself, her world transformed by the
sudden sure and certain knowledge that Simón loved her.

'We'd better go and find out what's happening to poor
Paco,' she said, drying her eyes.

'After I've kissed you.' This time he held her gently,
and kissed her with the tenderness which had under-
mined her defences on the roof.

'When I saw Jack holding your hand, I had a terrible
feeling that he was telling you he loved you. I felt ready
to murder him,' he said against her cheek. 'Was that
what he was saying to you?'

'Yes ... but he's guessed how I feel about you. I hate
to hurt him. He needs loving so badly.'

'But not by you, darling girl. Someone will turn up
for Jack. Maybe, on a temporary basis, Toni will ease
his pain for him.'

'Toni and Jack? I thought she was marked out for
you.'

'Toni is like a sister to me. She wouldn't mind a few
rolls in the hay with him. She said so this afternoon.
She likes macho blue-collar or no-collar guys. But I
doubt if she'll ever attach herself to any man perma-
nently. She earns enough money to keep herself and she
values her independence. The only thing that might
domesticate her is if, in a few years' time, she gets the
urge to reproduce before it's too late. But I shouldn't be
surprised if being godmother to our children isn't enough
for her. I'd like to have a large family, if that's all right
with you.'

'I should love to have a large family. But what if your mother doesn't approve of me? I'm not the sort of girl she must have hoped you would marry.'

'My mother will adore you. You're *exactly* the sort of girl she hoped I would marry. She's despaired of my ever finding you,' he told her, smiling.

In spite of Simón's repeated assurances that the former Marquesa de Mondragón would accept his choice of bride with enthusiasm, on the day they drove to Madrid to meet her Cassia was extremely nervous.

She knew how crucial it was to make a good first impression on the woman who, up to now, had held first place in Simón's affections, and who wouldn't be human if she didn't feel somewhat wary of the girl who had supplanted her.

If she were only half as nice as her son claimed, she would undoubtedly do her best to hide any reservations she might have inwardly and to welcome her future daughter-in-law with all the warmth she could muster. Nevertheless, it would be a daunting encounter, and one which had given Cassia several restless nights.

She had not been sleeping with Simón in the two weeks since his proposal. She had thought that he would come to her room, or take her to his, as soon as they were unofficially engaged. The official engagement had to wait until she had met his mother, after which it was his intention to marry her without delay. In the meantime he seemed in no hurry to claim the privileges that she was very willing to give him. She was still a little shy of him, and couldn't bring herself to ask point-blank why, when the embraces they did share quickly brought them both to a high pitch of arousal, he always stopped short of the point of no return.

Now that she knew he loved her, Cassia was impatient to experience every delight that love had to offer. She knew that he wanted her. She wanted him. She didn't understand why he was postponing the moment when they would be lovers in the fullest sense.

The Palacio de Mondragón in Madrid made the house at Castell de los Torres seem like a cottage. It was in the heart of the city, and as Simón slowed the car to wait for a break in the oncoming traffic, and she saw his family's coat of arms carved in stone above doors built to admit carriages drawn by four or more horses, she realised for the first time how immensely rich and distinguished he was. It made her even more nervous.

Someone must have been on the watch for them. Before there was a gap in the stream of cars, the great doors were opened by two liveried manservants, revealing the patio within, far larger and grander than any she had glimpsed in Granada.

'Don't panic,' said Simón. 'A large part of the house is now the administrative centre of my estates as a whole. The grandest rooms are, in effect, a museum, open to art connoisseurs by appointment. My private apartment is at the back, overlooking the garden, which is where, in all probability, we shall find my mother. She's always disliked Madrid and only comes here to see me.'

Cassia's first sight of the former *marquesa* was from a window in his apartment while she was in the bathroom, freshening up after the drive from Castell. Looking down from the first-floor window, she saw a tall, slender woman, her hair tied back with a soft chiffon scarf, pacing the paving surrounding a fountain pool. She was simply but elegantly dressed in a white shirt and navy skirt with matching tights and shoes. Cassia knew from her movements and the way she kept checking her watch that she was nervous too. The knowledge calmed her own jitters.

When, a short time later, they finally came face to face, her anxiety evaporated. She saw at first glance that Simón hadn't exaggerated his mother's *simpática* personality.

They shook hands and smiled at each other, and then the older woman looked up at her son and said, with a catch in her voice, 'I thought you had to be exaggerating, but I see you weren't. She does put them in the shade.'

Then she turned back to Cassia, saying, 'The de Mondragón wives have included many famous beauties, some with characters to match their faces and some not. Simón told me you were ravishing, but that it was your other qualities he found irresistible. I was beginning to be afraid he would never find the right girl, but at last he has, and now I can stop worrying about him. My name is Joceline.'

She let go of Cassia's hand, but only in order to give her a more demonstrative welcome—a hug, and kisses on both cheeks.

On the morning of her wedding day, Cassia woke up in a bedroom at the Parador de San Francisco, the State-run *parador* she had always loved, originally a monastery founded by the Catholic monarchs after recovering Granada from the Moors.

In her many explorations of the Alhambra she had often peeped through the gateway of the *parador*, but had never expected to find herself staying here—and especially not as the bride of a grandee.

It had been Simón's decision not to have the big fashionable wedding customary in Madrid society. Instead, they were being married quietly in a city where she felt at home and where Señor Alvarez could take the place of her father.

Simón had organised everything. Her only responsibilities had been to choose her wedding dress and a trousseau for a honeymoon on a faraway island in the sun, where the only things to do would be swimming, sailing and making love.

She had spent her last night on her own in Room 305— a very small double room with a private sitting room in the tower above it. This, she presumed, was where they would sleep tonight—their flight to their secret destination having been arranged for tomorrow.

She had had breakfast in bed, and was up and dressed when Joceline and Toni came for her. All three were going to a salon to have their hair done. Toni had driven down from Castell de los Torres the previous afternoon. She was still staying there, painting pictures of windows.

One of them she had framed and presented to Simón and Cassia as a wedding present the night before. She had not brought Jack to the wedding. He was now in charge of a second batch of teenagers, and Cassia's place had been taken by a capable local girl.

Saying goodbye to Jack had left Cassia with an ache in her heart that she would continue to feel until he found someone to love him as he needed to be loved. Whether he and Toni now had something going between them was impossible to tell.

But a sexual relationship, however enjoyable, could only ever be second-best, a substitute for the real thing, thought Cassia as, walking down the hill to the city centre, she listened to Toni telling the former *marquesa* about a wedding in Paris that she had attended recently.

'I can't wait to see *our* bride in her lovely dress,' said Joceline, giving Cassia an affectionate glance.

In one of several recent heart-to-hearts she had confided that her first wedding had been a terrifying occasion. Having lost her own mother, she had been bullied by Simón's formidable grandmother into agreeing to a

Spanish ceremony of almost royal formality and splendour, made more daunting by Joceline's then inadequate command of her bridegroom's native language.

Her second husband had flown in the day before, and was now keeping Simón company at the Hotel America, also within the boundaries of the Alhambra. Joceline and Toni had hurried Cassia past it after leaving the *parador*. Although neither was really superstitious, they hadn't wanted her to be accidentally seen by her bridegroom.

Only the wedding guests were staying at the Castillo del Sultán, and there were not many of them. Simón had been ruthless in pruning the list to fewer than a dozen particularly close friends. Parties for other friends would take place at a later date. Today was to be the intimate occasion he felt a wedding should be.

It was late afternoon when Simón gave Cassia's elbow a gentle squeeze and said, 'Time to change, darling.'

Although they weren't really leaving Granada tonight, he had thought it would wind up the festivities in an appropriate way if, after changing their clothes, the guests saw them off in his car. But they would only be going as far as the cemetery, for Cassia to leave her flowers on the ledge of John Browning's vault.

Toni helped Cassia to change from her white lawn and handmade lace wedding dress into a summery frock. Although it was only just May, all Europe was having a heatwave, and here in the south the days were hot, the nights balmy.

'You look so radiant that I could almost wish someone would come and sweep me off the shelf,' she said in Spanish as she dealt with the hooks and eyes.

* * *

Even the short visit to her father's grave could not cloud Cassia's happiness. She felt that today was the real beginning of her life.

'Are you tired?' Simón asked as they drove back down the hill, past the place where the tour buses parked. By this time of day the last bus had gone, as had the rows of cars now to be seen all year round near the Generalife gardens where, only a few months ago, she had sat worrying about Simón's motive for asking her to dine with him in the Mirador suite.

'Not very. It wasn't that sort of wedding. But I'm glad the others will have left when we get back.'

Later this evening, when everyone had had time to rest, his mother and stepfather were hosting another party at a restaurant in the Albaicín.

'So am I,' he said, giving her a smile with a glint of devilment in it. 'Our engagement has been a test of restraint for me.'

She didn't pretend not to understand what he meant. From this day forward there would be no more subterfuge, no more prevarication. 'It didn't have to be, Simón.'

'I know, but it wasn't for long.' He glanced at the clock on the dashboard. 'We may just have time to look at the sunset from one of the Alhambra's *miradores*. Would you like that?'

The suggestion was unexpected, but she realised that, yes, she would like to begin their honeymoon by watching the sun go down from one of the balconies inside the sultans' palace.

'It would be lovely, but aren't we too late? I think they'll have closed,' she said regretfully.

Sometimes the Alhambra was open at night, but not always.

Simón drove through the arched gateway used by taxis and motorists staying at the *parador*. Leaving the car in a place where she didn't think cars were supposed to be left, he jumped out and locked the driver's door. As she got out she thought that he would sprint towards the ticket office. Instead he came round and, taking her by the hand, strolled leisurely towards the doors where visitors surrendered their tickets. Perhaps he was planning to slip the doorkeeper a tip.

'What about the car?' she asked. 'Won't you be fined for leaving it there?'

'You worry too much.' His dark eyes sparkled with amusement. 'Who'd fine me on my wedding day?'

'But we've nothing to prove that we are just married.'

'We shall have to hope they take our word for it.'

At the entrance, the attendant smiled and said good evening.

'I've left my car near the ticket office. Could you have someone take it up to the *parador*, please?' Simón handed over the keys.

'Certainly, Excellency.'

'How is it that he knows you?' Cassia asked. 'Do you have some connection with the Alhambra?'

'He saw me this morning, when I came here to arrange for us to watch the sunset. By special dispensation, we're going to be allowed to wander about unsupervised.'

'You arranged this! What a lovely, romantic thing to do.'

'A wedding night is a romantic occasion.'

He put his arm round her waist and they strolled through the deserted rooms with their honeycombed ceilings and walls inscribed with mysterious Arabic inscriptions.

With no one else there it was magical. No footsteps but their own. No other voices. Only the sound of the fountains and water courses, and then, faintly, somewhere far off, the music of Spanish guitars.

'As one can't rely on the nightingales, I asked some gypsies to play for us,' Simón explained as they looked across the ravine at the rooftops of the Albaicín. 'But they're not here. They're over in the other gardens. We shan't be disturbed. The whole Alhambra is ours, from sunset to sunrise.'

Much later, after the gypsy guitarists had returned to their caves on Sacromonte, he took her to a moonlit room where the pools of silvery light fell from star-shaped openings in the roof, and the diaphanous folds of a transparent tent of fine gauze were stirred by soft currents of air. Inside the tent was a wide divan.

It was like a scene from the *Arabian Nights*—baskets of scented roses in every corner, their heady fragrance mingling with the exotic incense from burning pastilles which would keep the room free of mosquitoes.

Cassia realised that these preparations must have been made while they were drinking champagne in the Tower of the Princesses, listening to the throbbing guitars and a fine tenor voice singing 'Granada' which, as it died away, was followed by another surprise. From the dark cypress groves of the gardens on the neighbouring hill came fiery meteors and sparkling cascades of colour— the fireworks which were a traditional celebration at even the humblest Spanish weddings.

When she was lying in his arms on the spacious divan, inside the misty folds of their bridal pavilion, Simón said huskily, 'Do you remember the night I walked you home? The thought of you all by yourself in that gloomy house kept me awake. Since that night I haven't wanted any other woman. Now that you're mine, I never shall.'

She knew that it was a promise he would keep. Walking back to this main part of the palace from the Torre de las Infantas, pausing to gaze at the reflections of palms and pillars in the still surface of a pool, they had both revealed thoughts and feelings not shared with anyone else.

Simón had told her how his grandfather's libertine ways had been the outcome of an arranged and loveless marriage. How he himself, as a boy, had admired and been greatly influenced by his grandfather, inheriting his attitude to women, but always with the secret hope that his own marriage would be different.

With her arms round his neck and his eyes burning with the ardour deliberately held in check until this perfect moment, she lost her last vestige of reserve and felt only a passionate longing to be his—body and soul.

'Make me yours...now,' she whispered.

As he began to kiss her, somewhere outside she heard a nightingale singing.

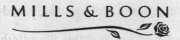

MILLS & BOON

For those long, hot, lazy days this summer
Mills & Boon are delighted to bring you...

*Stolen
Moments*

A collection of four short sizzling stories
in one romantic volume.

We know you'll love these warm and sensual
stories from some of our best loved authors.

Love Me Not	Barbara Stewart
Maggie And Her Colonel	Merline Lovelace
Prairie Summer	Alina Roberts
Anniversary Waltz	Anne Marie Duquette

'Stolen Moments' is the perfect summer read for
those stolen summer moments!

Available: June '96   Price: £4.99

*Available from WH Smith, John Menzies, Volume One, Forbuoys, Martins,
Woolworths, Tesco, Asda, Safeway and other paperback stockists.*

MILLS & BOON

Back by Popular Demand

BETTY NEELS

A collector's edition of favourite titles from one of the world's best-loved romance authors.

Mills & Boon are proud to bring back these sought after titles, now reissued in beautifully matching volumes and presented as one cherished collection.

Don't miss these unforgettable titles, coming next month:

Title #3   A GENTLE AWAKENING
Title #4   RING IN A TEACUP

Available wherever
Mills & Boon books are sold

GET 4 BOOKS
AND A MYSTERY GIFT

Return this coupon and we'll send you 4 Mills & Boon Romances and a mystery gift absolutely FREE! We'll even pay the postage and packing for you.

We're making you this offer to introduce you to the benefits of Reader Service: FREE home delivery of brand-new Mills & Boon Romances, at least a month before they are available in the shops, FREE gifts and a monthly Newsletter packed with information.

Accepting these FREE books and gift places you under no obligation to buy, you may cancel at any time, even after receiving just your free shipment. Simply complete the coupon below and send it to:

MILLS & BOON READER SERVICE, FREEPOST, CROYDON, SURREY, CR9 3WZ.

No stamp needed

Yes, please send me 4 free Mills & Boon Romances and a mystery gift. I understand that unless you hear from me, I will receive 6 superb new titles every month for just £2.10* each postage and packing free. I am under no obligation to purchase any books and I may cancel or suspend my subscription at any time, but the free books and gifts will be mine to keep in any case. (I am over 18 years of age)

1EP6R

Ms/Mrs/Miss/Mr _____

Address _____

_____

_____ Postcode _____

Offer closes 30th November 1996. We reserve the right to refuse an application. *Prices and terms subject to change without notice. Offer only valid in UK and Ireland and is not available to current subscribers to this series. **Readers in Ireland please write to: P.O. Box 4546, Dublin 24.** Overseas readers please write for details.

You may be mailed with offers from other reputable companies as a result of this application. Please tick box if you would prefer not to receive such offers. ☐

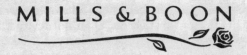

MILLS & BOON

Next Month's Romances

Each month you can choose from a wide variety of romance with Mills & Boon. Below are the new titles to look out for next month.

Available from WH Smith, John Menzies, Volume One, Forbuoys, Martins, Woolworths, Tesco, Asda, Safeway and other paperback stockists.